MIDDLE-AGED MAIDENS

MIDDLE-AGED MAIDENS

GWEN KELLY

SIRIUS

ANGUS & ROBERTSON PUBLISHERS

*Unit 4, Eden Park, 31 Waterloo Road,
North Ryde, NSW, Australia 2113;
94 Newton Road, Auckland 1,
New Zealand; and
16 Golden Square, London W1R 4BN,
United Kingdom*

*First published in Australia
by Thomas Nelson (Australia) Limited in 1976
This new Angus & Robertson Sirius edition 1989*

Copyright © Gwen Kelly 1976

*National Library of Australia
Cataloguing-in-publication data.*

*Kelly, Gwen, 1922-
  Middle-aged maidens.*

ISBN 0 207 16278 6.

I. Title.

A823'.3

Printed in Australia by Australian Print Group

CONTENTS

MIRIAM

1

I was nervous the week-end before my interview with Miss Spurway. I knew the decision was final. If I took the job at Etherington Ladies' College I should stay there, probably till death did us part, and Etherington meant not only a school but Meridale. Meridale for ever. Why not? I had been born here, the High School was my school, the Congregational Church was my church. Throughout the town my cousins and second cousins met and married and begat children in order to perpetuate the sense of family which is so strong in all of us, even though we are relatively humble people.

Meridale is old for an inland town, although if it comes to that we are barely inland. The map of New South Wales stretches away to the west of us but only a hundred and twenty miles through the ranges brings you to the sea. Yet for most of us it might as well have been five hundred and twenty. In my childhood the roads were barely roads; rocks, scattered along the centre to give a surface, and dust and potholes and hazardous mist-covered mountains. Very few of us owned cars. For me the sea was as remote as the summit of the highest mountain and much less concrete. Lift up your eyes to the everlasting hills. When small I did just that and believed Meridale, enclosed on all sides, was the world.

When I was fourteen I made the trip to the coast with

Father in a horse and dray and I shall never forget it. Rolling hills and green valleys fed by chronic fog, and on the edge of the plateau the first scrappy glimpse of the sea. But that was a rare occasion, although every minute detail and every change of colour remain. Green, blue, brown and, coming back, the wet enveloping white. But Father always said I had a painter's eye and it is true that I do like to sketch a little. Alternatively, I should probably have made a good carpenter. Piecing together with infinite patience the minutiae, the slivers of wood—and life.

In later years the sea I came to know well was the sea at Sydney and I did not like Sydney. I can remember my sense of release as the train chugged slowly up the range, for the bare trees and barren slopes offered me both freedom and security, the knowledge of roots in the earth that signify home. The roots were still there, but now the thought of permanent return oppressed me. I needed solitude to sort out my feelings. Perhaps above all things I desired some purpose outside my own home, a purpose that was not thrust upon me by others. All my purposes are second-hand.

That week-end I tucked Mother into bed, for her leg was worse than usual. It had been crushed by a tree half a century ago and she had been partially lame ever since; and even though I felt guilty at leaving her, for Father had died only six weeks previously, I pulled my hat over my ears to keep out the cold and prepared to go out.

Mother's eyes followed me round the room—they were soft with a melted grey that gives some old eyes a translucence surpassing youth; and her hair still curled, variegated grey, tipped with mauve, around her smooth face. Apart from the lines of pain creasing the edges of her mouth and forehead she was as pretty as the girl Father married.

'Must you go out this morning, Miriam?' I put on my woollen gloves and nodded without speaking. 'I suppose if you must, you must.'

I tried to sound tender, patient. I had to be patient, continue to be patient; it was a life sentence. 'Robert didn't have time to take me into town yesterday, Mother. We need food.'

'Robert is a man,' said my mother, 'with a family. He had to return to Danneworth today. A man must put his own family first. Parents can usually rely on their daughters in their old age.'

'I know,' I said, 'but I didn't do the shopping yesterday because Robert was going to drive me to town. It's a long way down the hill and the buses don't run very often.'

'As if I don't know that,' said Mother. 'I ought to know it, trying to feed and clothe you and Robert and your father—with a gammy leg, too. There have never been enough buses.' Her voice pushed through her lips like green shoots through poisoned blackberry. I straightened my coat. 'I won't be long,' I said.

She looked at me standing by the bed. Her voice strengthened again. 'You were always such a bony girl, Miriam, and tall like your father. Why do you hide your hair under the cap? Pull it out to frame your face. It would look much prettier.'

I picked up my bag. 'It's cold,' I said. I glanced, however, at the mirror, and I saw the large bones of my cheeks rising into my hat, Father's bones, big, strong. I suppose I did look gaunt, but my sandy hair permed on the ends was not attractive and I liked to be warm. Anyway I *am* gaunt, so why bother to hide it?

'Don't be long,' she said.

I looked at her lying frail in the solid oak bed that had seemed big even with Father in it. I felt pity. I hate pity; it unnerves, entraps. I prefer loyalty. 'I'll bring you a magazine,' I said. I looked at the buffaloes in the glass case, carved in wood by Father, for ever grazing in their prison fields of raffia. They looked back at me, bovine, unmoved.

She smiled. 'Thank you, Miriam dear. How could I manage without you? Would you mind changing my books for me? They're overdue.'

I walked down the long hill, Mother's bundle of books cradled in my arms. The wooden houses and the wooden shops were derelict after the neat modernity of Gunnedah. I passed the wooden reminders of my relatives—Hansen Brothers: Carpenters—only there were no brothers now, not carpenters, anyway. Father was the last, and he had been incapacitated by cancer for the last three years. It would be grey, I thought, fog on the ranges, creeping in, blotting out the sea—not white, grey—grey fog cells eating that gaunt strong body into submission.

Along the street Merrick's Mixed Business (Merricks always think in capitals) kept up a penurious existence on the outskirts of the supermarkets. Mother had been a Merrick, but these Merricks were only my second cousins. I crept past. I had not seen Aunt Myra since my return, except at Father's funeral, and that barely counted. 'Home for good now, I hope,' she had said. 'The last three years have been hard on Edith, particularly with her leg. Hard on me, too. Always having to pop in—as if I didn't have an old man of my own to worry over. We can't gad around the country for ever, can we?'

I said nothing. I suppose it was true, although I should hardly have called it gadding. Schoolroom after schoolroom, hot, cold, indifferent and all smelly with the flesh and worse of children; with the same uninterested faces in every one of them. It was true. I had never interested children *en masse*. If it came to that, I had never interested anyone very much within a group. I might as well come home as go anywhere else. But I didn't want to think about it—not now. On Bernard's Bridge I stopped for a moment, noting the patterns of the jetsam in the water and the incipient green of the bare willows. The water, scarcely more than a trickle, was stained with the effluvium of the gas works—like a disease. It could have been beautiful but it was not. It was Meridale, badly lit, haphazardly guttered, inadequately drained. Civic sloth personified. I dreaded it.

Yet I loved the creek because its winding patterns were the patterns of childhood—Robert and tadpoles. I curled my gloved hands around my handbag and I felt the bulge of Robert's letter.

'Muriel and I can't have Mother at Danneworth. As you know the Council pay is pretty lousy and we have four kids to keep. Might have been different if I'd been the clever one instead of you. Mother, after all, has lived in Bennet St all her married life.' (All her life, I amended. The Merricks were only round the corner on the highway.) 'It would be cruelty to move her. You've been teaching some time now. The Department could consider an appointment at Meridale.'

Good old Robert! You could always work it out, couldn't you? Miriam is the clever one, but Robert has his own skills. Once I tried to tell Father, I tried to say I know I'm cleverer than Robert, we all know it, but Robert always gets his own way.

'The big tadpole is mine,' he said. But he was swimming in my jar because I had scooped him from the creek. Black, lustrous, with blue-green sheen on his tail.

'I found him,' I said. 'He's mine.' Robert had straightened the wrinkled tops of his grey socks, to please Mother. She liked order, neatness. 'I gave him to her, Mother. She wanted to carry him up the hill so I let her—as a favour.'

'He's a liar,' I said. 'I found him.'

But Mother said, 'Give him to Robert, Miriam. It's mean to take his tadpole. After all he's only a little boy.' And Father said, 'What does it matter, Miriam? You get prizes and all sorts of things at school, but poor old Robert gets nothing. Let him have his tadpole.'

So I gave it to him and said nothing, but sometimes I wished I could come bottom of the class for a change. It was not my fault that I was born cleverer than Robert but he never forgave me. Poor Robert. I suppose it is hard for a boy to have the teachers throwing his sister up at him. I have heard lots of teachers banging the heads of siblings together. It's a professional disease. God knows I would have changed places with Robert willingly. As my father said, a boy must earn a living but it doesn't really matter for a girl.

'I'm afraid,' said his letter, 'we won't be able to contribute to Mother's keep. The youngest starts school this year and Billy needs dental treatment of a specialist kind. I know you won't mind, old thing. You've always been so generous, and graduate teachers do earn as much as most men. You certainly earn more than me.'

I continued to walk into town. I did not want to return to Meridale High School. I had tried it once. After the university in Sydney, the crowded anonymous streets, I wanted to come home—but it was an error. French and maths to the brothers and sisters of my school mates. I hated it. And I hated the schools that followed. Gunnedah was heaven by comparison. Only the best pupils took French and I had no maths. Even then the boys worried me. I like to teach girls. I believe boys need a man to discipline them. At Etherington Ladies' College there would be no boys. I began to hope they would want me. A boarding-school with insufficient money to pay its staff professional salaries was hard put to it to survive. They should jump at the chance of a graduate with training—less money but a limited number of fawn-tunicked little girls. I could stay for ever. For ever? Mother and me down there in Bennet Street for eternity. Miss Miriam Hansen, the school institution, the backbone of Speech Day.

Along the main street I passed the old blacksmith Kurt Hansen—dear old Uncle Kurt—his shop was now called Dunham, Hansen and my cousin Conrad Hansen ran it with Dick Dunham who had been Robert's friend at school. Few horses to shoe now, but junk and riding equipment for sale cluttered the window.

'Hi, Miriam,' called Dick as I passed. 'Home for good?' He's fat and middle-aged, I thought. How funny. Dapper Dicky Dunham—a wow with the girls—a real paunch. I nodded and said good day and hurried on. In the main store I passed Mena Furlonger, who was my third cousin. But she had married Maurice Furlonger of Furlonger's Hotel and we had ceased to be more than nodding acquaintances years ago. Her face in middle age was rigid with its repeated attempts to express gentility. But the hands testing the material on the counter were tremulous. Nerves, tension, bared twisted knuckles and anemone sensitive pink finger-nails. Perhaps Maurice Furlonger's money and position did not compensate after all for Maurice Furlonger. Rolling pink flesh, chin, chest, stomach. I blacked my thoughts. Never draw what you haven't experienced, said bald Mr Daley at the local adult art classes. Froggy Daley, we used to call him at school—wet, clammy hands that could draw the pastel reality out of the hills and paddocks and trees with delicate veracity.

I lifted my eyes from Mena Furlonger's traitorous fingers to her expensive genteel mask, and I remembered she had been educated at Etherington; for her mother came from the land and had hoped her daughters would be ladies, or at least indistinguishable from their landed peers. I wondered idly if all the girls from Etherington turned out like Mena. Repellent thought. Fawn-tunicked monsters in the making with lip-sticked ears and tractor tails.

To my surprise she spoke. 'Nice to see you, Miriam. I was sorry to hear about Uncle Thomas. How's Aunt Edith? I suppose you'll be home for good now.'

I nodded.

'Going to the High School?' She always pronounced 'High School' as if it were a slum. Her hen-like brown eyes ran over my cap, my sensible gloves and shoes. I was glad my eyes were green.

'Perhaps,' I said.

'I did hear you were thinking of Etherington. You'd find it so different there.'

'Nothing is definite,' I said, but I cursed the grapevine veracity of Meridale. They always had information and it was nearly always correct. Those who denigrate the reliability of gossip have never lived in Meridale.

'Hope you like it,' she said, flicking back to her velvet in cursory dismissal. Go lackey, bow your way out. 'My old school.'

'I know,' I said, and should have liked to say that this was one of the reasons why I still hesitated.

I bundled my purchases into my bag and walked into the park. Conscience said, 'Return to Mother, she's lonely. Nothing worse than lying helpless in an empty house.' But I wanted to think or maybe feel, perhaps even to *be*—for half an hour. To those who like colour and growth the park was not very attractive, but here at the end of winter I noted the grass withered with frost, the bony structure of the deciduous trees. I like gauntness, particularly the stripped-to-the-bone gauntness of late winter when I can already hear the potential of spring in the rising sap. I could hear it now as I sat in the sun tracing with the mind's eye the symmetrical pattern of branches on one of the poplars. I could see already the folded leaf buds and I knew, given a touch of sun, spring would burst out all over like the song. But the wind was cold. Around my feet scurried the fibres of grass gilded with dust, and the leaves overlooked in the autumn clean-up twisted in skeletal decay—ultimate. Winter had not gone.

I stooped to pat one of the perennial strays of Meridale. Thin, hungry brute, all prick and ribs, as one of my mother's uncles used to say. I stopped my thought. It is not nice to think too much in sexual terms. My uncle had been a vulgar man with several lady friends. I remembered that my father had disliked him. But he could be funny or at least I used to think so. Perhaps I was merely young.

I pulled a slice of devon from my basket. How inadequate. The long, rangy, half-collie, half-alsatian frame barely felt the impact. The eyes looked at me both hopefully and reproachfully. It was a look I met myself—often. It was the way I should like to look at Mother, but I could school my features into lines of uncommunicating rigidity. What is the use of duty if you couple it with reproach? I patted the head and argued: I have life, education, a university degree and a small talent for drawing, and I am a rural carpenter's daughter—a no-account girl to look after the house and Mother in her declining years. All told, my parents had been generous—but then it was so obviously useless educating Robert and I suppose it would have been silly to waste all that money .carefully saved for the son's education.

The dog laid his head on my lap. I liked dogs but we had never owned one. Mother hated dogs. Grandfather's dog had tripped her into the path of the falling tree at Andy's Creek timber camp all those years ago. And Grandfather shot it the same afternoon, shot it while they waited at the hospital. I hated Grandpa Merrick—roundball pretty, hard–kind–cruel —but I liked Grandpa Hansen, Danish blue, taut, dry, hard —but just. Always just.

I looked at the intelligent eyes of the head on my lap and I wondered if here were one of those working dogs that out-of-town graziers occasionally abandon when they have exhausted their usefulness. I felt my eyes melt into his and I thought this is the moment, he understands. The sun warmed my shoulders and through the mirror eyes of the dog the barren park was vicariously comforting. I knew then I liked Meridale, its scruffy non-fulfilment, its barren obstructive winter. Wherever I went it would go with me, making the growth of new roots impossible. Elsewhere there could be only hair roots, frail, easily snapped. Here was the transubstantiation of myself. I had to stay—if Miss Spurway would have me.

I was conscious of warmth. I would stay with Mother, not because Robert or Aunt Myra or any of my family ordered it, but because it was the necessity of my own being. Father had always stressed duty, the feeling for family that did not dissolve merely because it was personally difficult.

I felt grateful to the dog. I dropped the entire packet of devon at his feet, then slipped away while he devoured it with startled relish.

Miss Spurway's office was neat, trim, with polished desk and Venetian blinds—ordered, conventional, headmistressy, or at any rate what the Public Service or school councils considered headmistressy. I have always found headmistresses a mixed bag with overlays of pattern only. What authority epitomised was the overlay without the sloppiness, vindictiveness, irresponsible charm, petty jealousy, or mechanical efficiency that marked the Heads I had known one from another. Impersonality that missed all the tricks. The woman behind the desk was neat and orderly like the desk, yet the being that merged with mine across the polished wood was alien to the room.

She was little with silver blonde hair going grey but shrouded in pink mist. Mists are not pink, they are white, so this mist was an abstract, or perhaps impressionistic. Green rolling hills and pink mist on the range above the sea. It would be worth painting. She wore red-rimmed grotesquely curved glasses that mocked her prim mouth and through which her blue eyes looked with amusement—or was it uncertainty—on the world. Maybe it was the mist, maybe the glasses, but I felt immediately I could like her.

She was well dressed like the room—grey costume and beautiful, beautiful shoes. I have big feet with difficult arches and the doctor told Mother when I was thirteen that I must always wear good, strong, sensible shoes of a lace-up variety if I wished to avoid misery in my middle age. I have always done so, and my feet at forty are as good as they were when I was thirteen. I was proud of them, but no one ever saw them. Miss Spurway's shoes were delicate, grey, suede, perfectly plain but moulded to the foot as if they grew there.

She ran a pink-polished finger-nail over my references and tried to look as if she were studying them.

'You had first-class honours in French and maths in your Leaving?' I nodded. 'You'd be an asset backed both ways,' she said. 'Which are you best at?'

'Well,' I said, 'I came first in the state in French but only fifteenth in maths.'

'Only fifteenth. Well, well.' Her eyes were amused. 'The subjectivity of the examination system is very interesting,' she said. 'Did you take an honours course at the university?'

I shook my head. I found it hard to say I did not qualify for one. You can never explain starting a hundred yards behind all those slick metropolitan runners with no kind, keen-for-results paternalism to bolster you up.

'A pity,' she said, 'if you're as good as all that. Mind if I smoke?'

'N-n-not at all,' I said and she produced a curved tortoise-shell holder picked out in red like her glasses and the smoke from the longer-than-normal cigarette wreathed and melted into the pink mist of hair. I stuttered because I was surprised. I knew the Council of this school was stingy, narrow, petty bourgeois, and I admired her for ignoring their prejudices. The ash tray beside her right hand was overflowing, so apparently she ignored it regularly—a chain smoker. Father had told me it was an undesirable habit for a woman, because it injured her babies; but Miss Spurway presumably had no babies, and I imagined she was discreet in front of the girls.

The red spots glowed on the tortoiseshell like exotic fungi. 'A bad habit,' she said. 'I picked it up in the army. I was one of those AWAS girls. We picked up lots of bad habits, I'm afraid.' For a moment the blue eyes looked out of the red rims with mischievous memory.

I nodded sympathetically. My mother had told me a lot about AWAS that summer when I thought I should like to join myself.

'Why didn't you do an honours course?' she said, looking straight at me.

I fumbled, and could feel the skin on my neck deepening in colour. I cursed my sandy Nordic forbears. 'I wasn't good enough,' I stammered. 'I failed some of my first-year subjects and had to repeat.' Those cold impersonal benches hundreds of miles from home, day by day; and night by night the neat, smart girls in College who made me feel awkward and coun-trified.

'Bunkum,' said Miss Spurway. 'You took too long to as-similate, obviously. How old were you? A bare sixteen, I sup-pose.'

I nodded, and smiled at her gratefully. I knew then if I could only work for her I would repay her with unswerving loyalty. She walked to the window. 'Parents will never see,' she said almost sadly, 'that you can top the state and still be too young. Think of all those perpetual undergraduates teaching in our universities! It's a problem against which I bang my head ineffectually year after year.' She ran her fingers along the Venetian blind. 'They never dust properly, not one of them. I found the latest, a kid of sixteen, pulling the blind up and down the other day. It appeared she had never seen a blind in her life before. Lived in one of those out-of-town shacks, worse than the Aborigines. At least they have some sort of communal life. This type has nothing until Mum or Dad pack the children off to Meridale to earn a living as soon as they're old enough for the truant inspector not to ask awkward questions. The rural illiterate. There are more than you think.'

'You forget,' I said, 'I've lived in Meridale all my life. I'm well aware of the fringe-dwellers. Most of them are shocking, but you can't help feeling sorry, too.'

'Feeling sorry is not enough,' she said sharply. Then she shrugged. 'But they're not my problem. Only their richer equally illiterate brethren. The ones that make love to horses instead of books. Come here.'

The tone was peremptory, so I moved to the window and stood beside her. 'It is not a good school,' she said. I looked out at the straggling wooden buildings and the annexes of old brick houses cold with age. 'Derelict,' she said, 'but our Church is not the type to extract thousands from parents to build a new school; there is a love of purely private wealth in many non-conformist sects. We have the land, you know.' I nodded. Anyone born and bred in Meridale knew Zion. Ringed with trees overlooking the city, it stood a monument to Protestant faith. To the High School children it was a joke. It had been there so long. 'No Moses,' I murmured.

'Not even a Joshua,' she added. 'There are some who blame me for not getting on with the new building, but why should I beg for their money? I'm here to run a school not to conduct a charity drive.'

She sat down behind the desk and lit another cigarette. 'Our class-rooms are crowded, our dormitories inadequate, our general facilities are minimal. I have insufficient staff. I have no money and what I shall offer even you will be well below professional standards. I spend half my time black-mailing my staff to take less than they're worth.'

She looked at me through the glasses and I knew she was trying to sense my reaction. But I have a well-schooled face and I merely waited for her to continue.

She took the holder out of her mouth and watched the smoke wreathing to the ceiling. She spoke more softly. 'But we do try to rub off some of the rough edges from these country girls, to get the ones who are worth it some sort of matric. Perhaps we make it easier for them to pass from here into the world of the drawing-room, the large hospitals, the city offices and the urban university.' She stubbed out the cigarette. 'Do you still want the job?'

'You mean I can have it?'

She laughed almost maliciously. 'There was never any real doubt, was there? People like me have no choice.' She looked at my surprised face and her eyes twisted behind the glasses. 'My dear girl, how often do you think I get offered the services of a fully qualified, professionally trained, experienced full-time teacher?'

'You mean . . .'

'I mean just that. I have a few part-time grads—bored mothers looking for a short-term diversion from children and home, whose hours make one unholy mess of the time-table. I have one fully trained primary teacher who takes secondary English and everything else we can unload on her at a cheap rate because she has a chronic disease and the Department won't employ her permanently. Her husband has war injuries and she must work. One product of a Ladies' Music School, twenty years ago. Her Daddy could not bear the thought of anything so vulgar as a tertiary education for a girl on the threshold of marriage. Too bad she never crossed it. By now her mind and her music are forty years out of date. Oh, I

forgot, an ex-nurse to teach biology, to whom the more difficult girls give heart palpitations ("I'll really have to have the
day off"), and a few student teachers concerned with boys,
and exams, or both. I have to do so much teaching myself
that I interview parents with one mind on French verbs, or
vertically opposite angles, or Julius Caesar. Consequently the
school is badly run.'

I was embarrassed. I wished she would stop talking, although I had no doubt she wished to be honest with me and
I admired her candour. But it was hard to reply. I tried to
divert her. It did not seem quite loyal.

'What is your own subject?' I said.

She laughed without laughter. 'I am an honours graduate
in physics, but we don't teach it. Ironic, isn't it? So you see
we have mathematical ability in common at least.' She lit
another cigarette. 'Still want to come?'

There was a knock on the door and a girl entered with a
silver tray daintily arranged with a pot of tea and biscuits.
Miss Spurway poured me a cup of tea. I felt nervous with the
fine cup balanced between my big fingers.

'Now, salary. You may have guessed all my perambula-
tions lead to one point. I can't offer you much.'

I looked at her nervously but I could no longer find her
eyes. The glasses were like a wall between us. I sensed it was
deliberate.

'Whatever you say,' I said.

'Well,' she said, 'we usually pay a full-time grad. nine hundred a year. We could perhaps in your case make it nine fifty,
but of course I'd expect prep. duty at night for that.'

I cannot deny I was stunned. It was little more than half
my High School salary. For a second I wondered how they
got away with it. It was now I who wanted a wall between
us, but I had no glasses. I put on the expression that I had
cultivated as a guard whenever Mother spoke of Robert. I
knew I should protest, but my throat felt dry. Then I felt
sorry for Miss Spurway. A woman of her sensitivity forced
to make offers like this one. What was worse I wanted to

come. I thought of all those little awkward country girls waiting for someone to help them cope with the big world.

'I'll take it,' I heard my voice say. 'I must stay in Meridale and the High School is overflowing with boys. I don't like teaching boys. This will be a real challenge, Miss Spurway.'

The blue eyes emerged from the rims to mingle with mine once again. I felt a glow of happiness.

'Wonderful,' she said, 'wonderful. I feared when you heard the salary you'd run away. So few teachers have any sense of vocation these days.' She stood up. She reached my shoulder —just. 'Come along and I'll show you the school.'

As we passed along the dark linoleum corridors my feet lifted on a cushion of air. Exaltation. I knew it for the first time. I have never wanted to be a Catholic, being firmly convinced it is a foreign faith and not really suitable for an Anglo-Saxon. But I should at that moment have welcomed the long habit of a nun, the feeling of dedication symbolised by the covered heads. I bowed my own and saw below me the glimmer of blonde hair lighting the darkness. Miss Spurway walked like a saint before me. Here was peace and endeavour, a new duty to be carried out in the face of physical difficulties. It would lighten the burden of looking after Mother.

Mother had been difficult that night. For a week she had not left her bed. Her meal lay on the plate untouched.

'Really, Miriam, you know I'm not well enough for heavy diets. What made you buy chops, dear?' The mouth was petulant, the eyes translucent, melting. The favourite game, baiting Miriam.

I pulled off my gloves. 'It was the nearest shop,' I said. 'I'm tired. Chops are easy to cook. It seemed a good idea.'

'I realise that,' she said. 'You must put your own needs first. A working woman needs meat. Not like a poor old invalid with her nerves and sinews rotting away in bed.' Her eyes lit with the prospect of battle, grey battleships with all the gun-turrets open. I suppose she was bored. There was so little to

amuse her. My own game was to thwart her, to rob her of her
sport by non-reaction. Not even my eyes flickered. 'I'll make
you an omelet,' I said.

Her eyes dimmed with disappointment. She said nothing,
merely turned her head into the pillow, away from me.

I whipped the omelet, yellow fresco, fretted like foam ringing the sea. I looked into the foam of egg and felt the dis-
loyalty of Etherington edging like foamy scum on the sea of
the school. I had remained aloof, remote, building a position
of integrity, someone on whom Ina Spurway could rely. We
had already achieved a great deal, better organisation, better
results, at least from a minority. But even now the back-lash
of apathy in the school oppressed me. Apathetic girls, thirty
crammed desk-to-desk in class-rooms meant to hold fifteen,
so that it was impossible to move around them, girls sketch-
ing horses, writing notes, lazing in their seats. How often in
the past two years had I put down my chalk in despair.

'And what do you think you're going to do when you leave
school?'

'Be a lady of leisure, Miss Hansen. We don't have to work
in our family.'

I tipped the egg into the pan, watching it spread like a
wave across the non-stick surface. Non-stick. It described
those girls. But there were others, eager, intelligent, frustrated.
I shook my shoulders. 'You miserable eater of dirt,' I thought,
'walled in your own self-pity, your own frustration.' I wondered about Ann Denham. Did she feel frustration too? Fat,
round Denham. I had to admit she could teach. I wondered
if she swore in front of the girls. Probably not. She was not
a fool. But a unionist. I was glad Etherington had no union.
I have always found unions distressing, destroying the clear-
cut lines of loyalty, creating confusion. It was hard enough
for Ina with Ann Denham constantly undermining her authority in an attempt to get the staff to work together for better
salaries. I knew our poor pay was not Ina's fault.

Painting with Ina in the evening classes, I had come to
know her, to like her, as well as to respect her, and gradually

she had come to rely on me. There were bits of Ina quite like
Mother. Dependent, self-doubting. I have always been able
to organise; arrange time-tables, programmes, reports. I had
not meant to usurp Miss Cunningham-White's position. It
was simply that I did things so much better. I moved the
pieces around Mother's tray as if they were chessmen. The
pepper pot stood like a green knight ready to march right, left
on to Mother's egg.

She looked at it without enthusiasm. 'You were always self-
righteous, Miriam.'

Her unkindness wriggled snake-like beneath my defences.
The casual remark succeeded where her previous baiting had
failed. I felt the tears come to my eyes and I turned away to
the window.

'You feel good,' she went on, 'because you have made me
an omelet. But you didn't ask me if I wanted an omelet. You
didn't ask me if I wanted a chop.' The voice fell emphatically
on the *me*. Mother had always italicised 'me'. I pushed my
bony hands against my yellow nylon frock, practical and too
young, and felt a prick of electricity in my fingers. 'Don't eat
it then,' I said, and left the room.

I cooked my own chop and ate it. When I picked up
Mother's tray the omelet was untouched. 'Is there anything
else I can get you?' She shook her head. I straightened her
blankets and tucked them in. 'I'd like the lamp,' she said. 'I
want to read.' I fixed the lamp so that she was bathed in a
rosy glow. She looked curiously like Ina Spurway. 'I'm sorry,
Miriam,' she said as I walked to the door. 'I don't feel well
today.'

'That's all right,' I said.

In the dining-room I spread out my books for marking.
The table was large, commonsense but made with the perfection, the concern for detail, that Father gave to all his carpentry. I missed him; but regret is pointless.

Through the figures on the paper I could hear the hum of
staff-room voices. They drifted around me, wisps of air with
little meaning, the bubbled comments of a comic strip. 'My

students were impressed. Such lovely stencils. I told them to thank you.' Pudgy Ann Denham and the eternally non-working stencil machine. That day it had stuck as usual. 'Damn, oh damn,' she said as she forced the sheets through the ill-treated machine. 'The bloody Manchus are covered in splodges.' I looked at the ink-stained pages: 'The Fall of the Manchu Empire'; but no child given those sheets would ever have found out why it had fallen. Once again I moved across to help her. 'I'm rather good with machines,' I had said my first day at Etherington.

I had not added, 'I'm a machine, myself.' Mother's robot, cooking meals, chasing groceries, a computer into which she feeds malicious questions in the hope of getting an emotional answer. The result: stereotyped answers and stereotyped apologies. Mother usually ended the evening by saying, 'Sorry.' Her mother had been fond of quoting the Bible: 'Let not the sun go down upon thy wrath.' Only there was no wrath, merely malice.

Denham with her bulging tyre of fat ought to have been stereotyped, too, a good solid middle-class mum, but she wasn't. She was vital, a good teacher, the backbone of the solid average passes we had been able to chalk up this year. Competent, but . . . my mind curled away from her disloyalty.

'So you like our pink-haired Head,' she said, feeding the tortured pages into her machine. 'You paint together and read poetry together. Tennyson, I presume. If I remember correctly she never goes past Tennyson. And you also paint every Wednesday evening and Saturday afternoon and she talks every other day about worthwhile jobs and professional vocations, and the redemption of the rural illiterate, but of course no rise in salary, not even as a reward for twelve months' bloody hard, bloody successful work.'

Her brown-green blasphemous eyes looked straight at me and I quivered beneath the lash of her treachery. 'You forget,' I said, 'I was one of the rural illiterate, too.'

'Probably,' said Louise Hillard, still in her twenties, town-smart, confident, 'probably that is why you have been such a successful little girl in this place. Why, I'm sure every time our Ina downs a bottle of Scotch she thinks of you with gratitude, a good solid workhorse for ever pulling his load and never asking for another wisp of hay.'

'Shut up, Louise,' said Ann Denham.

I drew a hard black line through the prose in front of me. Hopeless, hopeless. 'Mother says I must have French for my matric.' 'You, my dear winsome, fresh dew-face, have not even the minimum of English, let alone French. You are brainless.' My black line looked comforting, the obliteration of love-expectant youth. Damn them. Why should they expect so much?

My eyes flicked automatically over the next prose but even as I read it correctly I saw not words but Louise Hillard. 'I worked in the economics department at Sydney University,' she said the first day I met her. 'But of course that was well after your time.' I knew Louise had meant me to feel old and she succeeded. But why lie, Louise?

'She's a bloody constitutional liar,' said pudgy-handed Ann Denham. 'She worked there all right, but she forgets to tell you she was merely the secretary. Shorthand and typing were her specialty then. Odd thing though, she's a gifted economics teacher without an ounce of background. She swots it up.'

Lying, unscrupulous Louise. She was my problem now. What does a loyal teacher tell? Ina trusted me, Ina needed help.

Dear Louise, wooing girls to her honours courses with teas on Saturday afternoon; scented tea fragrant with the heavy innuendoes, girls melting before the cool gentle invitation to unburden themselves about their headmistress and other members of staff.

How could Louise be so like Robert? Robert was stolid, black-haired, with creases of stupidity in the dents of his nose —but cunning. Louise was cunning too, even though her nose was delicate, not blunt. Louise was delicate, like a piece of Balinese carving. Father had a piece of Balinese carving some long-dead friend had brought him from the islands. I wondered where it had gone. It was missing, like the integrity of Louise. Could I really ignore the whispered stories brought into Monday's staff-room after the week-end round of parties which riddle this town at certain levels like a disease?

The proses flicked away under my fingers—good, bad, indifferent. Tomorrow I had promised to approach Miss Spurway on behalf of Mona Edison. Full pay and a week's leave. Was it possible? I cursed Louise's news of Mona's skipping afternoon lessons. I do not like concealing laxness. I was weary of Mona's repetitive complaints, her tortured disloyalty; but in her case there was an excuse. And she was kind: jars of cream for Mother, fresh fruit from her orchard. That morning she had said, 'You will help me, won't you? She may listen to you. I have to see this doctor in Sydney, but I can't afford to take the time off. I need the money for Bill. I deserve the leave, anyway. Most of the people here aren't teachers at all, not like me and you. Not really.'

Her hands twisted like clematis around the cup, nervous, tentative tendrils. 'Louise Hillard talks a lot about being a graduate, but you and I know, don't we, that being a graduate is not being a teacher, now is it? I have my certificate. It makes a difference, doesn't it?'

She was one of those people whose questions clutch, drawing you willy-nilly into the whirlpool of their prejudices.

Her voice was defensive. 'I'm a trained primary teacher, but I have to teach English and maths to secondary pupils here. You see, the duller children have to have a trained teacher. Stands to reason, doesn't it?'

'I suppose it does,' I said. I tried to change the subject to free my spiritual limbs from the clutching voice. 'Why don't you see Miss Cunningham-White?' I asked. 'She's Deputy Head.'

Scorn lifted the lines on her forehead and the tiny waves of short-cropped hair rose with them. 'Don't tell me, don't tell me, Miriam. Do you always put in the Cunningham? Well, I don't. As far as I'm concerned she's plain Miss White. And is she really Deputy? Stay long enough here and they call you Deputy. It's a matter of habit. But you do the work. After all, what has she come from? Some little private school in Sydney and a Ladies' Music College. Not a day's training.'

'The Head has to rely on someone,' I said. 'Miss Cunningham-White is resident staff, after all.'

'She relies on you.'

Mona Edison's thin fingers stroked her cup, stroked her hair, ran in nervous patterns along the top of the table. 'Anyway, White's nose will be out of joint next month. There's a new resident coming. Mrs Dewey from England. God knows what she'll be like. I hate these pommies. They still think of us as some sort of superannuated convicts. I teach thirty-two periods. Do you think a new-chum could do that? I couldn't do it myself if I were untrained.' Her fingers quivered. 'Yet I'm the worst paid member of this staff. "So sorry," says pink halo behind the cigarette smoke. "I could do something of course if you had your degree, but as it is"—gentle shrug of her shoulders—"not a hope, I'm afraid." Liar! She knows I'm in a cleft stick with my kidneys and an invalid husband. Legs blown away in the last war. Trust Bill. Never did get out of the way of anything fast enough.'

I smoothed my frock, good practical nylon, easy to wash. It was too girlish, I knew, and the orange flowers spilling over a yellow background did not suit my sallow skin. But it didn't really matter; and I had sacrificed aesthetics to practicality for so long. I walked to the sink to wash my cup so that Mona Edison would not feel the chill in my face. Pity for her concealed my resentment; and I hate pity. I bent my head over the aged brown stain running along the bottom of the sink.

'Miss Spurway is more understanding than you think. She may not know.'

Over-thin fingers gripped my arm. 'She knows, she knows.' The pitch of the voice lifted with hysteria. 'She knows but she doesn't care. She's too busy trying to catch a man, enjoying herself at the perennial parties that go on in this town. She wouldn't even think of battling for her staff.'

I turned round and gently removed the hand. 'Mona,' I

said, 'I think we ought to drop this subject. Whatever a Head is like I happen to believe the staff owes her loyalty. Otherwise they should leave. Miss Spurway's private life is not my concern.'

'OK,' she said meekly, so meekly I was surprised. 'I understand. You have to be careful. You and me. You with your Mum, me with Bill. We can't afford to lose our jobs, can we?'

My brush pushed the curve round the canvas: it was like taking, I should imagine, a curve in a car, feeling the wheel turn automatically; and I knew it was good. I looked at the reality struggling through the boulders across a dry-as-dust creek into straggling trees. It was formless, pointless, one of the numerous roads of Meridale ending in the frustration of grids and fences. Yet I knew my brush had objectified that echo of harmony suggested by the curve of the road, repeated in the blue mountain barely visible through the trees—that knitted skein of form, scarcely perceptible to the naked eye, that gives meaning to existence.

'But the cow isn't blue,' said Mother. 'It's black. You must try to paint it correctly, Miriam. You're too fond of being silly.' 'Mine's black,' said Robert. 'But it *is* blue,' I said, 'like the rock. Safe and secure, planted on the red soil beneath its feet, and the sky is red and blue.' Was I silly? A gawky child trying to find some harmony in the reality around me. Poor Mother, life conditioned by a limp, a drag of the foot over the dust of living, bogged down in black landscapes speckled white with little Roberts.

I glanced across at Ina Spurway's painting. It was pink. A mist of pink on dusty red eucalyptus-trees, pink-edged serrated clouds hiding the mountains. Sunset clouds, or was it perhaps sunrise? I knew she had missed the curve, the hint of form that gives meaning to the endless repetition of shapes. But it did not matter; art is not everything. Her pink-misted pictures mimicked her pink-haloed hair, lost themselves in her red-rimmed glasses, and I loved her. Why did I think 'love'? Normally I thought 'loyalty'; but Saturday was love,

Monday was duty. Dear Saturday, caught between the fret and fever of the week, the nonchalance of bored children: Mr Daley's afternoon of practical art. The smell of petrol and leather in Ina's Mini Minor, the throb of hearts with engines, and later the smell of turps and the bronchial wheeze of Freddy's breath.

'Mrs Dewey comes today,' Ina said, pressing pink into the heart of a gum-tree. 'We'll have to meet the train.'

I nodded, pushing my hair behind my ears. I edged the mountain with blue-grey, then stopped—startled as a line of uncharacteristic grey streaked across Ina's painting, destroying the brolga-pink illusion.

'It will have to be you,' she said. 'Cunningham-White is inefficient.'

I completed the mountain. I painted slowly, deliberately, without emotion. 'As you wish,' I said, 'but Miss Cunningham-White is Deputy Head.' 'Miriam, Miriam. I thought I could trust you.' She waved her brush at me in admonition. The curve of my tree wobbled. I had to repaint it.

'You *can* trust me,' I said. 'I'll do as you ask.'

I was too loyal to worry her with my problems. Side-of-mouth Cunningham-White had not been pleasant since Ina had given me so many of her Deputy's duties. That they were duties which had slipped into my keeping unsought, unwanted, made little difference. The aside comments, barely perceptible at first, became a little louder as the year proceeded. 'There are those who usurp the rights of others'; and Mona Edison coming in like a refrain at appropriate points, 'Real organisation needs a trained teacher, Miss White.'

'What should I do about Louise Hillard?' Ina said.

I felt the rigidity of my muscles push against the taut skin. 'You are asking my advice?'

'I am asking your advice.' A second grey streak followed the first across the painting. She must be disturbed.

Robert had told tales. Telling tales was anathema to me; but what could I do? I was a member of her staff. She asked my advice outright, appointed me to positions of trust. And I loved her.

'Somebody,' said Ann Denham, watching the meths splurge across her stencil, unreadable splodges for the delectation of children, 'carefully carries stories from this room to our gay and charming Head. How else could she possibly know I had called her a bastard of the first order? Do you like those that tell tales, Miriam, my dear?'

The water splashed, plink, plonk, icy cold against the stain of coffee in the sink but my hands remained steady. 'My brother told tales,' I said. 'I never liked him. But loyalty is another matter. Sometimes it is necessary if you hold a position of authority.'

And Ann Denham flicked her stencils—intensely lovely odour of meths—through her fingers. 'Blank, blank, blankety blank,' she said. 'What an infernal machine! And that rather points the finger at you, doesn't it, Miss Cunningham-White? The only one with that sort of authority amongst us. Deputy Head, but the little ant has been busy undermining you, too. Somehow I don't think our informer is you. You'd better watch out or you'll be plain White, my dear. Of course, I must be fair. It could be the lovely Louise; or poor, poor frightened Mrs Ellis looking in vain for a class she can control; but somehow, Miriam, I don't think so, I don't think so.'

'Don't put any more grey,' I said to Ina. 'It spoils the illusion. Here, give me your brush.' I jabbed at Ina's painting, watching the blend of paint eliminate the jagged edges.

'I should dismiss Louise,' I said. 'She is a trouble-maker.'

Ina Spurway pushed her stool away and lay full length on the eucalyptus-nutted ground. She lit a cigarette. 'I thought so,' she said. 'Tell me.'

'It doesn't sound much, but it is,' I said. 'Personal, private blackmail for increased salary, failing to turn up if thwarted, discussing staff with girls, anything for first-class honours in her subject even if they fail elsewhere.' I hesitated. 'What's more, she drinks.'

'True, oh true,' said Ina; 'but so do I and so does Denham.'

I felt awkward, hot. 'She spreads stories about you,' I said defensively.

The blue eyes retreated behind the lenses. She jabbed the burning cigarette against an ant. I almost said, 'Don't.' I wished she wouldn't indulge these impulses of cruelty, but it was not my job to criticise. Anyway, I knew she was testing me. She watched my face. I said nothing and she threw the cigarette away.

'Stories,' she repeated. 'Such as?'

'Your drinking all her Scotch at a party. Making up to men.'

'Do you believe her?' she said.

'Of course not.'

She sat up, raised her brush and slashed a line of black across her painting.

'Don't!' I said. 'You've spoilt it.'

She laughed. 'What a peculiar girl you are, Miriam. You let me torture an ant unprotesting, but you yell your head off if I harm a painting. Perhaps you ought to believe those stories, dear Miriam. They may be true.' Her eyes were lost to me altogether.

I put down my brush. I knew I looked gaunt, ungainly. I could see the rugged outline of my hip bone through the nylon frock. 'I respect you,' I said. 'Even if they were true I should respect you. But, true or false, no teacher with any sense of loyalty would repeat them in a staff-room.'

Her eyes came back. She laughed. 'You are right,' she said. 'I shall dismiss her, but I shall have a fight with Council. Are you willing to support me if I invite you to the meeting? They respect you.' I hated the thought of standing before my pot-bellied contemporaries as a sort of Judas, but I agreed. Ina came first.

Daley stood behind our stools. His frog eyes popped over our work. I remembered them popping over a frog we dissected in fourth year and I wanted to laugh. I knew he liked my painting even though he criticised the black sky. Good old Froggy, the perfect delineator of local landscape in regulated techniques for ever and ever, landscapes reborn in all the canvases under his tuition. Mine made him uneasy, but he could not deny the flash of perception. He had it himself.

He looked at Ina Spurway's painting. 'Pink illusion,' he said, 'joined by hard black reality. So unnecessary, don't you think, my dear, when you have all these lovely trees and creeks and hills to depict? Such wonderful shadows here on the tableland.'

The edge of Ina's lips moved. I knew she was laughing inside. 'Thank you,' she said gravely. 'I'm improving, though. Soon I shall be able to paint just like the rest of you.'

Jocular Daley's fingers moved over her shoulder. Freddy Daley had always had tactile fingers tangling in Hazel Livingstone's hair from the desk behind her. Even so, I, in the seat across the aisle, gingerly unnoticed, getting all my sums right, had always liked his hands. Ina Spurway moved her shoulder and the hand fell to his side.

'Well, Mr Daley,' she said, 'I think we'll have to pack up. Miss Hansen and I have to meet a new teacher on the day train.'

I did not like Mrs Dewey. Cockney English trying out the colonies. She was the oddest-shaped woman I had ever seen, an excessive posterior tacked onto an overdeveloped bust. I doubt if she were five feet.

Miss Cunningham-White edged over to me. Her protruding but not over-protruding eyes indicated she was speaking, but the voice that came from the side of her mouth through the fine white teeth was barely audible. Miss Cunningham-White always spoke like that when she had something private to communicate.

'She is not a lady. You can see that. Such coarse hands.' The confidential stoop became more pronounced. Her cheek almost touched mine. 'You know, I don't think she owns a pair of gloves.'

'Gloves are not important,' I said. The ridge on her lip closed a fraction over her solid well-bred teeth, the lip of a pedigree dog. 'You know what I mean,' she said. 'I wouldn't mind, but music is so essential for young ladies.'

I remembered the time-table. 'Come, come,' I said. 'She is only taking the choir, after all. You can have all the private lessons.'

For twenty years the choir had been streaking 'Over the Hills and Far Away', and frolicking with the 'Nymphs and Shepherds' under Miss Cunningham-White's superbly lady-like baton.

'Mrs Dewey,' said Ina, 'has her MusB(ac). I'm going to give her the choir. It needs a little pep.'

Miss Cunningham-White looked stonily at me. 'Ever since Miss Spurway came my jobs have gradually disappeared. Sometimes, Miss Hansen, I think you ought to be a little more honest.'

I felt the flush in my neck, but my voice remained steady. 'Imagine she's Mother,' I said to myself. 'Keep calm.'

'Miss Cunningham-White,' I said, 'I am a teacher. Miss Spurway is our principal. I merely follow her decisions.'

The previous evening Robert had thumped the table. 'You were always the same,' he had said. 'You could never bear anyone else to have anything. You tried to take my tadpole, remember?'

'I found it,' I said. He was in his forties now, big, swarthy, stupid, and still full of resentment over a wretched tadpole. He put his hairy arm on mine.

'Say,' he said, 'let's talk this over sensibly.'

'Mother needs an operation,' I said. 'It is only fair we should both contribute.'

'Fair!' he yelled. 'Fair? There's nothing fair here, Miriam. You're a wealthy old maid with no dependants and you try to take the bread and butter from my kids' mouths.'

I looked at him stiffly. Why should I discuss my private affairs with Robert? At Etherington I earned half my former salary. There were no increments. I had approached Ina from

time to time, tentatively, probing, but I knew her problems
with Council. It was not much use.

'Good little Miriam,' said Robert, 'so good. But you've
never loved anyone, have you?'

'I shall do my duty,' I said.

'It's all very well for you,' said Cunningham-White; 'you have
your mother, you have your job. You have everything.'

I banged down the edge of my desk. 'Mrs Dewey,' I said
as the little woman came through the door, 'could you let me
have the practice evenings for *The Gondoliers*? I'll have to
rearrange the prep. time-table.'

It was a terrible spring even though the rest of the staff
later referred to it as the exciting year, but all through winter
I had felt the simmer of poisoned life beneath the surface of
staff relationships. Mrs Dewey worked hard and Ina Spurway
liked her. Good pat-you-on-the-back Gladys; but somehow I
now sided with Miss Cunningham-White. I had not previously been susceptible to her genteel snobberies, but Gladys
Dewey was not a lady. Still, she worked hard. *The Gondoliers*
added a dimension of inner tension to the school. We floated
through winter on a cloud of gauzy costumes, paper flowers
and streamers. Dewey stood at my shoulder as I pointed out
my stage arrangements—an unexpected warm day in July
and the sweat spread in an ugly splotch under her arm-pits.
Ina had not come to our art classes for a fortnight. Saturday
was bare. I marked books and dug the garden.

'Sorry, Miriam,' Ina said, tucking her beautifully shod feet
under her on Mother's sofa. 'Gladys is here for a year only.
Someone has to show her round.'

I smelt Dewey's stale breath near my face and her tiny eyes
probed through my shoulder. She gave my drawings a cursory
glance. 'I have no worries in this connection, Miss Hansen.
Miss Spurway tells me you do everything competently—
utterly reliable, she said.' I turned to look at her, and the pin-
prick eyes stared unsmiling out of their wads of flesh. I felt
belittled.

As I looked at the sweat-stained grey frock, the diminutive eyes, the grotesque shape, I was at a loss to understand Gladys's attraction for the rest of the teachers. They clustered around her smoking and gossiping, but when I opened the door there was always silence. Only fragments of vulgarity wafted across to me. Father had never allowed us to tell dirty jokes.

'Well, he kept the mermaid in the bath, see? But one day his wife came home early.'

'Good on her,' said Mona Edison. 'That's what all the bastards need. Go on.' Gladys Dewey's eye caught mine around the door. 'Get to the point,' said Ann Denham.

Gladys raised her voice. 'Oh, the point. Why, he simply pulled out the plug and the mermaid swam away down the plug hole.'

'Is that all?' said Mona.

'That's all,' said Gladys Dewey.

'No, it isn't.' Mrs Ellis thrust her nervous squirrel-like nose into the group. 'My husband told me the rest. When he went into . . .' I saw Ann Denham's foot touch Mrs Ellis's leg while Gladys pushed her aside.

'Got those seats yet, Miriam?' We looked at each other. 'They're ready,' I said. 'I've been working instead of worrying about mermaids that go down the plug hole.' I sat beside Miss Cunningham-White who was embroidering hats for the gondoliers. The voice slipped in a comic-strip balloon from the side of her mouth. 'I hope you don't think, Miriam, that I listen willingly to these stories.'

'I don't think anything,' I said quite audibly. 'I'm far too busy.'

I was never invited to Gladys's room, or should I say THE ROOM in capitals? The front room of staff cottage was big and airy, even if derelict like the rest of the cottage. Gladys was lucky to get it. She was always slipping across to her den. There were times when the staff-room was empty. Gladys's room was the staff rendezvous, but they never invited me.

Miss Spurway arranged her delicate cups on her silver tray.

'Glad you could spare a moment to have tea with me,' she said. I remembered our first interview. Her red glasses still lit the blue eyes, her hair, newly rinsed, shone palely.

'I was glad to come,' I said. 'None of them are in the staff-room. They're having morning tea at the cottage. I'm the ugly duckling. Mrs Dewey never asks me to the den.'

'I'm sorry,' said Ina. 'I should think most of them simply ask themselves. It's your air of responsibility, Miriam. They stand in awe of you.'

'Oh,' I said.

Ina lit a cigarette. 'You need some vices, Miriam. Still, I'm glad you're not like the rest. I need someone I can trust.'

I said nothing. Ina leant across her desk. 'What's worrying you, Miriam?' I forgot the staff. I saw Mother's face cramped with pain, I heard the slivers of malice that punctuated her conversation the minute I came in the door.

'Mother needs an operation,' I said.

Ina's eyes were sympathetic. 'I'm sorry.'

I felt all the ridgy big bones in my body. 'I need more money.'

I saw the eyes retreat, although the mouth still expressed sympathy. 'I'll do my best, Miss Hansen,' she said, 'but you know our difficulties. If I give you a rise they'll all want one. They always do.'

I looked at my shoes, my well-kept feet shod in ugliness. Why should they know? I thought. Then I regretted my dis-loyalty. Of course they always knew. 'That's all right,' I said. 'I'll manage somehow.' I felt unbearable pride.

The eyes came back. She came round to my side of the table and put an arm on my shoulder. 'You're too thin, Miriam.'

'I have always been gaunt,' I said. 'I take after Father.'

'You know I couldn't manage here without you,' she said. I felt my fingers shaking. 'I was about to give up when you came. I'll do my best—honestly, Miriam. It's not my fault. We *have* got somewhere, you and I.'

My rise did not come through. Ina Spurway carefully

avoided the matter and so did I. Avoidance is an art. I was skilled at it. Avoiding the bathroom door while Father showered, spilling the water like waterfalls over his body and . . . well after the first time I avoided it Father usually remembered to shut the door. I avoided the sounds in the night, the creak of the bed that Mother oiled frantically every day, and I avoided the knowledge of indecencies that Robert tried to force upon me. Watch the birds, Miriam, watch the cock. I was glad when we ate them with their redcombed sexuality. So Ina avoided the subject and so did I. I had reasons, too. I saw the tiny creases of worry on her forehead. I saw her twice in town with Maurice Furlonger and I knew he was head man on the school Council. I am sure nothing but worry would have driven Ina to spend even a minute with him. It was hard to avoid Maurice Furlonger and his reputation.

Even so she was at her gayest for the annual cocktail party between staff and Council. She wore blue and changed her rinse to match. I have always wondered at the susceptibility of even intelligent people to the propaganda of advertising. She would have looked just as lovely with grey hair—grey wisps of smoke, grey fog, grey rocks above still streams, lovely softness of grey. But I smiled tolerantly. My own sandy hair would have resisted any rinse. Who was I to judge?

Almost reluctantly, I admitted its effect. Ina Spurway was an illusion of haze, a spinning tiny figure, not quite real. Her new silver-framed glasses lifted her eyes and they shone blue and sparkling. I felt proud of her. She stood posed in the centre of the room with the councillors grouped around her, great squat moths near a lovely lamp. I ran my eyes over Maurice Furlonger, jowled and balding and arrogantly confident. I felt my flesh crawl as his coarse hand ran surreptitiously along Miss Spurway's arm. I suppose you cannot snub the head councillor.

I heard sober Jim Graves say something and her blue eyes flashed up at him. 'What an interesting idea, Mr Graves.' Her soft voice melted with appreciation. Good, sober old Gravesy plodding his way through Latin proses. I had sat with him for

Latin in our fifth year. 'Gosh, Miriam, I won't copy it exactly. Old Buck out there will never know.'

Of course I had refused. I remember screwing my hair perplexedly in a tight ball, because I liked him but I did not believe in copying. 'No,' I said, 'but I'll go over some of the points with you.' Somehow it never seemed to help. He had failed his Leaving. He nodded to me as I passed. 'Good to see you, Miriam. I bet you stop the little so-and-sos copying.' I smiled. Every time I met him I was struck anew with the complete unimportance of academic achievement. It was not central to life at all. His coat was crumpled as it had always been crumpled, but his general air was prosperous. Why shouldn't it be? He ran one of the best motels in town. He could afford to patronise me, sandy-haired dux of the class teaching French for a pittance to his dumb kids. Gravesy would die rich. Not that he was the ambitious one; that honour belonged to two-timing sweet-scented Della. Dumb Della. I don't know at what point she sensed that slow Jimmy Graves had the aroma of success. But she did. Slow Jim and dumb Della. Always plaguing the school, blaming Spurway, blaming us for their kids' failures. I nearly lent Jim a book on genetics, but it would probably have been as ineffective as my help with his proses. 'Gosh, you're a brick, Miriam. Thanks. I'll take you to the farewell social.' But he hadn't taken me. He had taken dumb Della and I had sat in a ridiculous frilly pink frock with my back glued to the wall except for the farewell dance when they had hauled along a reluctant fourth year with bad breath to dance with me.

I watched Della trying to edge her now middle-aged dumb prettiness into the group around Ina Spurway. It was like a rather blatant sunbeam trying to compete with silver, blue-silver, moonlight. Five minutes later she was back with the women, sulking disconsolately. I walked over to talk to her. Della was more dangerous than Ina knew.

That was our role at the cocktail party. The teachers kept the wives happy while Ina courted the men. I set my face into lines of efficiency and listened to their daughters' problems once removed. Good sensible Miriam. Their fourth, sixth, tenth cousin once removed, whom they now patronised as fee-paying parents after spitefully pitying her from the desks of High School. For a moment I hated their motherly togetherness, their polite no-longer innocent eyes, their child-preoccupied minds. I clenched my glass too hard and the sherry which I did not normally drink spilt over the rim.

'Really, Miriam, can't you be careful?' Mena Furlonger's hen-like brown eye flicked over me, but her own hands were shaking.

'Sorry, Mena,' I said. 'I am naturally unsteady.'

'Liar,' she said. She did not look at me. Her eyes moved up and down her husband's back—click, click like a computer—as if she could record his patent infidelities. 'Look at him,' she said. 'Look at him. I'll get rid of that woman if it's the last thing I do.'

'That woman,' I said, 'is my headmistress.'

'And Maurice, dear Miriam, is one of your employers. For God's sake drop the green-as-grass mannerisms for once in your life. You can't be as dumb as all that. Everyone knows.'

'Knows what?'

'That Maurice has been running around with that gold-digging pink-dyed principal of yours for weeks.'

I was genuinely shocked. 'Don't be silly, Mena!' Then irrelevantly, 'Anyway, it's blue.'

'Don't be stupid,' she almost shouted. I could see the hairs on the lobes of her ears prick.

'Sh!' I said. 'Everyone will hear you. You don't want a scandal.' I placed my hand on her expensive arm. She pushed it away and banged her glass on a nearby coffee table. It was cedar, good cedar. Only a barbarian like Mena could treat it with such carelessness.

'Everyone, except apparently poor dumb you, knows already, cousin dear.' She spoke quite audibly and I could feel the current of repressed curiosity in the backs of those nearest to me. 'You can tell Maurice, when he ceases to paw that elevated governess, that I've gone home.'

The heads in the room except those centred on Ina Spurway turned as Mena walked firmly from the room. The eyelid
above the hen eye was twitching. I was disturbed, not by the
accusations of Mena Furlonger. I did not believe them. But
she was vindictive. I wanted to warn Ina, but I stood stiffly in
the middle of the room.

The voice of the staff washed over me in familiar rhythms.
'Next year we'll be getting one of the Croziers. You know the
big store people in Sydney? I thought you'd be interested.
Having the right people in the school is so important, isn't it?'

Cunningham-White, I noted, exulting to a captured grazier.
The record switched to Ann Denham. 'Of course Jean will
get her damn first level. She couldn't miss, not with her brains
and my teaching.' Delighted laughter from Jean Dennis's
parents. Good old Ann. I had rather liked drinking tea with
her. I did not know she liked Louise. 'And what did happen
to Louise Hillard? Mary's economics has been going down
hill ever since she left?' Old whingey Mavis Drew, whose first
teeth never fell out. It was a wonder she even remembered
the child took economics. When I first knew Mavis—in kindergarten I think—she remembered nothing of importance.
Her memory had remained as childlike as her teeth. Your cue,
Mona. 'She wasn't trained. In the final count, it is training
that matters. What Mary really needs . . .' I pushed past to
the centre group. I wondered if Mona would ever know how
like a stuck gramophone needle she sounded.

Maurice Furlonger was breathing down Ina Spurway's
neck, but I managed to hiss into his ear, great hairy baby-
pink caterpillar, like his nostrils: 'Mena's left. She asked me
to tell you.'

'God,' he said, but he did not even turn his head. I could
have been a voice on a two-way radio. He made no move to
depart.

The next day the difference with Ann Denham flowed into an
open quarrel. I don't know why Ina Spurway allowed her to
give her own history prizes unsupervised. We always chose

the girls' books so carefully, books on which we should be proud to place the school crest, books which embodied or at least did not disgrace the principles for which we stood. Ann Denham gave three history prizes and told the winners to choose their own books at the local bookshop. I have never believed that children should be entrusted with decisions that belong properly to an adult. They have a natural aptitude for rubbish or even worse.

That morning it was my job to prepare the books for the annual prize-giving. They lay in front of me, a semi-popular novel by a semi-popular novelist, but it did at least deal with a satisfactory theme, the destruction of the world by nuclear war. There was a volume of detective stories, and *Lolita*. I hesitated. I read detective stories myself, but I knew that Miss Spurway considered them of no literary importance. I had heard about *Lolita*. I had never read it and I never wanted to read it. It was the sort of book that no Church school could adorn with its school crest. I went down to Ina's office.

She glanced at the pile. 'We certainly can't allow the detective stories. We are an educational institution. And the nuclear war novel is rather lightweight for the school crest.' She picked up *Lolita* and smiled. 'This one is a classic.'

I stirred uneasily. There were times undoubtedly when Ina ceased to be a headmistress, when her natural feeling for propriety became lost in some private world of her own. I tried to be tactful, although a pulse twittered uneasily in my throat. 'But hardly suitable for a schoolgirl,' I said.

She glanced at me. I felt the blue eyes focus gimlet-like on my neck where the pulse twittered and I found myself pressing it down with one finger. 'But, my dear Miriam, that book is about a schoolgirl.'

'So I've heard.' I tried hard to italicise my naturally flat voice.

'You mean you haven't read it?'

I blushed, but I stuck to my point. 'I am glad to say, no. And with the Church President from Sydney coming and with his wife presenting the prizes—' I paused significantly.

She leant forward. 'Dear Miriam. How you do protect me. You mean my employing authority might not like an ex-banned book in the hands of our innocents?' She laughed. 'It would be amusing,' she said. Then she stood up briskly. 'I bow to your judgment, Miriam. You have an instinct for non-conformist niceties. Send the girls back to the bookshop and tell them to change them for more suitable fare. What about Dickens?' Her tone was ironic. 'If they go immediately there will still be time for you to process the books before the ceremony.'

Barbara Anderson, who owned the nuclear war novel, agreed readily. Meryl Davies, who had a taste for detection, co-operated sulkily. But Gretchen Dutch stood obstinately on the threshold of the staff-room and refused to go. Gretchen was tall, clear-eyed, insolent, and had a first-class mind. The 'Dutch' was an Anglicisation of Deutsch, camouflage for a background which, according to rumour, placed Daddy in Hitler's SS.

I was one of those who liked Gretchen, but I did not trust her. We need migrants, it is true, but I can only regret the necessity for imposing foreign patterns on good Australian stock.

Gretchen held *Lolita* firmly in her hand. 'I do not understand,' she said. 'Miss Spurway was talking to me yesterday and she said it was an excellent choice.' I cursed for the first time our pink-haloed Head.

'I'm not going to argue,' I began. I put out my hand to take the book and Gretchen thrust it behind her just as Ann Denham came round the corner. Her well-fleshed face was attractive that morning. I could hear her singing to herself as she came.

Gretchen turned to her. 'They won't let me keep my book, Mrs Denham.' Ann Denham laughed. 'Don't be silly, Gretchen. You're a mature girl. It's well within your scope. A good choice, I thought.'

I looked significantly at Gretchen. 'I think I should talk to you alone, Ann. This is a Church school, you know. There are moral standards.'

The good humour vanished from her face. 'You, of course, are our expert on morality?' She thrust her jaw close to mine. 'Are you trying to tell me that my prizes are to be bloody well censored by you, Miss Hansen?'

I saw Gretchen's rather thick brows rise with interest. I tried to shut the door. Ann put one foot in it. 'Not yet, Miriam dear. This is one fight you're not going to wage behind closed doors. Where are the others, Gretchen?' Gretchen, with the insidious eagerness of the young anxious to please, said, 'Barbara and Meryl were ordered to change their books, too, Mrs Denham. They're down at the shop now. But I wouldn't go.' There was a note of vindictive triumph in her voice as she glanced at me. 'I should bloody well think not,' Denham answered.

Mrs Dewey moved across to the door. She took the book from Gretchen's hands. 'Run off now,' she said. 'Mrs Denham will see you later.' Gretchen left reluctantly. There was something in the pudgy eye of Dewey that did not encourage disobedience. She shut the door; only the drop of sweat spreading across her strained grey silk arm-pits indicated her anxiety. I was grateful to her. She had some sense of school discipline. I was doubly grateful as Ann Denham continued to shout, oblivious of her surroundings.

'Just occasionally,' she said, 'very occasionally we are given in this dump of a place a human being with the spark of real intelligence. Gretchen Dutch is one. I don't care if she's rude, I don't care if she's arrogant. She has that divine spark which is given to us as teachers to nurture. She is nearly eighteen. The comicality of sexual perversion may make you crawl, Miriam Hansen, locked in your tight Australian villa with your maidenhead intact, but I assure you that to Gretchen's family who knew the horrors of the Russian invasion of Austria, who scrabbled for pieces of food on the street, the obscenity you shrink from is only an aspect of reality.' To my relief her voice softened. 'I can't expect you to understand the literary issue,' she said nastily, 'but perhaps you could explain, while you're on the topic, why Meryl was also forbidden to enjoy her creepy stories. Not even you could find *them* obscene.'

I felt on safer ground. I could not move, for Ann had edged me back against the wall. I said primly, 'I enjoy a detective story myself, but we can't give lightweight material as prizes.'

'You talk like an assistant in the drapery department,' she said. 'Nothing lightweight, madam, only good old heavy tweeds. And so, dear Miriam, we load them every year with a stack of books that most of our girls will never open. For your information, dear Miriam, Bierce, Poe, Ellin, Chandler and West are all American short-story writers of the first order. You see, my dear Miriam, a High School course in English hardly befits you to make lifelong judgments on literature in the name of others.'

I could feel my neck getting hot. I fought not to cry. My English teacher had had stringy grey hair dyed a streaky brown, a long heavy chin, and a tongue like an acid drop. 'I have no doubt you are clever, Miriam Hansen, but there is only one word for your own literary efforts, "banal". "Dux" is not a synonym for "educated", you know.' I had felt the enjoyment of a class watching the kill, the discomfiture of the paragon.

Ann Denham leant her well-padded rear against a desk. 'What is more, Miriam, I paid for those books. Why wasn't I informed of this decision?'

'There was no time,' I said. 'I have to process these books for the ceremony this week.' My hair began to rise like the fur of a cat along my neck. 'You part-time women don't do it, oh no! You have to trot home to your precious houses and husbands as soon as you drop the last word of wisdom in front of the swine. That's how you think, isn't it? Let old Miriam process the books, organise speech day, collect the sports cups, see that they are polished, draw up the time-table. Where were you at 9 o'clock? Tell me that.'

There was a silence in the room which isolated Ann and myself. The others watched as if suspended in a play set.

'I was bloody well where a phone could have reached me in two seconds flat.' Ann's shoulders hunched like a cat ready to spring. 'And allow me to tell you, Miriam, that if the jobs fall on your shoulders you have only yourself to blame. Yes, Miss Spurway; No, Miss Spurway. Miss Spurway would like this, Miss Spurway would like that. Who got Louise the sack, tell me that? Who carefully edged poor old Miss Cunningham-White into an inferior position? Who refused to join in our attempt to form an industrial union?'

I pushed her back. 'Get away from me,' I said. 'You have no loyalty, any of you. You accept a salary to do a job and you bicker and gossip and undermine the school every minute of the day. It is my duty to run things as Miss Spurway wants them.'

Ann Denham was shaking. 'If you were not totally ignorant of history, Miriam, you would recognise the classic argument of the German High Command. Doesn't it ever dawn on you that loyalties may conflict, that you may have a duty to humanity as well, even if it does not pay you? You may not know it, but Louise Hillard's job here kept her sane. Her personal life was a mess, her husband an impossible sadist. She committed suicide last week in Sydney. I wasn't going to tell you that, but I think now you ought to know.' She walked to the sink and picked up the kettle. It wobbled in her grasp. I stood unmoving.

Gladys Dewey took the kettle gently from Ann. 'Come over to the cottage,' she said. 'I've just restocked the wardrobe.'

'Thanks, Glad,' said Ann. 'I need it.' They moved to the door, brushing my arms as they passed. At the door Ann paused. 'If Gretchen does not receive that book,' she said before shutting it, 'my resignation will be on Spurway's table tomorrow. Believe me, Miriam, she can't afford to lose me as well as Louise.'

My nylon shirtmaker clung unpleasantly to my body and I knew I was sweating. Shapes of tiny Louise lying dead swirled in grotesque patterns within my head; Louise with blood trickling down her glasses from a shattered eye, Louise turning blue from poison, Louise dangling with pointed Oriental feet from a ceiling, Louise a contortion of limbs. 'Thank you, Miriam,' said the voices. 'Thank you, thank you.'

'I didn't know,' I said.

'Know what?' The question came from Mrs Ellis. The bell had just ended the morning session and she fluttered, all palpitation and heart-beats. I did not answer.

'What has been happening?' she said. 'I was giving a lesson and Ann Denham's voice came through quite audibly. In fact Lesley Durham looked up from her work. "Mrs Denham swore," she said. I was most embarrassed, but I shut her up. I must say, however, it did seem a little odd.'

Mona Edison looked coldly at her. 'Forget it, Janet, forget it.' I saw her head move imperceptibly in my direction. Janet moved across to her. Miss Cunningham-White came over to me. 'I'm sorry, Miriam. Ann Denham is not a lady. That is quite obvious. I agree with you entirely. Both she and Louise Hillard have been giving the girls most unsuitable books.'

'Louise is dead,' I said.

'Well, it's not your fault,' said Mona tartly.

My mind clutched at an irrelevant fragment. 'Why wardrobe?' I said. 'Why did Mrs Dewey invite Ann to her wardrobe?'

Mona Edison laughed. 'I guess you had to know some time, Miriam. The wardrobe is Mrs Dewey's private cellar. Well stocked, too.'

Miss Cunningham-White quivered, nose, hands, even feet. 'You mean they drink?'

'Well,' said Mona, 'they don't wash in it. Sorry, Miss White, we didn't tell you because we know you are a teetotaller. Obviously you wouldn't be interested.'

'Of course not,' said White happily.

'And me?' My voice sounded as if it came from somewhere a long way off. Mona shrugged. 'Let's face it, Miriam. It

would have worried your conscience. There was no point.
Duty would win.'

'I see,' I said.

'I must say,' added Mona, 'that old sweaty-horse mixes the
best gin sling I've ever tasted.'

Mrs Ellis giggled. 'I prefer her brandies and lime,' she said.

'And Council?' I asked. 'What would have happened to
Miss Spurway if the Council had found out? Her innocence
wouldn't have saved her. They'd have held her responsible.'

Mona laughed and Mrs Ellis stuttered, 'Th-th-that's all
right, Miriam. She comes over for an odd nip, too. Things get
her down occasionally. "It's good," she says, "to get out of
that madhouse even for a minute".'

'I suppose she likes gin slings, too?'

'Oh, no,' said Mrs Ellis. 'The best Scotch only. Gladys always keeps a bottle of the best Scotch just for her.'

'I don't believe you,' I said.

'Don't be daft,' said Mona. 'It may be a staff cottage,
Miriam, but it isn't a convent. What we do in our own time
is our own business.'

'Mm,' I said. 'Apparently in school time, too.'

I began to stamp the books automatically, mechanically.
Lolita. It went through with the rest. Why should I care?

I walked home. The willows were heavy with heat waving
across the parched brown of the paddocks. The summer dust
on the houses added to my depression. When Robert arrived
truculent, assertive, with a new armoury of arguments to prove
he had no responsibility to Mother, I did not even argue. I
rang Dr Carmichael and told him to arrange a date for the
operation next year.

That night in bed, I cried. I could not remember when I
had last cried. I had not cried at Father's funeral. I had stood
on the bleak hill facing the mountain's purple, blue-clear out-
lines, and watched the red clay fall clump by clump while
Robert and Mother and Aunt Myra wept. 'Why doesn't
Miriam cry?' one of my tiny cousins asked. And my aunt said,
'She was always a hard girl.'

It jangled and cracked into my dream, the reverberation of dreams, and Ina Spurway stood against the wall and the guns pointed at her. Only the soldiers weren't really soldiers. They were members of the staff dressed in red coats and blue trousers and Janet Ellis was saying, 'When I count five!' The drums began and I flung myself between them. 'No,' I said, 'no no no!' And Ann Denham, fatter than ever in her army uniform, said, 'What we do in our time, Miriam, is entirely our affair.' And the noise of the drums grew and grew—and the body that oozed blood on my feet was not Ina's but Louise's body.

'Miriam, Miriam!' Mother's voice and the ringing of the doorbell swelled and swelled. I struggled to consciousness.

It was a police officer. Eleven thirty. Not late, but it felt late. What is it that creates the primitive fear, the guilt of the criminal at the sight of an official uniform? I nearly said, 'I haven't done anything.'

In fact the figure was Henry Beresford. I knew him well. His big brother had been a year behind me at school and I think we were some sort of remote cousin.

'Sorry to trouble you, Miss Hansen,' he said. 'There's been an accident—one of the girls, a teacher. We couldn't find Miss Spurway and we've wasted ten minutes already.'

'Serious?' I asked. 'I'm afraid so,' he said. 'I'll come,' I said, 'straight away.'

Ours is a treacherous town; narrow streets, jagged tar edges, corner fences, hedges high with age. Street-corner accidents were common. The car was Gladys Dewey's. Someone had pulled her from it and the odd-shaped body lay by the side of the road. I turned away. It was no longer a face. I thought, 'She won't be going back to England now.' Out of the corner of my eye I saw an ambulance man cover her with a canvas sheet.

I looked at my feet and saw a trickle of blood brown with dust near the toe of my shoe. I followed the line to where a girl was lying on the edge of the footpath. It was Gretchen. The tops of three of her fingers were missing and the red stream flowed from her twisted hand. I knelt beside her near the ambulance officer who was bandaging her wrist. Someone had tied a tourniquet around her arm. One of the other girls, Narelle Atkins, was screaming, but Gretchen did not scream. Couldn't someone dam that smooth stream of red? 'You must stop her bleeding. You must,' I said. The ambulance officer looked up at me and I saw it was Danny Jones, local boy. I had taught him. He was not very bright. 'I am trying,' he said. 'I have already tied the pressure point.' Dr Mallinson came between us. 'Thanks, Danny,' he said, 'I'll take over. I can't do anything for that woman over there.' Gently he began to move his hands over Gretchen's body. The girl looked at me, her lips clenched with pain. She was brave.

'Miss Hansen.' It was barely more than a whisper. I bent over her. 'I cannot see—' she said—'my hand. I can't see it. You are honest. I know I can trust you.' I looked at her mangled hand, the topless fingers, and I saw part of a little finger lying on the grass edge like a bad practical joke. I took her other hand and I felt it tighten in mine. 'It is injured,' I said. 'It looks as if you have lost a couple of fingers. I'm not sure about the rest of the hand. I think it will depend on the doctors.'

Dr Mallinson raised it in his. 'Don't worry, girlie,' he said, 'we'll do our best.' He was and always had been a kind, affable shoulder-patter. Gretchen looked only at me. 'Thank you,' she said. She turned her head away so that I could not see her cry. I said nothing. I merely sat there, her hand in mine. I heard a screech of brakes and I saw Ina Spurway running across the road. She knelt beside Gladys, but one of the men pulled her away.

'What happened? What happened?' Her voice was hysterical. Standing near her I could smell whisky. She caught my shoulder in a grip so hard I winced. 'Don't look like that, Miriam. For God's sake haven't you ever smelt alcohol before? Everyone drinks a little. I'm sober. Dead cold sober. I've been out with a friend.'

'I'm not interested in your private life,' I said; 'but Gretchen is injured and Gladys is dead. Someone has to get the rest of the girls home. Can you do it?'

'Why did I let them go to the play? Why, why, why?'

'Don't be silly,' I said. 'They go to plays regularly. This is an accident.'

'But I knew Gladys was the only one with a car at school. I knew she was not reliable. I knew she shouldn't drive.'

'Gladys is dead,' I said firmly. 'We cannot alter that. The ambulance will take Gretchen. I shall go with her. The doctor is checking Karen, Narelle and Susan now. In my opinion they are suffering from nothing worse than shock. You must drive them home, put them to bed and see they get hot drinks and sedatives.' I realised I was speaking slowly as if to a child. Words spelt out in a dark night, and the woman I admired was standing on the road behaving like a child.

'I can't,' she said, 'I can't. Not after this.'

I shook her and the blue hair flopped over the blue glasses. 'It's your duty,' I said. 'You take them.' I propelled her across to the girls. 'Miss Spurway will take you back to school,' I said.

She said nothing. 'You can rely on her,' I said. 'She is your headmistress.' I pushed her elbow hard. 'Yes,' she said. 'Yes. We must get the rest of you to bed.'

Karen said, 'Mrs Dewey!' and began to scream. I slapped her. At the same time I put my arms round her shoulders.

'She'll be all right,' said Ina Spurway. 'Don't worry, girls.' And I thought, 'Why do you lie?' Lies everywhere. I looked straight at Karen. 'Mrs Dewey is dead,' I said, 'and Gretchen is injured. You are lucky. The only way you can help us is to control yourself. I am going with Gretchen.'

Karen squeezed my hand. 'I understand,' she said. 'I'm sorry, Miss Hansen.' 'That's all right,' I said. 'You couldn't help it. I wanted to scream too.' They climbed into the car. I turned back to Gretchen.

That last week before the summer vacation was chaotic. Mrs Dewey was not buried in Meridale, so we were spared the horrors of a school funeral. After three days of X-rays,

and false hope, they amputated Gretchen's hand. Her father
and mother arrived, a tall arrogant man with eyes like Gretchen and a little Jewish-type woman whose hair was bleached
snow white.

Ann Denham also went to see Gretchen. On her return she
came up to me in the staff-room. We had barely spoken since
the *Lolita* affair. Her soft skin rolled into her too fat neck,
but her eyes were kind. 'Gretchen said, "Please thank Miss
Hansen. She is honest. I could not have borne that night without her." ' I pushed my hands against the bones of my face. I
was conscious of pain like neuralgia, but it was not physical.
Can the mind feel pain? 'By the way,' said Ann, 'thanks for
me, too.' 'It was nothing,' I said. 'It was my duty. I was the
teacher present.'

I saw Ann's pudgy face pucker. 'Oh, damn you,' she said.

I wrapped a puce scarf around my face because it was
windy and my face ached. I watched the silk slip through my
hands and I thought, 'My God, why didn't I burn it? Puce and
ginger!' Only Robert's little girl had given it to me and I
always try to use a gift. I walked out into the playground.

That afternoon Ina Spurway sent for me. She was dressed
in grey and her blue-grey hair settled like a mist on sea.

'I am resigning, Miriam.'

'I am sorry,' I said. 'We have achieved a great deal together.'

'The Council does not think so,' she said. 'The Furlongers
and the Graves are apparently dissatisfied. The accident, of
course, makes my position quite untenable although I was
not to blame in any way. It gave them the excuse they needed.'

'You are not to blame,' I repeated, 'for either Gretchen or
for Gladys. She's dead. She drove badly.'

'A Head is blamed for everything,' she said. She looked at
me wryly. 'And not unjustly, Miriam. I encouraged Gladys. I
knew she drank too much. It suited me to forget about it that
evening.'

I felt frozen. My features did not move.

'My dear Miriam, don't look so shocked. I'm glad to go. I'm going to travel. There's a job in Algeria.'

'Algeria?' Africa? To me it was the equivalent of the end of the world. She laughed. 'Such lovely masculine Arab-type men. I'm a real perv. about Arab-type men. They have a High School there. My French is good.'

I tried hard to control the tic in my features. She had never spoken coarsely to me before. Even so, I thought I understood.

'I hope you will be happy.'

'Thanks, Miriam.' She smiled and took my hand. 'Thanks for everything—loyalty beyond duty. I did enjoy painting with you.'

In the staff-room their speculations spilt around me, but I said nothing. Miss Cunningham-White edged over. Only her teeth moved. 'I told the Council about the wardrobe,' she said. 'I thought they ought to know there had been drinking on Church premises. Don't you agree?'

I picked up my purse. 'Miss Cunningham-White,' I interrupted. Quite audibly for the benefit of the entire staff. 'You ought to know by now I never speculate and I have not the slightest intention of discussing our principal with anyone.'

'Bravo,' said Denham.

I closed the door and walked out of the building. Summer stretched ahead. In the clear light I felt free, as if the atmosphere had lifted. The poisons of Etherington were buried inside the brick walls.

At our front gate I felt with my hand through the letter-box. I tore open the envelope before opening the door. Mother's operation was scheduled for the end of January. I should write to Robert that night indicating his portion of the cost. After all, he had always claimed his share of everything.

INA

2

Miriam Hansen was my salvation. Without her I should have sunk from sight in that glug-pool of non-conformist morality long before I did. From the moment she sat down in my office, her sensible lace-up shoes black and shiny with polish, planted squarely beneath my desk, I chuckled to myself. 'Dear God,' I prayed (I usually prayed even though I didn't really believe there was anybody up there), 'dear God, don't let the lousy salary deter her.' To myself I said, 'Play it cool, Ina, probe her weakness. No honours degree and a dependent mother. Well, well.' The lines of duty were already embedding themselves around the eyes and mouth. They deepened as she clenched her jaw and drew together her sandy brows. I was to know that look well in the months ahead. Good old duty. The key to freedom for people like me.

I do not dislike dutiful Puritan-bred types. A matter of contrast, perhaps. No, similarity. A dog returning to his vomit. It would be interesting to ask a psychiatrist, but I have never dared to lie down on one of those couches—not yet, anyway. I guess there is still time.

He would probably say that duty appealed to me because I had rejected it the night I slammed the door in Mum's face and joined the AWAS. Good old AWAS. Such dingy khaki uniforms. Only masochism or desperation could have persuaded any girl to don one when she had a university degree. 'Your university career,' Mother wailed. 'Your Dad and I have sacrificed everything to give it to you.' It was, of course, a lie. The old dear had thought of me, it is true, but she had a fair wad of good suburbia left for her old age. Our neat respectable cottage on the outskirts of not quite old Adelaide stood for all those Mums and Dads resolutely putting their children through High School and the university. Frankly, it was the end. No prospects in that quarter. So I slammed the door and went in search of Dad, who was already serving in the Navy, pretending he was thirty-five not forty-two.

I slammed the door. I was a smart cookie, a neat doll. 'Ina's a gay girl,' they said. That repulsive khaki hat looked good on my fair hair and not even that tunic could hide my neat figure. I took care of my skin, too. I had a dressing-table overflowing with creams and lotions and a row of gloriously scarlet lipsticks. How dim my modern counterparts look today with their sickly pale glows and silvered lips!

And so I joined the girls serving King and country who banged a typewriter from nine to five just like their civilian cousins. I suppose we hoped for extracurricular benefits. After all, the army is reputed to contain a lot of men. They were good girls. They taught me to smoke and to dance and to drink a little. But when it came to sex something went wrong. You can slam a door, you can leave your destitute mother wailing on its farther side, you can head for a glamorised Dad, but you cannot shed the inhibitions of a lifetime. Not easily, anyway. I think perhaps it was a pity I took up the minor sins. They consumed all my moral energy and when it came to the major one I had nothing in reserve.

There were chances, plenty of them, and my companions were not always too particular. That was one of the problems. I had been taught to be ultra-clean. I still clean my teeth after every meal and I have never once tumbled into bed in my whole life without thoroughly cleansing myself first. There were Aussies and Yanks to spare, not to mention an occasional Frenchman, and my heart throbbed at the sight of every one of them, but my nose and training revolted. Men do smell, particularly around the feet. Still, as I said, I was a gay girl and I compared notes on my adventures and swapped stories with my mates—only most of mine were false.

Luckily for me—or should I say unluckily?—I had a natural instinct for a gentleman, or was it simply an incurable moral sense? I tried, I really did; and when I met the American from Texas I said to myself, 'This is it! Farewell virginity.' He certainly thought I was willing. To my dying day I shall see his bewildered face in that hotel room we had booked as I sat firmly in the chair buttoned securely into my uniform and talked physics for half the night. Finally he said, 'For God's sake, Ina honey!' and I said, 'I know, I know, but my parents are good Methodists. It takes time. Give me till your next leave to think it over and I really will, Bill, I really will —only I need time.' And he simply said, 'Time, honey, is just what I haven't got. It's in short supply.' But it made no difference; I just couldn't do it. Finally he said, 'I'm getting a drink' and went out—I thought to the bar—but when I looked there later he had gone.

Perhaps if he had told me he was leaving for the Pacific it would have been different; but he was one of those guys who took the myth of military secrets seriously. As far as I know, he never came back. He certainly didn't write to me and so I continued to be a gay girl. Whenever I felt my resistance rising I drank frantically to counteract those background Methodists; but it made no difference. I merely fell asleep a bit sooner and either way I just couldn't undress. Not in front of someone else.

Which is probably why I am sitting here as headmistress of Etherington with a perfectly good honours physics degree but no husband.

Still, I like men. It's not the men on the Council who worry me. It's not even their suety kids. It's the wives sitting at home with nothing better to do than to invent infidelities for their husbands. Not that they need much invention. There's usually plenty of raw material for them to work on in this town. At our very first Christmas party Maurice Furlonger offered me a drive to the lookout and Clinton Amos, editor of the local paper, made a perfect fool of himself in a paper cap for my sake. But I could never prevent their wives taking over when they reached home. Getting a man to yourself alone in a double bed after midnight gives you an initial advantage. The trouble is I find matrons are either bores or hypocrites or a bit of both, for ever mouthing maternal concern over the off-spring they dump on my doorstep with a sigh of relief at the beginning of every term. It is hard to be a successful head-mistress if you don't like mothers, and I don't like mothers.

Which is one reason I value Miriam Hansen. You can thrust the most unpleasant contacts on her and she handles them with dignity and ease. Miriam never complains. She interprets 'duty' very broadly. You know where you are with the Miriams.

I have never trusted the rest of the staff. Not that Ann Denham is dishonest, but I never feel quite easy with her. She has the arrogance of the first-class honours Arts graduate, that flick of amusement that dismisses the sciences as some sort of non-culture. As if everyone couldn't get an Arts degree if he wanted it. I was always top of English at school and Mother bought me all the Romantic poets when I was fifteen. I have always liked Tennyson and Browning, but when I offered my Tennyson to Ann Denham for a lesson she said, 'No thanks. I'm reading Carl Sandburg and Louis MacNeice this lesson', and I know she picked them because she knew I had never heard of them; so I said 'How interesting! But I hope you don't neglect the older writers. The children must learn something about their great heritage', and Ann looked at me intently and said, 'Get lost.'

One thing I learnt long ago was to withdraw myself behind my glasses. It's the only thing to do when you have the sort of staff members that tell a Head to get lost; and I did it then, so that Ann would know that I just wouldn't be bothered with her. I can withdraw even without glasses, a slight glazing of the eye and an inner concentration, and I can go a hundred miles away in one second. It used to be handy with Aussie sergeants who got too fresh. I did not aim to go to bed with a sergeant.

I did not expect at first to like Miriam, not really. I expected to depend upon her, not to like her; but after we went to Froggy Daley's art class together I found that in art we had a real affinity. Not that I like Miriam's paintings. She uses such odd colours, plain depressive, but they are the sort of paintings that people look at twice. Critics at our art shows always like them. 'Boudoir pink' the last judge called mine, although I think it may have been a compliment after all. He squeezed my elbow as he said it and I could tell by his eyes that he knew all about boudoir pinks. I suspect he was an ex-private.

The trouble with Miriam is intensity. Even if you like her, you can only take so much at the time. It's like inviting your conscience to walk around with you. I must admit it was a relief to escape Miriam's dutiful adoration and to skip off occasionally for an evening at Louise Hillard's. 'Forget that old school,' Bill Hillard would say, and we'd settle down together to a few glasses of Scotch and send old Meridale sky-high. Louise was one of those people who know the worst there is to know about everyone and she had the gift of mimicry. But then Louise was such a liar. She would sit on her lounge, her dainty tiny feet tucked under her, watching us thoughtfully as she sipped slowly at a brandy and ginger while Bill and I drank Scotch. We were friends. It was true I did finish the bottle the time Bill was away, but Louise knew I was low that night. That was why she had said, 'Come over' in the first place. She put the bottle on the coffee table near my elbow and said, 'Help yourself, Ina, while I rustle up some dinner. I know you're blue.' I was blue and I did finish the bottle and Louise did have to drive me back to school; but the whole town could not have talked the way they did unless Louise had told them. What was worse, she literally black-mailed me.

'I must have a little more salary, Ina. I know the Council

is difficult; but we both know how hard it is to manage, particularly if one is prone to depression.' More salary or else, she meant. And of course the Council did purr over those first-class honours in economics. Silly old snobs. They valued them more than a pass in the overall exam, and Louise had only to absent herself for a day and one of the Council would ring her and offer her the world. Behind my back, too. Louise usually told me about it before the Council got around to it. They never knew what hell they created for me with Louise boasting about her rise in the staff-room and all the others arriving silently on my doorstep to ask for rises, too. At least they arrived secretly. They knew and I knew that rises only came at Etherington through personal pressures. I was the pressure point. I was the one who knew both that their salaries were a disgrace to any school and that the Council was broke. A lovely situation for me.

That is where Miriam is so reliable. Miriam could see that Louise simply wouldn't do. Ann Denham is too soft when it comes to a showdown, but Miriam is like rock, granite rock. Good granite, scattered around the western river-beds of this district, blue-grey outcrops of solid stone. Miriam is a local girl. Once that whisky story began to spread at the Saturday parties, I had no choice but to dismiss Louise; but I doubt if I should have been successful on my own. Miriam's strong, honest, reliable face, draped with her unprepossessing sandy hair, reinforced her verbal testimony to the Council. Meridale men are inclined to believe a local rather than a foreigner, particularly a local with whom they shared desks at school. They'd never look at her as a woman. After all, she could beat them at school in any subject you care to name; but for that very reason they referred to her intelligence as masculine. If Miriam Hansen said it was so it was so: she was one of them.

Miriam also meant I could deflate that snobbish bitch, Cunningham-White. God knows how I stuck my first year in that place. 'I thought, Miss Spurway, you ought to know that Margaret Mason's parents own Tinterden. You can't be too

careful when choosing your prefects.' How the little pink
tongue tripped across the little pink words, ladylike poison.
'Family is so important in a school like this. You must have
the right sort of background in a head girl.' Blah, blah, blah!
Every damn thing to do myself from time-table to dormitory
arrangements. 'I couldn't do that, Miss Spurway. I have always held a senior position on this staff.'

Thank God Miriam is different. Miriam can do anything.
Her ex-school mates are right there. What is more, she's used
to being some sort of slavey around the place. Occasionally I
have felt ashamed. Her only night off and a crisis in the school
and the one decent party in Meridale for months. I had only
to say, 'You do understand, don't you? I really can't let the
Dennises down, such important parents', and good old work-
horse Miriam would slip on one of her frightful frocks, hide
her hair beneath one of her unbelievable caps, and return to
school for the evening. Of course, I did what I could. I always
picked her up and brought her home and, when all was said
and done, she was never going anywhere. She did worry about
her mother but the telephone was next to Mother's bed and
all she had to do was lift the receiver. I always let slip the
magic word 'duty' when Miriam was reluctant. Holy, lovely
word. You had only to say 'duty' to Miriam and she came
immediately, big-paws lolloping all over the place, tail wag-
ging. It was only Ann Denham who looked me up and down
and said, 'Duty is such a reversible proposition, isn't it, Ina?'

Funny how long it took Miriam to call me Ina. Art class
after art class. I really do believe she thought it was indecent;
but of course I did have less social contact with her than with
Ann and Louise. I always liked Ann's parties, good food, good
drink, good company. Louise, on the contrary, relied on all
grog, and it took me six months to find out why. Nothing
better than unadulterated grog for commitment purposes, for
promoting those remarks people shouldn't make that Louise
found so handy the morning after. But I beat her, the little
liar, I beat her with Miriam, although I did feel bad about
Ann and Miriam. Funny how white Ann goes when angry.

Not red, white. I should paint her stark white with pink red effluences in the background.

'You know damn well Miriam tells tales. And you capitalise on it, Ina. You encourage her.'

I retreated behind my glasses. 'Mrs Denham,' I said with emphasis, 'if you have come into my office to insult my staff and to swear at me, I must ask you to leave.'

'Don't be so bloody righteous,' she said.

I stood up. I can look dignified even though I am small. 'I will not endure your criticisms of staff members who have a high sense of duty.'

It was then she said, 'Duty is so reversible, isn't it, Ina? So conveniently reversible.' And she slammed the door. Still, I don't worry about Ann. When someone can teach like Ann, you take it. Just a tiny flip occasionally to put her in her place. I must admit that this town is corrosive. Too little entertainment and too many true life tales to take its place. Insulated, oyster-tight little groups, carefully excluding one another. The old families, damn them, really water-tight, unless they want a drive for one of their favourite charities, or a working-horse secretary for one of their damn committees. Enough of them to do their own drinking and fornicating without ever admitting a single stranger. Sometimes I've been bored stiff, and, let's face it, lonely. Gay-girl Ina sitting on her dainty middle-aged rear drinking tea alone in a non-conformist school.

Strange to say, I enjoyed a meal at Miriam's. I like Miriam's Mum, the caustic edge sharpened into corrosion by physical disability. The old girl enjoys a game of cards, provided you let her win. That is one trouble with Miriam. She always wins, playing doggedly and obstinately and honestly with that clever mind of hers. I have sat on Edith Hansen's bed smoking cigarettes and playing God knows what games for two hours at a time, and every time the old girl won those magnificent grey eyes would light up and she'd really begin to talk. Quite an achievement on my part. I can't say I like Robert. I only met him once but he struck me as mean and calculating, pulling the wool over the old girl's eyes, sponging on Miriam's sense of duty. Not even pulling his weight with his mother. Still, it isn't simple. He may not be mean, only unintelligent. His wife draws the line at Mother, and if I had a house and kids to save for on a working man's income I'd probably draw the line at taking on Mother too. Did I say unintelligent? Who knows? Such a quaint old house. High-vaulted wooden walls, shut in on itself like so many older Meridale houses. Did they build the houses to keep the weather out or to close themselves in?

A few superficial parties, an occasional dinner with staff, cribbage with an old woman: hardly exciting for a girl used to Adelaide, Melbourne and the joys of World War Two army life. I don't think I could have stood it as long as I did without Maurice Furlonger and Gladys Dewey.

Get Maurice away from pursy-mouthed Mena and he's an amusing chap. Council meetings are the horror of any small private school Head. There they sit, the graziers, some of them barely removed from the animals in their own paddocks, but astute, oh, astute. Of course, I put my foot in it the very first meeting when I called Olaf Denton a farmer. After all I don't come from these parts. I'm a city girl, and I'm damned if I can see the ultimate difference between the cow-cocky who milks the cow and the grazier who slaughters it. It was Maurice who turned it into a joke. 'You can see she's a new-chum, can't you, Olaf?' and they all laughed; but Mervyn Harris, who is a dairy farmer, wasn't amused.

But it's the up-and-coming tradesmen who are the worst, the motel owners, the garage proprietors, the up-and-at-'em town dignitaries with their roots in the mud of small trade. They want to run the school on a shoestring, otherwise they can't afford to bring their kids up to mix with the graziers. It's a damn back-biting assembly. Whatever you do is wrong. If it hadn't been for Maurice I'd have thrown in the ruddy job long ago. If it isn't salaries, it's results; and once you get the damn results looking respectable (Ann and Miriam were marvellous there) it's the blasted sleeping quarters or the peeping-toms. I really don't know how *I* am to stop dirty old men looking through the windows when the Council won't provide new dormitories. It's not my fault some of the girls are sleeping on a louvred veranda, and it's not my fault that Gretchen Dutch has no inhibitions whatsoever about undressing with the blind up.

Somehow, that evening I'd had it. I was standing by the fire with my head on the mantelpiece and I didn't hear Maurice come back for his scarf. He put his hand on my shoulder and before I knew it he had his arms around me and I wept while I said silly things like being bloody well sick of it and having no one to appreciate me and so on, and he patted my hair and said he knew but not to give up, all those who knew me thought a lot of me. Then he said 'I've been wanting to hold you like this for a long time', and it was so nice and warm and comforting when I'd been bloody lonely for a hell of a time and we sat on the lounge and he made me a cup of tea and we laughed and talked for almost an hour.

He may be fat and he may be balding, but he was nice; and of course it was all really quite respectable. He was treasurer for the year and there was no reason why he shouldn't stay an hour or two after each meeting to talk over accounts; and what if we did cuddle up a bit on the lounge? No harm was done. I don't blame him. That long-nosed phial of vinegar would never cuddle him, and it was a long time since I'd felt the warmth of a man's arms and that delicious prickle of repressed chin stubble brushing against my face. There was nothing more. I have never taken off my clothes for anyone. It was all perfectly respectable. Miriam, of course, warned me though I doubt if Miriam knew what she was warning me against.

She said, 'Ina,' as she splashed her ridiculous colours across a perfectly normal landscape, 'I know I have no right to interfere and I know as far as money is concerned Maurice Furlonger is a most respected man, but this town talks and Maurice was . . . well . . . rather a gay lad and I think it is my duty to warn you that Mena is vindictive. She is my distant cousin.' And I said, 'Thanks, Miriam, I appreciate your

thought. But the accounts have to be worked out, and I really
can't discuss salaries and repairs unless I understand something about them. But I shall remember your warning.' And
we went on painting.

I must admit the arrival of Gladys Dewey made life easier.
From the moment her squat, travel-stained form alighted on
the railway platform, I knew she was my sort. After Gladys
came, the school took on a gayer note. We ran a musical for
the first time. We joined one of the boys' schools and the local
Training College on the Gilbert and Sullivan circuit and we
were as good as any of them. We all enjoyed the production,
even Miriam, although she did insist on making a duty out of
every little thing she had to do, taking sets home for painting,
designing programmes and God knows what else. But even
Mother came to the show, and Robert almost came, which
was something of a triumph.

But that was the professional side of Gladys. Her interest
for me was the non-professional. Good old wardrobe. No one
could ever accuse Etherington Council of wasting money on
staff. Miserable, pokey little staff-rooms and freezing derelict
cottages for living quarters. Still, they subjected their own
offspring to much the same conditions in the name of education, so I never worried about it, and most of the resident
group were young.

Gladys was a sport. She could sense my bad days. She stood
in my office, the sweat spreading in thick bands from her arm-
pits even in winter (but of course she *was* English), and said,
'You're driving yourself too hard, Ina. It isn't worth it. No
one will thank you when you're gone. Drop over to my room
for a minute.' And I said, 'For God's sake, Glad, this is working time', and she said, 'Nonsense, this whole collection of bits
and pieces is your prairie and the good Miriam is upstairs
brooding over the school like a guardian angel. She can hold
the fort for us with her beautiful innocence and her boundless
duty'; and we both giggled and I felt better already.

Gladys's room had an old-fashioned brass bed, and a magnificent cedar wardrobe. Amazing how much lovely cedar,

usually under layers of paint, lies buried in our country towns. I'm a perv. about cedar.

Gladys opened it. 'Scotch or gin?' I must have looked disbelieving, because she said, 'I'm not kidding. I have to keep it in here because Cunningham-White has the ears and eyes of a ferret, but she's too much of a lady to rummage in my wardrobe. Not that I shouldn't have a drink or two in my own time.'

'I agree,' I said; 'but, let's face it, the councillors are a little grim-faced and the wardrobe is school property. I think gin for a change.'

It was the best long drink I had ever tasted. That funny little woman with her protruding rear and exuding sweat mixed the most superb long drinks that have ever come my way. I fingered the lovely cedar and murmured, 'Lovely, lovely', and Gladys, her little darting eyes twinkling above her whisky, said, 'Yes, far too lovely for shapeless garments like mine. Such cedar is fit only for a coffin or a drink cabinet. If I stay here until death do us part you can carve it up for me.'

Good old Gladys. What fun we had in that room. 'Help yourself,' she said, 'when the councillors get you down.' And I did. What fun we had, too, on the nights that Cunningham-White and Miriam were either on duty or at home. In that room, mellowed by the contents of the wardrobe, I made the contact with the staff that any good Head should have. The school was ticking over perfectly, and there was Maurice on Thursday, and occasionally on Friday as well.

After all, what was the harm? Mena was a fanatical golfer and Maurice liked a drive. I am not a bad fisherman and those trout streams are cool and restful. Bread and sausage for lunch, with an occasional fresh fish on the coals and a few cigarettes smoked together on the warm rocks. I liked Maurice because in the beginning he never wanted to undress me. Just an odd cuddle and kiss. After all, affection was what he needed, and if I could help him in this way it was not much to do in return for all those accounts. But Mena had a suspicious nose and, let's face it, she may have been educated at Etherington but she was not well bred. No lady would have behaved in public as she did at the staff cocktail party. I was enjoying it, too. I had a new tint and a new frock and I was making those contacts so important for a woman in my position. After all, the fathers pay the school bills and an impression of charm and efficiency at the top helps to win the new men of the town. Men mean pupils, I believe. And there was Miriam to support me. An air of stolidity, reliability, to assure both the Mums and the Dads that this was the very school for their precious offspring.

Elevated governess! It was not I who was elevated. I could have had a post in any school or even the university in Adelaide, but I was damned if I was going to be Mum's and Dad's pet drudge in their old age. It was Mena Furlonger who was elevated. Cousin of carpenters and descended from carpenters. Funny how a bit of the good earth creates delusions of grandeur.

And there was really no need for Miriam to breathe all over Maurice. 'Mena's left.' We all knew she had left. We couldn't fail to know it, not after the way she banged that door.

It was not important, but nevertheless the rot started from that moment. Nothing went right after that party. I know Miriam was worried over her mother, but how the hell could I offer her a rise? The Council was even jibbing at new staff and in no mood to pad the pay cheque of settled members.

As Maurice said when I told him, 'Miriam does a hack job, not a director's. She can't expect a director's wage. The Hansens have never really amounted to much and if old Hansen did nothing about his wife's limp I don't see why Etherington should pay. We have a duty to the parents to keep fees at a reasonable level.' Good dear Maurice. He made it so easy to see everything in its right perspective. Even so, I had to live with Miriam and undoubtedly she was getting more difficult every day.

There was that horrible row with Ann Denham over books. I really think it was a storm in a teacup. No one on our

Council ever looks at the books we give the girls, let alone reads them. But of course Miriam had to interfere. 'It is our duty,' she said, 'to see that the girls receive wholesome literary prizes', and the bloody Council was being so buggerish at that moment I decided to back her. I suppose I also took the easy way out. I should have guessed Ann wouldn't like it. She had not been speaking to me ever since Louise Hillard's death. What the hell I had to do with Louise swallowing sleeping-tablets I don't know. Louise was always a liar and it merely proved I was right to dismiss her. I don't believe she meant to kill herself. She was trying to blackmail someone as usual. But why Ann had to tell Miriam I don't know, even if she were upset over Gretchen's prize. As if it really mattered what precious book Gretchen finally took home!

I'm sure if it hadn't been for Miriam and Ann I shouldn't have gone that evening to Gabo pub. I was so sick of everything. I thought, 'What the hell?' I was even prepared to take the final step. For some reason Maurice was like all men in the long run. He was beginning to hanker for more than company and a few kisses. Until Miriam stood in my office saying over and over again, 'Louise is dead', I had intended taking the girls to the concert myself.

'Louise is dead and we killed her and Gretchen must have her prize.' What the hell! I did not kill Louise. She killed herself. And it was Miriam not me who made a fuss about Gretchen's prize. Suddenly I was sick of them, sick of the girls, sick of the whole wretched outfit. I knew Gladys was never reliable by 8 p.m. after an afternoon left to her own resources, but I had to get away for the evening or go stark raving mad. If it hadn't been for the neurotic bunch of them screaming, yelling all over my office, I'd never have gone with Maurice that evening. But I thought, 'This is it, Ina. Make the break once and for all. Sleep with him if he asks you or remain for ever a taut little ball of authority in some run-down girls' institution for the rest of your life.' It was crisis point and I was ready to face it. I'd even begun to allow Maurice to pull down the zipper on my frock when the telephone call came through.

It was Ann Denham, saying, 'For heaven's sake, Ina, where have you been? Gladys and the girls have had an accident. A serious one. I couldn't find you anywhere, but finally I tried to reach Maurice Furlonger and Mena Furlonger said, "Try Gabo." Of all the God-forsaken spots!'

And my mind said, 'Mena? How did Mena know?' and I heard my voice say, 'Accident? Good God, is anyone injured?' And I barely heard her say, 'Gladys Dewey and I think one of the girls', because I was thinking, 'I won't have to do it after all', and I said, 'For God's sake, Maurice, get the car. I have to get back to Meridale immediately.'

We drove faster than I can ever remember driving. I was conscious only of the stark lovely trees appearing and disappearing in our headlights, the odd rabbit that crushed beneath our wheels. At the edge of the town, Maurice left me and I took the wheel. I could feel myself crying, partly from anxiety, partly from frustration, partly from relief. I should not see him again. I knew that. Maurice would not risk exposure in this town, not his town built on the sweat of his dead ancestors. I looked at the zipper on my dress. I thought, I'll never do it now, never. The tears coursed down my cheeks.

At the roadside I felt superfluous. Miriam was in charge. One girl was screaming. One lay on the side of the road. The others were huddled together. I heard my voice blaming Gladys, saying anything to justify myself, trying to explain; then I saw the canvas-covered figure and I stopped. I thought stupidly, 'Her bottom is sticking out, just as it always does. She isn't dead really. Not with that bottom.' But Miriam's voice said, 'Dead', and I knew Miriam did not lie.

I glanced at the girl beside the road and there was blood trickling through the dust and a finger lying on the grass. I saw the blood was Gretchen's and I turned away feeling sick and knew that I was no use at all. I heard Miriam say, 'Take the girls', and I said, 'I can't drive. I can't. Not after this.' But she looked at me hard, forcing my eyes to hers. 'It's your duty,' she said. Her eyes were the eyes of an Old Testament prophet and somehow I did it. I drove those girls up that hill and I supervised their hysteria, reducing it to instant coffee and biscuits and bed.

Good Miriam. I did it. I said I liked Puritans. I do. You can rely on them. She allowed me no grief, no pity. Simply reminded me of my duty and bundled me into that car with a stack of girls and I had to drive, not think.

I resigned, of course. There was no point waiting for the Council meeting. I knew they'd ask for my resignation. Mena would see to that. So I resigned first and I beat them. They had to say how sorry they were to lose me, to farewell me with congratulatory speeches. They obviously hoped I should find it difficult to get a new job. They never thought of Algeria. Perhaps even I will manage to undress in that climate. It was good to see all their faces, staff and Council. Poor Miriam. Proper people don't go to Algeria—proper people stay and do their duty. Poor old dutiful Miriam. I wonder what would happen if some genie whisked her off and dumped her in Algeria. I have no doubt she would dust down her shoes, smooth her nylon frock, poke her sandy hair under her cap to keep out the dust, and say to the nearest camel, 'Please conduct me to the capital. I must be on duty by 10 a.m.'

MIRIAM

3

That vacation Mother was difficult. She was scared, and for once I pitied her. To make matters worse, Robert and his wife came for Christmas. I liked the children. They gave life to the rooms, brightened the garden. They laughed tumbling the fruit from the old trees into their laps, gobbling the gooseberries from the vines, bringing me armfuls of daisies from the untamed, rampant plants sprawling across the yard. Old commonplace yellow-centred marguerites, but in our garden they bloomed and bloomed, tangling with the iris bulbs that multiplied in unchecked fertility in the corner of the yard.

Mother was irritable. Hospital is a frightening experience for an old lady. The children worried her with their self-evident vitality and Robert's wife fussed and fiddled around the kitchen.

'Good old Miriam,' said Robert. 'A real old maid, Muriel. She doesn't like you in her kitchen. She never liked anyone to touch her things. Even as a kid.'

'I'm sure I was only trying to help,' said Muriel. Such wispy faded hair and eyes. So shrewdly stupid.

I put the plates in the sink. 'Of course,' I said. 'I appreciate your help. Take no notice of Robert.'

He grinned. 'I thought you might be glad of help, Miriam. You were better at maths than at cooking.'

'I've had plenty of practice at both,' I said tartly. 'After all, Mother has been my sole responsibility for some time.'

'I'm sure it's not our fault,' said Muriel, and I hated her whining voice. 'You can't expect us to take Mother, not with our responsibilities. Robert didn't ask to be sent to Danneworth.'

'No,' I said, 'he didn't ask. He was just lucky. It lets you out, doesn't it, Muriel? Still, I may as well enjoy my holiday now. I won't be in your way. I'm going out.'

As I walked to my bedroom I was aware of her indefinite mouth slipping open in surprise and of the narrowing of Robert's eyes as he tried with his limited intelligence to calculate my motives. I pulled a crushed scarf from my drawer and wound it round my head. Outside it was warm and windy. At the front gate my niece, Kerrie, met me. 'May I come too, Aunt Miriam?' She had a piquant plain face. Muriel's wispiness translated into elf. Even her sandy hair did not rob her of sweetness. She was Robert's second daughter. I knew no one cared about her very much. Daughters are not important to men like Robert when the perpetuation of their idiocy has already been ensured by sons. I wished to be alone, but I said, 'I'm going to walk fast, very fast. You can come if you keep up.' She came, walking and running in little quick bursts to keep pace. I felt ungracious.

We strode past the open paddocks. The sheep scattered away from our coming, woolly bundles of anxiety. The wheat-coloured grass blew wispily against the wire fences structuring a delicate buff-coloured fence of its own, harmonious with the yellowed paddocks and harvested wheat fields.

'I could paint that,' I said.

'Why?' said Kerrie. We sat by the road and chewed the stems of paspalum. I could feel the grit of dust on my teeth and I thought it ought to rain. The country needed it. I looked at the child. 'Because,' I said, 'it is harmonious, peaceful, and it shields a herd of frightened sheep who don't know that the fence divides us from them. Fear behind harmony. I should try to convey both in my painting.'

The child dragged her feet across the dust. 'You say queer things, Aunt Miriam. Mummy says she doesn't understand you.'

'Oh,' I said. 'And what does Daddy say?'

'Daddy says, "Don't worry about old Miriam." '

'Oh,' I said again.

'He reckons you have it pretty easy. He says you earn a good salary and have only yourself and Mother to spend it on.'

My throat tightened. 'And you, Kerrie, what do you say?'

'I like you,' said the child. 'I reckon you spend it on us, too.'

On an impulse I put my arms round her and hugged her, feeling the thin, taut little bones beneath her inadequate flesh. 'You're full of bones, too,' I said.

She pulled away, embarrassed. 'Are we going back now?' she asked.

I was depressed. Ina, Gladys, Gretchen. The darkness remained within me. Somehow I had let Ina go without a gesture of friendship. I had offered duty when I should have offered love. I shuddered. Next week our new Head was arriving. A woman from one of our biggest girls' schools. She appeared to be a virtuoso. Languages, music, carpentry. I had seen the applications. The Council had even asked my opinion. 'After all, Miriam went to school with us.' I suppose one achieves a position of respect—in time.

It was a pretty face. In a remote way. She must have been forty at least, but her hair hung limply and uncurled across her shoulders just like the hair of a contemporary teenager. It was black, stringy with the gelatinous look of greasy hair, unwashed for at least three days. She held it back with a band that pressed her ears close to her rather pointed head. She had prim, taut lips and eyes that did not see throughout our first meeting. In fact, she looked straight through me like a woman without sight. It was only later that I knew she was short-sighted, extremely short-sighted, but too vain to wear her glasses. I remembered Ina and Louise flaunting their glasses like chunky jewellery, and I wondered why a woman whose clothes were plain and haphazard cared so much about her eyes.

'There is a lot to do,' she said in her clipped English voice (she *was* English). 'This building is totally inadequate and the teachers' cottage is shocking. One look would drive any self-respecting woman away.'

I was surprised, then amused. The cottage was a replica of thousands of Meridale cottages, weatherboard inside and out with tapering verandas and old fuel stoves. Our own home was not dissimilar. I believe in absolute values, but the relativity of values struck me at that moment. Philippa was like the town matron talking about the impossibility of living without sewerage to a community that had never seen anything but a pan. It was an old story and I had heard my uncles and father laughing about it many times. The timber cutters of Andy's Creek, their primitive wives, and the impossibility of non-sewerage! I forced my attention back to Miss Ormiston. 'So you see,' she was saying, 'I am painting the walls. It's amazing what a few gay colours can do. You can help me. We'll have it ready by the beginning of term at that rate.'

Mother was still in hospital and I had plenty of spare time. I agreed because she was my principal and I believe in duty, yet I was uneasy. As I watched Philippa Ormiston at work, thin, frenetic, pixie-headed, I knew that my duties were going to multiply indefinitely. Was 'multiply' the right word? It would be an arithmetical progression. In that month we painted walls, varnished chairs, rearranged the garden, cleaned the blackboards. Only once I mentioned the possibility of official cleaners, but she looked at me without looking at me, pulled at her gardening gloves caked with the good earth, curled the edge of her mouth with well-bred arrogance.

'My dear Miss Hansen, this school needs buildings, grounds, staff. It needs money. Desperately. It is so silly to waste the little we have on small chores that we can do ourselves.'

I sighed, but not audibly. The rest of my summer holiday

slipped away painting, painting, painting. I did not even ask for a day off until Mother returned from hospital.

When school opened the staff-room was a whirl of new young faces. Twenty-year-olds looked through their dangling hair, blew smoke through their pale lips, and spread uncovered thighs, lusty muscular flesh, across our old chairs. Ann Denham, tippling tea, looked cynically at Cunningham-White, Mona Edison, Mrs Ellis and myself.

'My, we are full of youth and enthusiasm this year,' she said. 'Our apathy will blossom like the wilderness. The girls, our dear old solid average and below average seniors, will lead classes and discussion groups and brighten the lives of the local aged citizens with their little charitable acts of kindness.'

'It's worth trying,' I said.

Ann smiled. 'And how many hours overtime have you worked already, Miriam dear? The same old rates. New buildings, yes; new staff, yes; even new girls. But watch the well-bred withdrawal at the mention of money for staff.'

'For God's sake, Ann,' I said, 'give her a chance.'

Miss Cunningham-White cut in. 'I agree, Miriam. It is nice to have a lady in charge and we should give her a chance. Even so, Mrs Denham has a point. There is a limit to the extra duties I, for one, can perform. This morning I had to take the girls out for breakfast to the local forest—at 7 a.m., mind you. And what did we eat? Fungi! To be quite frank, I'm still a bit worried about the puff-balls.'

'Puff, puff, puff,' said Mona. 'Pfft! No more Miss Cunningham-White.'

Even I smiled. 'I'm quite sure Miss Ormiston won't ask you to eat anything poisonous,' I said.

'No,' said Ann, 'she's one of those naturally folksy ratbags the English produce so effortlessly. She is a well-bred lady who knows her edible fungi to the last stem. But let me warn you—she sulks. She hasn't spoken to me for two days because I doubted the ability of dear little Susie Graves to conduct a forum on foreign affairs.'

I studied the stain in the sink. It was still there. 'I believe,' I said slowly, 'that when the scheme was put to you, your precise statement was "Rats".'

'Exactly,' said Ann. 'Anyone is rats who thinks those 4B dimwits of whom Sue is the shining light are even remotely interested in foreign affairs.'

'She'll learn,' said Mona. 'But I tell you one thing. She's just as mean as Ina. I'm still asked to take all the dumb-bunnies for secondary science and I'm still to be lowly paid because I haven't a degree. I pointed out I was one of the few trained teachers on the staff, but she looked me up and down and said the great public schools of England had managed without trained teachers for years.'

I did not mention my own rise in salary, unsolicited by me. Philippa Ormiston had sent for me, her black hair dangling incongruously, child-like, around her sallow yet lovely English skin and ageing eyes.

'Do you get overtime, Miss Hansen?'

'I have never asked for it,' I said.

'I see,' she said. 'There is so much part-time work here that rates are confusing. The Council, however, ought to be made aware of those who really work without grumbling.'

Next week I received notification of my increase. It was small, but with Mother's bills yet to come in and Robert's contribution sure to be indefinitely postponed, I was grateful.

Mother was not an easy convalescent. She could now walk with the aid of a stick but I had to provide grips to enable her to pull herself up. The frustration of partial mobility irritated her even more than her previous immobility. She would continue to pull herself around the house long after she ought to have gone to bed. Every evening it was a struggle. No longer could I tuck her in and shut the door. She persisted in sitting in Father's old chair, grizzling away while I tried to mark books. She bickered and picked at me, complained and ranted. Sometimes I was forced to lift her bodily and undress her, taking her gown and slippers away with me. For-

tunately I have always been strong in a wiry sort of way—
like Father.

Philippa Ormiston had a car, an open ramshackle affair
that she called Tom. She was the sort of person who names
everything, even a pressure-cooker. 'Poor Tom,' she said, the
first time I drove with her, 'he needs a new choke.' It was
also the first time I really saw her laugh, her sallow smooth
skin crinkling around her black eyes. I had said 'Tom? Is he
your brother?'

Life was busy, so crammed with activities that our previous
crowded year of *The Gondoliers* seemed like a period of relaxation. There were meetings after school, charity drives,
working bees, drama evenings, forums on everything under
the sun. I even attended a couple of breakfasts. I did find it
difficult with Mother, particularly when I had to stay back
for what Ann Denham called the 'late, late show', namely the
weekly social get-together over a violin, a piano, and a cello.
I have never been musical. Robert could sing and he and
Mother used to sing duets when he was a boy. 'Bull-frog,' he
called me. 'Why?' I asked. He laughed. 'Because they croak
like you.'

Philippa did help by driving me home afterwards. To my
horror I noticed she rarely wore her glasses in the car. The
roads of Meridale are makeshift, pot-holes treated with a dab
of tar to hide their cancerous erosion. The result is a line of
bony ridges or sunken depressions. I am not a praying woman
but I prayed regularly riding in Tom. Sometimes as we hit a
particularly high ridge, my head would touch the roof, but
Philippa Ormiston was never disturbed. At intersections we
missed other cars by inches. She would shake her head bound
in a self-woven scarf and laugh gaily.

'Funny thing, you know, I didn't see it.'

'Why don't you wear your glasses then?'

She looked at me for a flicker of a second and her eyes
held the arrogance of Cunningham-White's lip, only more so.
'They are not necessary at my age,' she said. 'I can see quite

well. It is a matter of mind over matter.' I did not pursue the topic.

One night as Tom squeaked to a stop in front of our gate I said, 'Come in and meet Mother.' She walked awkwardly down the hall. I stopped at the glass case. 'Father's buffaloes,' I said. 'He made them. He was very artistic with wood.'

She laughed gaily. 'Aren't they quaint?' she said. I wondered why she avoided 'odd' or 'eccentric', any word that expressed her inner feeling. Philippa Ormiston would weave scarves, dress up for charades, sing madrigals; but she did not carve bulky buffaloes into rough coated shapes of wood and put them in glass cases. My mental fingers stretched out towards my dead father and I felt he was solid, earthy, fundamental.

Mother was sitting in her chair. The fire in the fuel stove was burning warmly and the shadows of red light gyrated across the worn wooden walls of the kitchen.

'How folksy!' said Philippa Ormiston. She meant 'how primitive'.

She took Mother's hand. 'I'm so glad to meet you,' she said. 'Thank you for Miriam. I don't know how I'd have managed without her the last few weeks. All that painting.'

Mother looked up with her luminous, gentle eyes. 'You're welcome,' she said drily. 'Miriam is naturally useful. She has always been a clever girl.' Her voice curled with tiny twists of mockery.

I got up abruptly. 'I'll get a cup of tea,' I said. 'In this house the fire is always burning and the kettle is always on the boil.'

On the way back to school Miss Ormiston drove straight into the creek. Somehow Tom missed the road. In the darkness the ribbon of water did resemble the asphalt, particularly when the viewer was a near-blind woman too vain to wear her glasses.

When the policeman appeared at the door I felt again the horror of the previous year. 'No harm,' he said reassuringly, looking at my hands clutching my dressing-gown. 'Merely a very wet lady.'

I took her in and dried her, dressed her in one of my night-gowns and gave her hot milk. When she had dried out mentally as well as physically I called a taxi. She was remote, polite, grateful; but I felt we should never now be friends. We agreed to call one another Philippa and Miriam, a sop to gratitude, but I knew indebtedness was something Philippa Ormiston could not tolerate. She had been able to thank Mother for me because she thought of me as a useful inferior.

'Who was that?' called Mother. 'Sometimes, Miriam, I think you don't care if you keep me awake all night.' I told her. To my surprise her lines of petulance deepened into mirth and she laughed and laughed. 'Oh dear,' she said, 'my poor leg. Serve her right. The Hansens don't need patronage.'

'Don't be ridiculous, Mother,' I said. Nevertheless I tucked her up quite tenderly for once. I almost felt liking.

At the end of the week Philippa sent for me. She was wearing green stockings and a green and purple hand-woven skirt. I looked at my lace-up shoes, my down-to-earth two-piece costume and for once I did not feel awkward. My soul rejoiced like David in the Lord. 'I am normal,' I thought. I waited patiently.

'Miriam,' said Philippa, 'I have decided you must learn to drive.'

I merely stared.

She moved her hands nervously together. She made a cult of nervous hands. I held my long fingers unmoving on my lap. 'I must have a reliable teacher on hand at all times,' she continued. 'Quite obviously, I cannot always be free myself to run you home.'

'Quite obviously,' I said.

She looked at me suspiciously, but she said, 'You appear to understand perfectly.'

'Unfortunately,' I said, standing up to leave, 'I have no car, so that puts an end to the idea, doesn't it?'

She pushed back her dark hair from her face with an impatient hand. 'Don't be silly, Miriam. You must buy a car, of course.'

'Oh,' I said.

She must have seen the lines of obstinacy on my face, for she put her hand on my arm, a friendly gesture. Her eyes, I noted irrelevantly, were grey-green, not brown. Normally they were shadowed by her black hair into a semblance of brown. 'I must paint them,' I thought.

'You are wearing yourself out, Miriam. You have duties at home, you have duties here. It's too much for you. I need a reliable teacher on hand some evenings. I know it's unfair, but at least I can lessen the burden. I tackled Council again on your behalf.' She drew out a paper from her drawer. It was a copy of a letter to Council saying that she knew I had already received a small rise, but in view of the fact that she needed my help after hours it was not enough. It stated that I was the hardest working, most trustworthy member of staff. She suggested what seemed an enormous rise in salary. I looked at her. For once my own eyes must have reflected my incredulity. She laughed. 'Don't look like that, Miriam. They agreed.'

I felt curiously grateful. No one had ever sought my welfare before, not without my asking. It was true she needed my help but . . .

'Well, that's settled,' she said briskly, before I could say anything. 'A second-hand car. It won't be too difficult to make the payments. We'll go down tomorrow and look around.'

I nodded dumbly—determined not to cry. The next day we bought the Morris. I liked its nice compact shape. Within six weeks I had my licence. I have always been dextrous. As I left for work each morning I felt a new exuberance, a top-of-the-world feeling I had never known before. Mother now listened for the hum of an engine instead of footsteps. So agonising, trying to pick an engine coming down the street. It gave her something to do.

Activity, activity, activity. What a year! We varnished chairs, we sang—girls and staff—in two-part harmonies, we took on charities, everything from bed-jackets to egg-warmers and Sunday-afternoon visits to the surprised aged. We even had mornings; crisp, cold Autumn mornings, the air crackling with premonitions of winter, when we ate breakfast beside the local creeks. I did not mind, now that I had the Morris. Fungi galore. Cunningham-White was right. Philippa Ormiston knew the lot. Puff balls were eaten under the eye of Philippa and we prayed her knowledge of non-poisonous fungi was as good as she thought it was. Some of our younger staff turned pale at the sight of cacti. I remember pointing out a particularly prickly giant to one of our young science teachers. 'For God's sake,' she said, 'don't show it to Miss Ormiston or we'll have it for breakfast.'

Excursions multiplied. We waded in the local lagoons for all forms of small life. We scrambled through the mossy slippery paths of rain forests identifying the flora and fauna. It was perhaps unfortunate for Philippa that we had no girls like Gretchen that year. Our junior school had suffered from poor staffing for some time, with the consequence that the quality of our new seniors was poor. Their academic ability was so low that they discovered discarded beer cans rather than tadpoles or frogs in the lagoons, and were more interested in a group of schoolboys also exploring the rain forest than in the decayed mosses or staghorns that festooned the trees. Perhaps they were merely normal. At any rate the renaissance of thought and creativity envisaged by Philippa did not burst upon us, and the increased freedom and the over-young teachers produced, instead, a weakening of general discipline.

Yet it had its pleasant moments; and, even though I am one of those who consider that children come to school primarily to work, I must admit I enjoyed some of our activities. Shakespeare evenings, Milton evenings, Wordsworth evenings (how those poets loved an evening), and those of us who stayed sat with the girls after supper on the carpet in Philippa's drawing-room and sang to Philippa's guitar or listened to her cello, soft and lovely in the fire-light.

I think Philippa Ormiston was lonely. At first she looked at our senior staff as if we were encumbrances she hoped would disappear. The pudgy competence of Ann worried her, also her cynicism. Philippa's activities to Ann smelt of folk-dance societies, campaigns to preserve derelict buildings. 'In other words,' said Ann, 'the whole pack of folksy, semi-adolescent, conservative English. I'm allergic to them.' And so, at first, the good critical mind of Ann and the fine aesthetic mind of Philippa slid away from each other when they should have met for the benefit of the school.

I felt sympathy for Ann. I, too, found it difficult to absorb the crop of brash untrained youth that flooded the staff-room. Mona Edison sulked in her corner as she discovered that each new graduate, untrained, inexperienced, received more money than she did. 'What use are they?' she wailed. 'A few fancy ideas about English and history and French. What do they know about getting children to learn?'

I avoided such discussions whenever possible. I had my duty, the job of helping a new Head to organise a school and, while my own academicism, my age, my instincts, pulled me by nature to the side of Ann and Mona, I resisted the temptation to fraternise in hate sessions. My job was not to decide what sort of school Philippa Ormiston should build. My job as Deputy was to assist her to build in her image.

There was one thing. Miss Cunningham-White grizzled less. Check stockings, purple frocks, hand-woven tweed scarves notwithstanding, our new Head was a 'lady'. She had been educated in England with the best people. On official occasions she never forgot her gloves, even if she had knitted them herself.

Philippa rumpled her untidy hair. 'We must have youth, Miriam. Girls in a boarding-school need young staff; it gives them deeper security, a feeling of home with bigger brothers and sisters.'

'Sisters at any rate,' I said, 'and not too many parents, eh?'

She missed the irony in my voice. 'Exactly. Take Rachel.'
We took Rachel. Rachel was attractive. She laughed frequently. Her blue summer-sea eyes melted long-lashed to tone
with her shoulder-length blonde curls. Not even fashion or
hair spray could rob Rachel's hair of curl. She taught sewing
and craft, part of the new wider policy of the school to make
sure that girls had the necessary womanly arts, and she was
barely twenty. She wore the knee-length socks of her contemporaries, the calf-filling boots, the bottom-flipping little skirts.
And Philippa loved her. She also smoked cigarettes with the
senior girls behind the old gym., and covered up for them
when they went to town without a pass. She carried notes to
Grammar boys and in general behaved like the teenager she
almost was. I did manage to drop a hint to Philippa, but she
only said, 'Dear me, she is a naughty girl, isn't she? Such fun.'
When Philippa loved she allowed no facts to intrude between
her and the object of her affection. Her love for Rachel was
obvious. Some of the other young staff members were plainly
jealous. Rachel was invited to the office for cups of tea;
Rachel had to help with the assembly; Rachel had to sleep in
the best room; Rachel had to have the easiest dormitory;
Rachel sat at the feet of Philippa when she played the cello
or the guitar. Some nights when the last notes had drifted into
silence her hand would stroke Rachel's hair as if it, too, could
draw music down. Orpheus, I thought. A purple robe and
notes of music tangling in the hair of a nymph. That would
be the way to paint it. Or perhaps Saul and David.

'I feel so responsible,' said Philippa. 'All these young things
in my charge. Away from home, too. Rachel, I mean. She's
so young.'

'I think she can manage,' I said. 'The Rachels can usually
manage.' For some inexplicable reason I thought of Robert's
wife. A pale wisp and a lambent flame. But there was something in common.

'You are so hard, Miriam,' said Philippa. 'You have been
shut up too long with old people. You should get out and
enjoy the young.'

'After so many years of the young,' I said drily, 'I can well dispense with them in my spare hours.' Philippa's black hair flapped witch-like around her, but the rocky lines of my withdrawn face must have warned her to try no spells. She changed the subject.

Meanwhile the resentment in the staff-room grew. The younger ones resented the favours shown to Rachel, the older ones resented their seasoned opinions being ignored in favour of youth. Each tended to find her own favourite amongst the young, and there were days when staff members did not speak to staff members because of fancied insults to favourites. Ann's badly printed stencils continued to roll off the press, and she carefully ignored the Coventry to which the Head persistently sent her as a mark of displeasure.

'We are beginning,' she said, wiping the surplus carbon from her hands, 'to resemble an Oriental harem. If you don't stop bickering over these ridiculous young women I shall have to leave.' She looked balefully at Mona Edison and Mrs Ellis who were defending their protégées against Rachel.

In the meantime Rachel accepted the Head's affection as if it were her due. She was the spoilt only daughter of a Melbourne merchant. People had paid dues to Rachel ever since she could remember. For that very reason I knew Rachel, in time, would hurt Philippa. I was there when it happened.

'It's an invitation to play at the local musical group,' said Philippa. 'I can take a member of staff with me. I know Rachel would love to come. This Saturday.'

I thought of the local group. Froggy Daley who combined horns with art; my own cousin, Michael Hansen, spare, tough, stringy and Puritan, who could tear the guts out of a violin; gentle Mrs Mersey who had followed me around at High School and now fluted away with notes like herself, high-pitched and somewhat hysterical. A typical country town group, middle-aged or old, but not bad musicians for all that. I wondered what they would make of Philippa.

'Why don't you ask Ann Denham?' I said. 'She likes music. She knows the group. In fact, she once played the violin with them. Or Miss Cunningham-White?' Philippa's black eyes looked at me opaquely. She had a curious crocheted orange band tied around her black hair.

'It is youth we must encourage. Youth, always youth, Miriam. Faith in youth is essential. I'll send for Rachel now.'

Rachel Hutton was not unkind. She was young.

'Thanks awfully, Miss Ormiston,' she said. 'I'd love to come, of course, but it's Saturday. I'm afraid I have a date.'

I watched the frost creep up the face of Philippa Ormiston. Instead of simply saying, 'That is all right, Rachel', and dismissing her, she sat for a moment drumming her fingers on the desk while a nerve twitched in her cheek.

'This is important,' she said. 'You can break your date.'

Rachel Hutton was young, but she had the obstinacy of the spoilt.

'I'm sorry, Miss Ormiston. It is my night off, and David's. I'm afraid we've already planned our evening.'

'David who?'

Rachel looked surprised, but answered, 'David Payne. He teaches at Grammar.'

'I'll ring Mr Emerson,' said Philippa. 'He is headmaster. He can tell David you're working.'

Rachel's blue eyes hardened to agate points of black. 'I'm sorry, Miss Ormiston. If you do that I shall have to resign.'

'I see,' said Philippa.

'May I go?'

'Yes. You are dismissed.' The voice and the manner suggested an English lady who has just finished discussing the menu for the day with the cook.

I, too, rose as Rachel left. I looked at the tic in the otherwise frozen face and I was sorry. Impulsively I touched her arm. 'Youth is like that, Philippa. Thoughtless.'

She ignored me. 'I thought she liked me,' she said as if to herself.

I smiled, and felt it was rather a stupid smile. 'Of course she likes you,' I said; 'but it is natural for a girl of her age to have a date with a boy.'

She pulled her arm away and almost viciously pushed me aside. 'Don't touch me,' she said. 'I hate to be touched. And did you have dates with boys at that age, Miriam? Did you put your dates before your duty?' My neck flushed, and I hated her for making me say it: 'I never had the chance,' I said. 'I've never had a date in my life. For one thing, I have never looked like Rachel Hutton.'

She looked me up and down. The big bones in my fingers looked bare and raw, my bony face felt more ridgy than ever. She smiled. 'More fool them,' she said. 'I have never had much opinion of the male sex.' I could have said 'I always preferred my father to my mother. He was big, capable, creative.' But I said nothing, and I discerned some subtlety of tenderness grow towards me in Philippa.

I thought the matter was ended, but it soon became obvious that for Philippa it was not. I was on duty the following Saturday evening. I had spent that afternoon alone on the edges of one of our local gorges, painting; and I was still imbued with a sense of timelessness; the bottomless gashes in the earth, the streams embedded like crystals in rock thousands of feet below. I had been humanity impaled on eternity, Alpha and Omega or Zeus and Hades. I had tried to paint my sense of God, the heights and depths of the eternal nature.

Week-end duty should have been Cunningham-White's, but I obliged. A sense of God could not survive the attacks of Mother's carping earthiness; and God knows poor old White deserved a few outings. Here at school, with the girls absorbed in creaking Hollywood 32 mm and Philippa buried in the depths of her flat with her cello, I could at least huddle over the staff table and continue my dreaming.

It was late supper that night. I stayed and Philippa poured tea behind a silver teapot while the girls mastered the art of genteel traymobile service. I could see the flicker of nervousness in Philippa's fingers and the silver pot wobbled, spilling the tea over the saucer. A social sin. She was dressed in some flowing medieval garment which could only be called a tea gown. (No one should play a cello in short skirts.) She flowed in vivid green like a black-topped willow, and the silver teapot wobbled.

'Do you mind waiting for a while, Miriam?' she said as we farewelled the last prefect.

'It's late,' I said.

'I know. Rachel isn't home.'

'It's not late for the young,' I answered; 'barely midnight.'

'Rachel,' she said in a voice strangled like the sound of a concertina, 'went for a picnic with David Payne. They must have had an accident. What could you do at Point Summit at midnight?'

It was obvious of course. Youth could do a great deal at Point Summit at midnight. Modern cars are not cold, not even at 5,000 feet. I had listened to the giggling stories of my contemporaries.

'The young stay late,' I said. 'I'm quite sure David is a competent driver.' She clapped her hands impatiently. Behind her neck floated a green chiffon scarf, attached to the collar of her gown. Her face was black with jealousy. I shook myself: too much heaven and hell in those gorges. What was jealousy? A normal emotion. But why should a middle-aged headmistress be jealous of a twenty-year-old girl?

'I'm ringing the headmaster of the Grammar school,' she said.

'You're unwise,' I answered.

'I cannot risk an accident.'

'Of course not.'

'Get me the number, Miriam.'

Obediently my fingers found the holes in the telephone dial. A somewhat grumpy voice answered, 'Yes?' I suspected he had crawled from bed.

'Mr Emerson?'

'Yes.'

'Miss Ormiston would like to speak to you.'

I heard him mutter, 'What the hell?' before I passed the receiver to Philippa.

'One of my teachers is missing,' she said. 'She should have

been home long ago.' Pause. 'David Payne. A most unreliable young man.' A longer pause. Philippa's black brows met in a straight line. 'The girl is barely twenty, Mr Emerson. I am responsible for her. No—she was not on duty.'

This time the pause was a very long one. Mr Emerson must have made his feelings quite clear, for Philippa stamped her foot. The hysteria was replaced by anger. 'If I can wait around here in a state of anxiety, Mr Emerson, I don't see why you can't get out of your bed and do something.'

I was standing on the other side of the room but I could now hear the man's voice quite clearly.

'My dear Miss Ormiston, it is not my business, nor, if you'll excuse my saying so, is it yours. They are adults. Off duty. If he wishes, he can do what he likes with her without any interference from us.'

She turned pink, a faint purple-pink that ran into the roots of her dark hair. She put down the receiver as a car drew up.

'Come here, Rachel.'

The girl was creeping along the corridor, shoes in hand. She stopped, startled.

'What have you been doing at Point Summit at this hour?'

The girl's face hardened. Beneath her mini skirt her lovely long legs were brown. A few twigs clung to the back of her brown hair and along the fibres of her woollen jacket.

'That is my business, Miss Ormiston.'

Philippa was shaking. Her words tumbled, barely intelligible, from her lips. 'How dare you worry me like this? How dare you? I didn't know what had happened to you.'

'Didn't you, Miss Ormiston? Do you really want to know?'

Philippa was silent. Rachel's blue eyes passed contemptuously over the flushed face. 'Perhaps you can imagine it for yourself. Or perhaps you can't. A young man held me in his arms and kissed me again and again and again. You don't like that, do you? You can't bear the thought of young men touching me, can you, Miss Ormiston?'

Philippa's hand tangled in the dangling drape. 'Get out,' she said. 'Get out! I never want to see you again.'

Rachel shrugged. 'Suits me,' she said. 'I'm moving over to Grammar soon. David and I are getting married next week.'

I could see Philippa was sorry she had asked me to stay. I put on my coat and pulled on my cap, my face registering non-interest. 'I'll see you on Monday,' I said.

She did not answer, and I realised with horror that she was crying, eyes and mouth open, while the tears coursed down her cheeks into the drooping neck of the green gown. I closed the door.

And so Rachel left to be joined in holy matrimony to the man of her choice. But they did not live happily ever after, and later I wondered how far Philippa's jealousy had been responsible for that unfortunate marriage. Rachel, beautiful, spoilt, with parents who contrived to give her everything but mental independence; and David, small-time schoolteacher, resentful, possessive. In two years they were divorced. Rachel had already run away with a ship's officer. Six months later David blew his brains out. Where does tragedy begin? Rachel's infatuation was undoubtedly fed by Philippa's 'don't'.

As far as the school was concerned, the marriage was beneficial. Philippa, of necessity, began at long last to trust her experienced staff and to value Ann Denham. They became friends, and it was a friendship which lasted at least until the school Council parted them and (I hope) beyond that. I like to think of angular Philippa and chubby Ann exchanging letters wherever Philippa may go. I myself would never be close to Philippa. Pity was our only point of contact. We were different. I like a school to be disciplined. I believe that people send their children to learn, to pass examinations, and, if they are clever, to win scholarships. I do not believe that children suffer simply because they are expected to work. To the lonely, work can be a relief. Philippa's school needed high-powered pupils, and at that period they were few. We collected the intellectual flotsam and jetsam of the district primary schools; the daughters of expatriate Victorians or Queenslanders, dedicated with blind zeal to private education;

the children of graziers, in love with their horses and long
lazy sunny afternoons in the saddle. It is nice to dress up,
nice to act, nice to sing, nice to be a lady, to take the bundle
of woollies to the poor rejected old, in the twilight home on
the hill: but Etherington parents came from good stolid Protestant stock; they wanted something concrete for their money.

And so the school flitted on its way, pretending much, and
satisfying few. The pupils stayed up later, they went out more
often. In the dormitories the transistors blared, the sickly
odour of cosmetics permeated the atmosphere. On Saturday
they waltzed round the corridors like creatures from Mars,
with their hair rolled into ridiculous shapes pinned beneath
coloured nets and the masts of the ever-present transistors
jigging above their heads. They were not clever girls, and with
the growth of freedom they undoubtedly grew ruder, particularly in the junior school. Poor Mrs Ellis sat in the staff-room
palpitating beneath the strain. 'Feel my heart, Mona,' she said,
pressing Mona's hand to her woolly breast. 'Feel it. It begins
pumping away at the very thought of taking second year.'

'Little beasts,' said Mona.

She was wrong. They were not little beasts, but they often
behaved as if they were. They were undermined, swung off
their tees, by a surplus of junior staff, half of whom should
have left with Rachel; a staff that allowed girls to loll on their
beds while they giggled through anecdotes of their own parties
and boy friends. I have always contended that the deteriora-
tion of modern youth began then, and not, as some would
have it, two years later.

To make matters worse, Etherington began to look like a
foreign bazaar. The school has always been short of good
teachers, denying any connection between cut-rate salaries
and non-dedicated staff. So Philippa solved the problem in
her own way. They were taught science by a girl in a soft
draped sari, with delicate expressive hands, who spoke English
with an intonation I could not master. The pupils mastered
it less well than I did. Music flowed from the hands of an
expatriate Pole, Paul Pilsudski, whose wife had been mis-

laid somewhere or other. The strains of Beethoven, Mozart, Brahms, drifted like oral incense along our corridors, and Ann Denham forgot to turn the handle of the duplicator while she listened.

I am not musical (I take after Father), but I tried hard to be sympathetic to Mr Pilsudski. He was gaunt and spare like myself, with hair the colour of certain rodents, woolly grey-brown. I said so to Ann, and Ann looked at me and said, 'You have such an apt subconscious, Miriam', which was not really fair. I am sure my subconscious is quite normal.

His own musical compositions were divided into parts. Strange atonal cacophonies named nut, bolt, screw, etc. He asked how I liked them. I try to be pleasant. I have always encouraged the creative, and I know only too well the dampening effect of non-appreciation. Anyone who lived with Mother and Robert is familiar with denigration. So I said, 'Most interesting. I like the first one best. Nut, wasn't it?' Mr Pilsudski's pale-blue eyes reddened and he hissed above my head, 'Zere is no first one, Miss Hanzen. Zere is only unity. The soul at one with God.'

I brought my hands together, clapping them lightly beneath his nose.

'In my Father's house are many mansions,' I said.

'You are a non-believer,' he replied, which was ridiculous: as I have attended Church every Sunday all my life.

He was a great performer, but unfortunately he was the only one who played the piano during the children's lessons. Occasionally I found his pupils in the playground. They had slipped away while he played, but he never missed them.

'You do not understand, Miriam,' said Philippa, when I reported his negligence. 'He is an artist, a creative artist.'

'No doubt,' I said drily. 'But I cannot imagine Della Graves accepting that explanation when Isobel fails Grade 4.'

Philippa did not reply. She sat looking at me gravely, unspeaking as if she hoped my too solid flesh would melt, as Ann Denham used to say. So I did just that: melted away. I had done my duty.

French in the junior school was now the province of a Greek reared in Algeria; a sweet woman in her mid-thirties with a thoroughly commendable sense of duty. She read French very well, but could not render a line of it in acceptable English. '*Regardez les fleurs dans le jardin*' was translated as, 'Regard the bloomers in the park.' She played the flute very nicely and the Saturday evening entertainment benefited. The children's French declined. I liked her, but I was not sorry when a lonely Greek snapped her up for immediate marriage the following May. They had met at a migrants' club in Sydney.

'You're a dark horse,' said Miss Cunningham-White slyly.

Miss Nikolides came to Ann Denham. 'Why does Miss Cunningham-White refer to me as the black animal?' Indignation mingled with her sweetness, but we farewelled her with music and gifts without the point ever being clarified.

Ting-a-ling went the flutes, boom-boom went the cello. We were all so active, yet Philippa was lonely until her friend Margaret Kersten arrived.

'The school has needed a carpenter for a long time,' she said. 'I have a friend. A woman. She has been minding my dog.'

'A carpenter?' I said.

'Why not?' said Philippa. 'I am sure, Miriam, you were quite capable of mastering your father's trade.'

'You have a point there,' I said.

Mother, of course, thought the idea ridiculous. She banged around the house with a great deal of unnecessary noise. 'I suppose you must continue to work in a school with women carpenters,' she said.

'You know I must,' I said.

'You career women!' said Mother. 'You take the bread out of men's mouths. No wonder Robert finds it difficult to manage.'

'Robert is not a carpenter,' I said, wearily stoking the stove.

'You know quite well what I mean, Miriam. He never had

a chance with you around. You encouraged your father to treat him as an inferior.'

I filled the kettle and carried it to the stove. I took care to appear unperturbed. 'He was inferior,' I said, 'in fact, plain dumb.'

She lashed out at me with her stick, but I sidestepped her, grabbing the crutch from her hand as I went. She was forced to sit down. 'If you do not behave yourself, Mother,' I said calmly, 'I shall put it on top of that cupboard over there and carry you to bed.'

She bit her lip and sat in her chair, refusing to talk. For half an hour we sat there, the old woman grasping the arms of the chair and I, her daughter, clasping her staff in my hand. In the end she could bear it no longer. Perhaps she was about to fall. Anyway, she apologised and I gave the weapon back to her. I was glad Mother was mobile again. I could now thwart her nastiness whenever I wished, and somehow I seemed to wish more often than I once did. When she took up her bed and walked again I was freed partially in spirit.

I don't know what I expected from a woman carpenter. Perhaps at the bottom of my heart I secretly agreed with Mother. I certainly did not expect Margaret Kersten. When I first came into the staff-room for our monthly meeting I did not notice her. Then I heard a man's voice say, 'Am I supposed to be part of this ritual orgy, Philippa?'

I turned around, surprised. A short stocky blond man was standing near the door. I saw the stain on his tweed trousers and smelt the leather of his belted coat. The short hair was wavy and brushed straight back from the forehead. A cigarette dangled from the fingers.

Philippa smiled. Her mouth twisted with fondness. 'I'd like you to stay, Margaret. You may as well meet the staff and get it over. I assure you our ritual is brief and comparatively harmless.'

Philippa beckoned us over one by one and a hand roughened with work took mine. I smoothed my semi-bruised fingers as I looked into the clear pale-blue eyes. She merely said,

'Glad to meet you, Miss Hansen', but I felt one of those moments of instant liking that come to you three or four times in an entire life.

Ann Denham caught my eye and grinned. 'She nearly caught you out that time, Miriam,' she whispered.

'I don't understand,' I said. But I did. From under my lids I studied them all. Cunningham-White was obviously flabbergasted. Her adam's-apple, over-prominent at any time, palpitated in her throat with jugular disapproval. Mrs Ellis looked as if there were things other than second year that sent the heart pounding dangerously.

'We are thrilled you are here,' she said. 'It's most relieving to see you. I simply could not imagine a woman as a carpenter.'

'Oh,' said Miss Kersten. 'You mean you're delighted I'm a man?'

Ann Denham choked beside me as Mrs Ellis tried to flutter her way out of the impasse.

Mona Edison, rangy and masculine in a feminine sort of way herself, merely said, 'I suppose you are a trained carpenter, Miss Kersten', at which the deep voice which I realised now had the mellowness of Philippa's cello, replied, 'Yes, I can assure you I'm qualified.'

'I'm glad to know it,' said Mona. 'I'm a trained teacher myself.'

She cast a look of triumph at the young graduates, the sari, Miss Cunningham-White and Mr Pilsudski. 'I fear,' she said, 'we have a great number of untrained people on this staff.'

With Margaret Kersten came Dido, although she was not present at that meeting. It was strange, for later Dido attended every staff meeting and every Council meeting. Margaret Kersten had a tiny cottage next to the school and Philippa invited us to meet Dido that afternoon. She was a female Dalmatian with huge black spots and a broad slobbery mouth. She was ten years old, over-weight, over-exuberant, over-well —over everything. I have always liked dogs. I had always wanted a dog of my own, but of course Mother hated them.

Dido came slobbering over and I patted her head. She stood with her paws on my shoulder.

'Down,' said Margaret sharply.

'No, don't!' I laughed. 'I like her.'

'It's just as well,' said Margaret. 'I assure you she'll do it whether you like her or not. She is obstinate, dirty, sensual, and I like her, too.'

We laughed.

Dido was a friendly dog, with followers. She was never without an attendant train of dogs. She obeyed Margaret as a rule, and she loved Philippa. She was supposed to stay in the carpenter's workshed with Margaret, but she followed Philippa around the school. Shut out from a class-room, she leant with her head against the door and wailed in a curious sort of howling chant like a recorded singer involved in a duet with herself. I am lucky. I have good control in my class-room. I have always found discipline is no problem provided you keep the girls busy and active. Apart from an initial giggle, my girls soon grew used to Dido.

'It's only Dido,' I said. 'Now get on with your prose.' They did. Ann Denham also had no problems, but apparently Dido's laments disrupted junior classes, particularly those in the care of the young and inexperienced. Mr Pilsudski suffered most, for Dido could not stand nuts, bolts and screws, either disparate or unified. She sat outside the music room and howled, with her muzzle pointed upward, until Mr Pilsudski would rush out pulling at his hair and screaming, 'You must shut up ze dog. I have never been so insulted. I left my wife for lezzer insult than that.' Both Dido and Philippa remained unmoved, and in the end Mr Pilsudski would retire to continue with the next creation, presumably hammer and nails.

Margaret Kersten's shed was a haven of scented shaved wood. I watched her strong hands fashion the leg of a table. She was wearing a polo-necked sweater and blue slacks. There was no trace of make-up on her face. I felt moved by the lack of artifice, that barrier of deceit that stands between almost all women and their inner selves. I felt a contact with the reality I was accustomed to associate with men rather than with women. Her fingers moved with the steadiness of a fox after prey. Hair lines of pleasure modified my own gauntness as I watched her. I picked up a tiny bird in full flight. She had carved it from wood and it balanced on my hand like the essence of all falconry.

'Why?' I said. 'How?'

'No secret art,' she said. 'I simply like wood. I always have. I was born in a timber camp in Gippsland. My father was a cutter. My mother died when I was two. He decided to raise me himself. He never liked my mother's sisters. I suppose it was a strange life. A camp of men and a little girl. But I did not think so.'

'My mother came from Andy's Creek,' I said; 'but timber did nothing for her. She hated it.'

'Some women do,' Margaret said. 'Men don't. They taught me to live like a man. Perhaps to think like one. It made me impatient with most women. They live buried in kitchens and miss the forests.'

'All Marthas,' I said. 'Still, I suppose we have to eat.'

'I suppose so.' She laughed.

'If you like men, why do you come to a girls' school?' I asked.

'Father died,' she answered. 'I had to earn a living. Not many carpenters employ women. A girls' school seemed an ideal solution. Then there is Philippa.'

'Where did you meet her?' I asked.

'School before last. She had just arrived from England.'

I stroked the wing of the bird. 'I see,' I said. 'But you're not alike. Quite the opposite.'

'I don't know. You could be wrong there. Philippa is a gipsy at heart; a forest creature. Then again, she is a musician. A St Cecilia, someone to offset the damn loneliness of institutions like this.' She ran her plane along a surface of cedar. I saw with a remembered delight the beauty of the grain. 'It's strange,' she said, 'how often the human race commit their young to loneliness in the name of doing what's good for them. It's a bloody shame.' I nodded, and put down the bird. I realised with interest that strong language no longer disturbed me. It was my debt to Ann Denham. 'It is lonely,' I said, 'but I like solitude.'

'The solitude of open spaces, yes. Human institutionalised alienation, no.'

There was vehemence in her voice and I felt embarrassed. I picked up the bird and stroked it. 'It is lovely,' I said. 'I like it.'

'Keep it.'

I hesitated, and she laughed, put down her tools and lit a cigarette. I held my breath so that I should not inhale the fumes. Father always regarded smoking as a filthy habit and the new research on lung cancer certainly justified his attitude. Margaret breathed out and the little bird floated on a white cloud.

'Morning's minion,' said Margaret. 'Keep it, Miriam. It shall be your minion, too. I'll expect a return some day. One of those deep, black, depressive paintings you're working on at the moment.'

'The gorge?' I turned my face away in case my own feeling should surface in my eyes or skin. 'But . . .'

'I'm a pryer,' she said. 'I watched you, last Sunday. I did not intrude. It was not my business.'

'Thanks,' I said.

I took the bird home and it stood poised on top of my bookcase. I did not bother to show it to Mother. Somehow I could not have borne her criticism.

The same month, Philippa decided we should plant a rose garden. We prepared the earth the week after Miss Nikolides was married. She had asked us all to Sydney for the wedding, but Mother became ill the day before I was due to leave so I did not go. Miss Cunningham-White confided sidewise that it was white and sumptuous and just a wee bit vulgar. I was sorry I missed it.

By the August vacation, the soil was ready. 'The roses must be planted. Any volunteers?' asked Philippa.

Ann Denham shrugged her coat over her plumpness. 'My dearest Philippa,' she said, 'you must be joking. I do not plant school roses in my vacations. In fact, I propose to don the nearest thing to a bikini my ample form will tolerate and bask on the sand of an ocean resort.'

In the end there remained only Philippa Ormiston, Margaret Kersten and Miriam Hansen. The loyal trio. Monday to Saturday we worked and Sunday we rested. I helped to turn the cold brown earth once again, while Margaret fashioned the winding paths and built the bird-baths and Philippa shaped the pools and painted the lattices. The day of the planting we had a picnic.

I was happy that day, in an old brown shirt and my solid brown boots, and a pair of khaki overalls Margaret lent me. I spread the roots over the mound of earth while Margaret held the plants. I could smell her stained grey trousers and see the lines of her neck through the blue shirt. She was seasoned by sun like a man who works long hours in the open air. Her indented weather-beaten face was kind, and the blue eyes, vivid and alive, smiled down at me. I have never desired to kiss my suffering fellow humans, male or female. It is an unhygienic habit. But I did feel in that moment a wave of love that suffused my being. I wanted to put my arms around her, to feel the security of her taut, hard lines. Philippa stood beside me in tartan slacks she had woven herself. An old felt hat was pulled over her forehead to protect her from the sun and the ends of her matching tartan ribbon straggled out with the lengths of black hair. She was sallow but her skin was soft. She was Margaret's friend. What would she have thought if she had read the desire behind my eyes? I frowned and bent my head to concentrate on the spreading roots, while Philippa stood ready with the watering-can. It was sufficient, after all, simply to be included, to feel part of them. Perhaps the Holy Ghost in the Trinity felt something like I felt that day.

The water sprinkled from Philippa's can. I watched it soak into the earth. 'We had roses at home in England,' she said. 'It was a run-down little cottage but a wonderful garden. My mother and sisters worked very hard after Father left. We had lavender and pansies and mignonette. Headier than perfume. It's funny how permanent is the memory of scent—but I liked the roses best.'

'You're a romantic,' said Margaret, striking her rose into a new section.

I said, 'I suppose your family is still in England.'

I meant to be conversational, to assert myself as part of the trio. I wondered why Margaret's knuckles whitened on the stem of the rose. Philippa looked at me with her chameleon eyes blankly innocent.

'Yes,' she said, 'they stayed there. I was the only one away from home during that air raid. I escaped. So did Father. But then he had deserted us years earlier. I've always been religious, but I sometimes think it is the wicked not the meek who inherit the earth.'

I bent my head above the next rose. I could feel the flush on the back of my neck. Margaret lowered the rose and I felt a reassuring flick of her hand over mine.

'There,' said Margaret, 'that's the last rose. We'll call this section "Miriam". Peace and Madame Butterfly will bloom in your honour.'

'Sounds like a tragic opera,' said Philippa.

'Peace,' I said. 'I like that.'

Philippa picked up the garden rake. 'I hereby name this section "Miriam".' She turned to the far square planted with reds and whites, Crimson Glory and Iceberg. 'You,' she said, 'are "Margaret". And this mass of Talismans shall be called "Philippa". I have always liked the multi-coloured and the gold. Would you believe it, when I was small I used to weep because my hair was not gold? Nearly all the princesses in the stories had gold hair.'

'You are gold,' said Margaret.

'There was Snow White and Rose Red,' I said. 'They had black hair.'

I suppose we looked ridiculous that late winter's day in the clear frost-blue light of the tableland filtered through a brilliant sun: three maiden ladies in overalls and trousers, planting roses and naming them after one another. But we were happy. The gold and the black looked at each other and I felt the telepathy of love between them, but I did not resent it. I was to remember that day. Those roses represented for me my stake in Etherington.

We packed up our tools and returned to Philippa's room for coffee and biscuits by the fire. Philippa played her cello and Margaret smoked endless cigarettes; and I sat and fondled Dido's ears while she slept noisily at my feet.

The roses took root and spring came. The school spun into the tension of third term; but somehow we continued to dance when we should have worked. Our results were less than good that summer. Philippa merely flicked her long black hair back with her fingers and said, 'Well, they can't have everything.' Ann's eyes met mine. We both knew that Philippa despised them, so there was no way of conveying to her that certain parents did in fact want everything and were beginning to grizzle about not getting it. We packed our books away, cleaned the desks, and set out for the summer vacation.

I missed Etherington that summer, or should I say I missed Margaret Kersten, who left with Philippa for a trip to Fiji and the islands. Sometimes I sat in our kitchen at home and looked at Mother without looking. Tap, tap, tap. What irony of existence forces two people without mutual liking to live together till death do them part? Even a bad marriage is your own choice. Or is all choice a mockery? Tap, tap, tap round the room, poking, prying, criticising. I found myself wishing we had left her in bed for ever. That tap, tap, tap and the voice whose spited edge drew nearer to the core of hate every day seemed to pursue me.

Sometimes I left her, taking the car and speeding away through the shadowed hills to refuges beside volcanic, boulder-strewn streams. Fortunately I had plenty to do. Philippa was aiming now at a cosmopolitan school, having exhausted the possibilities of a cosmopolitan staff. Already we had pupils from Nauru and Hong Kong, with another coming from Singapore the following year. And then she bought the poems of an Aboriginal poet. Philippa gravitated to charitable and religious organisations like a moth to flame, and soon she was attending conferences, joining societies for the assimilation of coloured folk. 'We are all guilty,' she said. 'Our ancestors took this land from these people. We must make amends.'

'Not mine,' said Ann Denham. 'They didn't arrive until 1860, then they sat down in Sydney and refused to budge, on a suburban square of earth that no Aborigine had bothered to look at for years.'

Philippa ignored her. 'We must have a scholarship,' she said, 'a scholarship for the Aboriginal girls of Meridale. They must have equal rights to attend this school.'

'I thought we had persecuted them enough,' said Mona Edison.

I sighed. It was not a matter of lacking sympathy for the coloured people, but I recognised the light in Philippa's eye. Brochures, placards, visiting speakers. We were already suffering from the after-effects of an urban science professor, who, bearded and romantic, had urged the importance of science during a long week-end seminar at a local school. Led by Philippa, we had responded like knights of old to the challenge of science. Most of our girls could be guided through history and geography, and with a stroke of luck get a pass in English or biology or perhaps art.

'It is a scientific world,' said Philippa, still hypnotised by the bearded expert. 'We must meet the needs of our expanding universe.' And the children of the Graveses and the Dentons and the Harrises were channelled to the laboratories, where they sank to their natural level, and failed.

As usual the parents blamed the teachers. They now forgot that Ann and myself, backed by Ina Spurway, had resisted the scientific pretensions of the mediocre children of mediocre parents. Fluffy Della Graves planted her blue-sandalled feet in front of me in the main street. Little lines of annoyance pitted the corners of her mouth, revealing her real age.

'I don't know what you've been doing, Miriam. Our Susie was just as clever as Annette Winters who went to High School. Or, for that matter, Brenda Missenden who passed last year from Etherington.'

'Brenda did not take science and mathematics,' I said. I watched the clock tower instead of Della's face and noted that it was fast. It was always fast. Slow Meridale took its time from a fast clock.

'Surely it's your job to advise the girls properly.' I could feel the edge of nastiness in her voice.

'Oh, we do,' I said, not moving my face, 'but some parents are so difficult. I mean if a father really believes his child is cleverer than its contemporaries, and he insists on a scientific career, he has the final choice. We are an independent school, aren't we?'

'Miss Ormiston encouraged us,' she said. 'It was your job to warn us.'

I was silent. I was remembering Della at a Meridale show long years ago. She had insisted on ice-cream and the tumble-bug. She had Froggy Daley in tow. 'You'll be sick,' I whispered, but Froggy, given one chance in a lifetime to partner Della, had said loudly, 'How would Miriam know? No one buys her ice-cream or takes her on the tumble-bug.' I remembered holding her head after she climbed out, no longer pretty, merely damp and cold and smelly. And she said, 'You should have stopped me, Miriam. You're older than I am.'

I looked at her petulant face. 'Still tumble-bugging?' I asked.

She gave me a queer look. 'Really, Miriam. There are times when I simply do not understand you. It is lucky you are a good teacher and a conscientious one.' She walked away and I felt a moment's unease for Philippa. Or was it unease for myself? If Philippa went away Margaret would go too. I could not bear the thought.

Science had failed. It was now the turn of the Aborigines. 'We must be in the vanguard of enlightenment,' said Philippa to the assembled parents on Speech Day. 'We, who have so much, must bring the original Australian into our midst. We must restore the birthright we have filched from him. Education is his passport to a better life, and so we are offering a scholarship to an Aboriginal girl to enable her to complete a secondary course.'

It had not been easy to choose. The Aborigines had lived in shanties on our ex-dump for years. They were there in my grandfather's time, and I must say that, as far as I can remember, they seemed reasonably content with their lot. Galvanised iron still sheltered many of them. For long years no one in our progressive town had asked awkward questions about schooling. It solved problems if they simply did not turn up. But now there was a sprinkling of children in the primary schools and we finally chose, after much heart burning, a twelve-year-old called Ella Middleton.

'It's a good name,' said Philippa. 'We already have white Middletons. They are related to the Quirindi Middletons, you know. The big stud owners.'

I rubbed my finger along my jaw bone. 'So is Ella,' I said. 'Her old man maintains his old man was a Middleton of Quirindi.'

'How nice,' said Philippa. 'They must be cousins. How nice for Ella and Anna Middleton.'

I looked at her in amazement, but Philippa was not joking. 'If I were you,' I said, 'I should not mention it.'

It was my job this summer to see that Ella had all she needed for school. 'I can trust you, Miriam,' said Philippa, as she and Margaret packed for Fiji. 'I know that you intend staying in Meridale this summer.'

'I always stay home,' I said.

This day in January, I left Mother mumbling in the kitchen and I put Dido in the car. I can't say Mother was particularly pleasant about Dido, but I ignored her anger. Philippa and Margaret expected me to look after Dido and that was that.

'You see,' said Philippa, 'Dido trusts you and you know, Miriam, trust is so important.'

Margaret patted the spotted head with her rough hand. Her

eyes held mine. 'She's a nice beast,' she said, 'even if she does snore. She's quite good company, really.'

The first evening Mother kept backing away with her stick held in front of her. Finally I took it from her and put it out of reach on a cupboard. She had managed to back into a corner, and crouched there helplessly, while Dido eyed her malevolently from the rug and growled in her throat. I admired Dido's growl. It had the richness of an operatic contralto.

'You hit Dido,' I said.

'Don't be ridiculous, Miriam.'

'You hit Dido with that stick. She only growls at people who threaten her.'

'This is my house, Miriam. The dog is savage.' Remnants of maternal dominance. But I pay the rent, Mother, I buy the food, Mother.

'The dog is not savage,' I said. 'But if you feel unhappy about her, Dido and I can go elsewhere. I'll get Robert to come up.'

'Robert is busy,' she said. 'You know quite well, Miriam, he can't afford to come up this year.'

'Then I'll pack your things and drive you down there,' I said.

Her lovely, moist eyes swivelled uneasily. She was caught and she knew it. She loved Robert, but Robert's wife was too busy to worry overmuch about her comfort.

'I would not dream of imposing on Robert,' she said.

'Then behave yourself,' I snapped.

She wept, but I ignored her. I could hear the little sputters of her grief. She sounded like a badly revved engine. 'I don't understand. You used to be a loving girl. All that education. No gratitude.' I let her sputter. After ten minutes in the corner she capitulated and an uneasy truce was arranged.

I took Dido, however, when I went to see Ella. I did not trust Mother. As I drove through the gum-trees into the fold of the hills to the east, I wondered at the beauty and squalor. Tiny farms and larger properties spread around me, the earth rolled in green shadows. I was pleased to note a number of the tin shanties had given way to tiny wooden cottages. But the settlement still looked like a camp rather than a suburb. It was a matter of uniformity, square wooden blocks with the same front door, the same front windows, the same tiny porch, the same tin roof. I suppose a blocked-in square is the cheapest way of housing people, and if the Aborigines were to be in any sense financially independent it had to be cheap. But I did wonder what strange fauna would live and grow in such uniform ugliness.

I edged the car along the street with great care. Children and dogs pressed on either side of it and Dido growled in her throat. 'Don't be ridiculous,' I said. 'You're a spotted ass.' She put her nose on my shoulder as I drove, and snuffled pathetically.

Ella Middleton's house was clean and tidy. The front room was a splendid expanse of radiant green linoleum and shining bright curtains. We moved through to the kitchen. Here the floor-boards were bare and scrubbed to the whiteness of bleached bone. Mrs Middleton looked as if she were my own age, but I could not really tell. The Aborigines never attended school in my time, so I had no record of contemporaneity. The same class, the same year, the same space and time, mould your companions so that they become fixed like flies in amber. You can collate them exactly.

Mrs Middleton was small and chubby, unwrinkled; but somehow time had worn both of us. My sandy face was marked by unfulfilled time, hers with the burden of fulfilment. Half her teeth were missing and her hair needed cutting. Three children smaller than Ella hung on the outskirts of the room. Two mangy dogs poked their noses around the door. Locked inside the car, Dido howled.

Ella stood beside her mother, her foot turned inward and her hair in her eyes. She had brown hair strangely streaked with faded blonde. I realised she was shy. I was again the girl in the unsuitable frock on the steps of Sydney University, and my identity reached out to embrace hers.

'You want to come to Etherington, Ella?'

She looked at me, then hid her face. Her head nodded but she did not speak.

'Yes, Miss Hansen,' said her mother.

Ella muttered obediently, but the words did not come through.

I turned to her mother. 'Did she enjoy the local school?'

The woman nodded. 'In the end,' she said. 'Ella always gits used to things in the end.'

'You will be the first of your people at Etherington,' I said to Ella. 'You will not find it easy. Some of the girls come from big houses and big properties.'

'My husband come from a property at Quirindi,' said Mrs Middleton. I caught the lilt of pride.

'I know,' I said. 'Is your husband home?'

'He's not been home for a month,' she said. 'He's lookin' for work on the coast.'

I said nothing. Mother would have said, 'I told you. I told you. You can't trust them. Those blacks go walkabout at the drop of a hat.'

I smiled at Mrs Middleton. 'Work is scarce in this town.' She nodded. 'It's hopeless for his sort. This town has few crops. All sheep and students.'

I nodded again and wondered if the juxtaposition of nouns had been an intended humour. She was right about the sheep. Our area did not use black labour to any extent.

I looked at Ella still standing beside the table. Something about the girl's slim figure with its shy contours attracted me. 'Would you like to come over and see the school?' I said. She nodded. 'Good.' I smiled at her mother. 'We won't be long.'

She and Dido understood each other immediately. Dido was a wise dog. One pat from the brown fingers and she knew this girl would never hurt her. My respect for the dog grew. She had been right about Mother too.

Ella and I walked through the empty dormitories and looked at the beds reminiscent of the absent owners. I felt fear. How would Ella fit into this close, almost secretive community?

The girls could be cruel. The refusal to talk, the removal of contact. The books that were not shared, the clothes carefully hidden away; the exclusion within a group in the very centre of conversation. I had watched it now for four years. They could toss phrases from one to another over the head of an excluded member with the ease of professional tennis players. I had seen plenty of small girls stretching on tip-toe trying to reach the tantalising lobs and in the end rushing from the group to weep in dormitories alone.

There was a glow in Ella's face. It appeared in the shine of her eyes, a warming tautness in her skin. She fingered the desks and touched the blackboards and looked with awe at the neatly quilted beds.

'I'll sleep here?'

I nodded. 'It will be lovely,' she said. 'I've never had a quilt before.'

There had been cleverer Aboriginal children in the primary school, but she had been selected because her school record revealed adaptability. Respectability also counted. Mrs Middleton was known to be clean, hard-working, honest. Her children attended school regularly. Ella was also a very good athlete. She could run, jump, as if movement had been built into her being.

For that reason my fears were not realised. Success in school sport is a passport to assimilation. The feeling of triumph as the sports trophies are pressed into the hands of the school captains, the joy in the defeat of other schools, is part of the communal consciousness of all schoolgirls. I have never shared it myself. I have never been athletic and I always despised the adulation of sporting heroes and heroines, the elevation of them to positions of power requiring intelligence rather than brawn; but as a teacher I learnt to appreciate the function of sport within a school.

The children did not exclude Ella. In fact she had the attraction of novelty. There were, of course, fringe areas of exclusion, the Graveses, the Wheatlys, the Middletons. But Ella's shy hang of her head, her sudden illuminating smile, her willingness to slave for them, made her popular. She was helpful. She would darn their socks for them, press their tunics, take up their hems.

'Ella, be a darling. I can't, I simply can't appear in public with my hem this length.' And Ella would laugh behind her hair, put out her brown hand, and within half an hour the garment would be back on its owner shortened appropriately.

Ann Denham was cynical. She clasped her biscuits in her pudgy hands (she always took three) and dunked them in her coffee.

'It must feel like home to the upper classes this year,' she said ironically. 'A permanent servant to wait upon them, a servant who never complains.'

Mona Edison waved her nervous hands. 'It's not right,' she said. 'This isn't a school for Aborigines. Philippa is asking for trouble, asking for it. Property owners don't pay fees for their children to be closeted with blacks.'

One of the young girls clenched her fist. Linda Skaines was new that year, straight from the university. 'And what is wrong with being black?'

Mrs Ellis palpitated. 'Nothing. Nothing at all, Miss Skaines. I don't think Mrs Edison meant there was anything wrong. It's well—they haven't much money, have they? I mean—she can hardly afford the same sorts of things as the Graves girls.'

'Jim and Della didn't begin with much,' I said drily. 'I remember Jimmy Graves at school. His mother used to send notes begging off the school subscription.' Then I felt ashamed. I should not have said that. Mona looked at me hard. 'Exactly,' she said. 'They knew their place. They went to state schools.'

Ann dunked another biscuit. 'Blast the Graveses,' she said. 'Upstart little motorised innkeepers. Even so, it's a dangerous experiment. I can't see what good it can do Ella. A set of values totally unrelated to her background.'

I watched youth bristle all over Linda. 'You make me sick,' she said. 'The lot of you. You're all fat and complacent and middle-aged. Any chance of an education is worth it for these people. It's their passport to a better life.'

Ann smiled. She looked horribly like a middle-aged cat. 'Now, now, Linda,' she said calmly, 'you can't call Miriam fat. Me, yes. Mona and Miriam, no. I admire youthful idealism, too. But passports to nowhere are useless. A good practical education at High School with a group of children who don't think of her primarily as a servant is what she needs. I have never admired misplaced altruism.'

She picked up her books and went out.

'Rationalisation of prejudice,' said Linda Skaines.

I said nothing. I knew Ann's fear was a real one. A coloured servant. But I could sense some dignity in Ella that resisted the role. Ella could iron and sew, but her dignity was her own. On the sports field Ella rose. As I watched her smooth brown legs swing over the high jump, I felt a poetry of motion and I knew the children felt it too. I have never been interested in the human figure; it has too many revolting aspects. But I sketched Ella. The girls admired her as an athlete; as a girl, they used her, but they were partly on the way to loving her, too.

In my case it was love. On an occasional Sunday I took her home. Mother sat, the embodiment of disapproval, but I did not care. In the afternoon Ella and I would drive or walk out into the country. Sometimes we painted. She had a facility with a paint brush that was not negligible. I felt her shyness slipping from her. I could feel the shine in her hair grow. It was true she was lonely. She missed her family, her mother, the milling children, the dogs; but she was not unique. 'They all miss their families,' she said. 'So many of the teachers never know how much.'

Rock-strewn gullies, grey dusty roads, limitless ravines, green rolled sheep land, streams crashing into waterfalls, we visited the lot and my fondness for Ella grew. In her silences lay wells of knowledge.

'Mrs Denham feels you do too much for the girls,' I said.

She smiled behind her hair. 'I do not mind. I do plenty at

home for the little ones. Mrs Denham is a good teacher but she is not always a help to us. Miss Kersten does all sorts of things for us. She makes us tiny wooden figures, little bowls, or anything. No one says she does too much.'

'You like Miss Kersten?'

It was an unprofessional question but I was curious. I knew that Philippa Ormiston had received a curious letter from Della Graves, objecting to the presence of 'sub-standard children' and 'women carpenters'. It was Margaret who mentioned this to me, not Philippa. Margaret had been repairing furniture at the time, and the fresh smell of the wood shavings enveloped me nostalgically as I watched her rough, capable hands hammer and plane. How powerful are the scents of childhood!

'It's not normal,' I said. 'Women aren't carpenters, not in Meridale. Della and Jim are so normal.'

Margaret nodded. 'So they matter?' she asked. 'You can imagine Philippa's reaction. She dropped the letter gaily into her wastepaper basket, muttered, "Such a silly woman, poor thing", and took out her weaving.'

I knew Margaret was asking me a serious question. The oldest inhabitant. The local girl. Margaret knew I should know. I watched the ash from her cigarette drip down her paint-streaked slacks. She was a person who tightened my honesty to breaking point. I could not have lied to her if I tried. The main street of Meridale ran east to west blindly into the sun. I walked along it mentally. The old stores, the new service stations, the budding supermarkets. The new superimposed on the old. But it still swung with the rhythm of the old.

'I think it matters,' I said slowly; 'in fact I know it matters. Philippa is alien to Meridale. In her heart she despises it. Her way of thinking is urban, folksy urban I admit, but urban for all that. Della Graves could make a lot of trouble if she tried. She belongs here. Jim is a local boy made good. The locals can buy a beer with him, pat him on the back. He smells of success, yet they can identify with him. It is very reassuring.

Yes, I think the Graveses could make a lot of trouble if they wished.'

Margaret hammered in a nail, surely, deftly. 'I rather thought so myself,' she said.

The following autumn I planted bulbs in pots. Mother watched with disapproval. She was well that summer and autumn. She had pottered round the garden all summer. She had even ventured in the car with me for a couple of outings. We drove down one Saturday to Danneworth to visit Robert. I could feel that both Robert and his wife were not pleased. Muriel welcomed us palely with thin tea and biscuits. It was disturbing for her to think that Mother was no longer landlocked in Meridale.

Robert fussed over Mother, tucked her up in the best chair. 'Glad to see you made it, old thing. The roads are dangerous.' Mother's luminous eyes collaborated with his dark ones.

'I cannot say I was happy,' she said, 'but Miriam is cautious.'

'That's the trouble with women,' said Robert. 'My apologies, old girl, but I never met a woman yet who could drive.'

I turned my head to speak to Kerrie. He knew I was ignoring him. Mother let the syrup of complacency run through her voice. 'I know what you mean, Robert. I never feel quite confident myself with a woman.'

Robert's wife ventured a remark. 'They are careful,' she said.

'That's the trouble,' said Robert. 'They're too scared to move. They crawl along, crowding the road until the competent driver is forced to overtake them.'

'A lot of cars did overtake us, didn't they, Miriam?' I could see by the translucence in Mother's eyes that she was enjoying herself.

'Yes, they did,' I answered; 'but only a fool talks of being forced to pass. A good driver passes only when it's safe, however inconvenient a hold-up may be.'

'With women at the wheel,' said Robert, 'it's never safe.'

'You know, Robert,' I said earnestly, seriously, 'you know, you worry me. Mother's safety should come first. Can't you try for a job in Meridale? Then *you* could drive Mother.'

He knew in an instant he had gone too far. Mother put her hard, possessive claw on his arm. 'That would be wonderful, Robert. I'd feel safe with you.'

He got up. 'Can't spend any more time yacketing away with women,' he said. 'There's a hundred things to do outside. You'll be nice and cosy in here, Mother. Muriel will look after you.'

Mother frowned. She was on the track of an attractive idea. 'Why not, Robert?' she demanded. 'Why not Meridale?'

'Because the Council needs me in Danneworth,' he said abruptly. 'Anyway, my home is here. It costs money to up-root a family. We can't all be choosers, Mother dear, like good old Miriam. A man has a family to consider.'

The joviality flowed from him like sweat, but he exuded uneasiness in spite of himself. He tried to smile at Mother and glare at me simultaneously. I went on talking to Kerrie, who was standing near my elbow. Robert pushed past and took Kerrie's elbow. 'Get the vegetables and help your mother,' he said. 'It's time you thought of others.'

'Don't kick the cat,' I said.

Mother nagged all the way home. 'You're driving too slow-ly, Miriam. . . . You nearly hit that car, Miriam. . . . There's a curve, Miriam.' Clickety-clack, clickety-clack, like knitting-needles.

When I came in after shutting the car in the garage, she was sitting in the kitchen clutching her heart and breathing with dramatic intensity. I began to build the fire.

'I can see, Mother,' I said, 'that you are too old to risk the perils of the road. In future you had better stay at home.'

So she stayed at home—I suppose in a sense Robert won that round—and made my life as miserable as she could with ceaseless complaints. She disliked flowers in the house. She said they gave her asthma, although no medical man had ever diagnosed asthma. And so I planted the bulbs.

When it bloomed the daffodil was perfection. It was the tallest daffodil I had ever seen. Long, straight stem and spreading blue-green leaves. It raised its golden trumpet high above the foliage. I found comfort in watching it, losing myself in the golden aura. Some evenings I sat contemplating it as the minutes ticked into half-hours and the half-hours into hours. It did not matter if Mother continued to talk. I did not hear. I was part of a gold centre of being, a tiny insect on the rim of the flower, until my very consciousness was itself golden, golden, golden. Mother usually ended by going to bed and I sank into the golden centre of the flower and dropped off to sleep in my chair. I needed comfort.

If it had not been for the daffodil I don't think I could have endured school that term. It was still a hive of extracurricular activity, but academic standards were slipping. There was a note of general unrest. Mrs Ellis had so many palpitations trying to control the third year that she finally resigned.

'They don't want to work,' she said, weeping. 'They don't care. They would be glad if I had a heart attack. Feel my heart, Miriam, just feel it. They defy me openly. If I punish them they run to Miss Ormiston and tell her I'm ill-treating them. And she supports them.'

Thumpety-thump, thumpety-thump went her heart beneath the dress. I was glad I should not need to feel it again.

'Miss Ormiston has provided them with plenty of activities,' I said. 'You must understand her viewpoint. She wishes it to be a home as well as a school.'

'For God's sake, Miriam,' said Mona, 'be honest for once. You no more agree with school policy than we do, but you run around like a white-haired angel trying to make it work.'

'I am a teacher,' I said. 'A teacher must have professional loyalties.'

'Shit!' said Ann Denham. I did not reply.

I could only regret Ann's language. It was not worthy of her; and yet our staff-room was trying, even to the most patient of us. It was again crowded with the young and transitory. There was also a navy reject from the United States.

Bill, we called him. His surname was inappropriately 'Musket'. He fed the children John Birch pamphlets and taught amidst a din like a thunderstorm. The girls turned their dainty feminine minds to devising ways of annoying him. Wherever he went the banners of disorder were raised.

I remember one hot afternoon in early summer. I was teaching in the fifth-form room. Below us there was a curious rumble like a subterranean storm, while outside the window the heavy lightning-flecked air gave warning of a thunderstorm. It was impossible to teach. Finally I put down my book. 'What is that noise downstairs?' I asked.

The class giggled. I liked fifth form. They were girls with a communal sense of humour, a trigger-like response that made contact with them easy.

Jean Dennis answered. 'That rumble, Miss Hansen? That's merely Mr Musket taking second year.'

For a moment of time their eyes held mine, and I know the laughter flowed into mine. I managed, however, to control my mouth.

'Go on working,' I said. In the midst of the uproar Dido's howl rose clear and melancholy, and I knew that Philippa was teaching sixth form in the neighbouring room.

Philippa listened to all complaints with chilly non-comprehension. Her mask of self-protection was as strong as my own. If she could no longer cope herself she would send for me.

'There seems to be some trouble in Mr Musket's classes. Do you think you could root it out?'

'Pick or shovel?' I asked. But Philippa did not smile. It was no joke, her look said, and it was my duty to help her.

Of course I tried, but no one can do anything for an incompetent man who is merely looking for a meal ticket to sustain him for a time in a world that has rejected him. In the face of disaster Philippa decided to see nothing. To parents she said, 'Mr Musket gives such an international touch to his lessons. He understands the need for a permissive atmosphere so well. So American in outlook.'

Her illusion of progress embraced even Mary Christoe. 'Such a delightful girl, Mary Christoe.'

I looked at Mary Christoe, young, untrained, reared in the aura of good local Sydney permissiveness. Her long dark hair dangled on her shoulders, her leather boots rose to cover her smooth knees. She made me think of storm troopers. I knew that she sat on the girls' beds at night, tête-à-tête with the seniors, encouraging them to try her cigarettes, to sip her drinks, to discuss the staff. Bill Musket's discipline was dissipated even further as he became the butt of her nightly mimicry. I pointed out to Philippa the moral danger in which her girls stood, but once again she was caught in the charm-net of youth. Rachel, however, had been a nice girl; Mary Christoe was not.

'For God's sake stop worrying about other people, Miriam.' Ann Denham was washing her splodged hands at the sink. 'Simply be grateful that you and I can still control the children. Philippa is right about the need for activities and a more permissive atmosphere, even if the children are a little out of hand. They'll settle in time.'

I wanted to say, 'That's all very well, but she expects me to rescue her from her excesses. If only she would give me some support, see through the Christoes, dismiss the Muskets.' She failed to support them against the children, but failed to dismiss them. I was too loyal to complain to Ann, so I said nothing. My job was to run the school as Philippa wished. As an escape, I spent nearly all my spare time chatting to Margaret Kersten or helping Ella with her mathematics. Margaret chattered of material things, of building cupboards, of making chairs, of planing surfaces. She was an oasis in the restlessness. Ella was slow but willing. I liked the sight of her dark streaky hair bent over her book, her dark hand clasped round her pen while she struggled to understand the intricacies of set theory. I knew she would never master it, but her willingness to try was also restful.

The simmer of discontent was bubbling in town. They talked Philippa into freedom of choice for their children, and then expected us to produce results where there was no talent. The glamour of being a progressive school was wearing off.

'The graziers don't care,' said Ann, 'and the petrol-pump pushers want High School results and private school contacts. Poor Philippa!'

Discontent spread and the older staff began to leave. Even Mona Edison took a new appointment. 'I want your advice,' she said. 'I have been underpaid for years. St Celia's has offered me more money. They need a primary teacher; and I am a trained primary teacher.'

I thought of the downcast eyes of the nuns at St Celia's counting beads and calculating the precise number of notes required to woo our teachers.

'You have a duty to the girls,' I said to Mona. 'Miss Ormiston is facing staff difficulties.'

Ann Denham interrupted me. 'Ignore the voice of duty, Mona. This institution has exploited you for ten years. You have the chance to get out. All I say is "Good for the nuns".'

'You're supposed to be a Protestant, Ann,' I said. 'Mona's a Methodist. How can we keep our schools going if people like you walk out?'

Ann laughed at me through a roll of cigarette smoke. She did not smoke very often so I must have disturbed her.

'Come off it, Miriam,' she said rudely. She patted Mona's shoulder with her other hand. 'I doubt if even Wesley would turn down all that extra money in the circumstances.'

'Very well,' I said, 'we'll forget Wesley. But there is Miss Ormiston. How can she run a school without staff? I thought you were her friend.'

Ann shrugged. 'Friendship has nothing to do with Mona's taking another job,' she said. 'She has that right. If they wish to keep her this Council should pay her properly.'

'Miss Ormiston won't see it that way.'

I was right. She did not see it that way. She ceased to speak to Mona for the remaining month, and her purple head-bands expressed mourning tinged with indignation for a staff capable of betrayal. However, she found her own solutions.

In the next few months our tiny staff-room resembled a crèche. Nursing mothers were enticed back into teaching by permission to bring the children. Miss Cunningham-White bubbled with annoyance.

'It's not funny,' she said, the words slipping like pellets from the side of her mouth. 'It's not funny to come into the room after a morning's teaching to find every chair occupied by a two-year-old.'

Privately I agreed with her. French proses punctuated with baby Williams's yells for his bottle, baby Souter's screams for her mother, baby Anderson's gurgles of affection.

In the schoolroom Mary Christoe and Linda Skaines increased the confusion. Linda incited the children to rebellion. The word 'anti' was plastered all over her: anti-religion, anti-pollution, anti-Vietnam. The pupil unrest culminated in an attack on Mr Musket and Mr Pilsudski with paper pellets. Mr Musket ran roaring to a member of Council. Mr Pilsudski shut himself in his room, refused to take any music lessons for a fortnight, and wrote three distinct and unified musical compositions.

Miss Christoe, on the other hand, was holding sherry parties with the seniors, just a small group late at night in her room. But the boarders became more exclusively boarders (they had always tended to snub day girls), and even Jean Dennis, nice girl, led the movement to let Isobel Graves know that she was excluded. I came upon Belle in the playground, screaming like a dervish.

'I don't want to go to your parties.'

Jean smiled. The rest followed her. Even Ella closed ranks against the girl.

The following week there was a special Council meeting. I was asked to attend. The sherry parties, I thought. But I was wrong. Their Meridale minds were more devious than that.

I thought as I entered how pompous my contemporaries looked. Maurice Furlonger was, if anything, fatter than ever. He was also balder. The local clergyman looked like a portrait of an English butler. Jim Graves was obviously in one of his less lovable moods, while Froggy Daley glowed as pink as a Spurway painting. In one corner Dido snored. It seemed the most appropriate comment, but every time the stertorian wheeze filled the air I saw Jim Graves's fingers twitch and Maurice Furlonger's eyelid quiver.

Philippa, dressed in a flowing gown, looked beautiful, but remote. I sensed her mood: She was the European celebrity who had dropped in to play the cello or the piano for a single evening, who could flick the Meridale citizenry off her garments like dust tomorrow. And I prayed to myself, 'Don't scorn them, Philippa. Don't underrate them. They look stuffy, but they are not silly. They know a snub when they see it.'

I expected questions on school discipline, the stories of sherry, the paper battles, the Polish inconsequence of Pilsudski, but they did not come.

Maurice half leered at me, then said, 'Miss Hansen, you are acquainted with Miss Kersten?'

This time the surprise was mine, but I kept an unmoving face. 'Naturally.'

'Do you mind giving your opinion of her?'

Dido gave a loud snore. I should like to have done the same, but more rudely. I am, however, well controlled.

'Miss Kersten,' I said, 'is a very fine person.'

Jim Graves leant over the table. 'But not exactly feminine?' I felt my skin tighten. A slight flush warmed my sandiness. I looked at him in a way which I hoped would make him remember his Latin proses.

'I am not in the habit,' I said slowly, 'of measuring my colleagues in terms of femininity. If it comes to that, I am not myself exactly feminine, as you call it.'

John Dennis smiled. 'Good for you, Miss Hansen.'

Furlonger now put his elbows comfortably on the table and said to me ingratiatingly, 'Let us put our problem this way, Miss Hansen. Doesn't it seem strange to you that a woman should be a carpenter?'

Dido snored.

'Unusual perhaps,' I said, 'but not strange. I could have been a carpenter myself.'

Froggy Daley nodded. Like Dido he was not awake. He rose to consciousness on the tail end of my words.

'Yes, yes,' he said. 'Yes, yes, we all remember Miriam's Dad. A fine craftsman. So was Miriam. She made us a small box for our chemistry club, remember?'

'Yes, yes, yes,' said Jim Graves, impatient acquiescence, 'but we're not discussing Miriam, Mr Daley. Our point is this, Miss Hansen. We feel that Miss Kersten is not a suitable person for a girls' school.'

'Oh,' I said, 'and what sort of person is that, Mr Graves?'

He was irritated. 'You know quite well what I mean, Miss Hansen.'

Dido groaned loudly.

'For heaven's sake, Miss Ormiston, I do wish you would keep the dog quiet.'

Philippa rose. Her draperies swirled around her. 'I shall shut her out,' she said, 'but I warn you. She will howl.'

For some reason her very movements that night suggested poise, culture, Europe. She made the rest of the room look like small-town hicks. Maurice Furlonger raised a hand. He looked weary. 'Please leave her where she is, Miss Ormiston. If Mr Graves has forgotten Dido's howl, I assure you and him I have not.'

'As you please,' she said. She sat down again and Dido's next snore vibrated across the surface. Jim Graves swore, beneath his breath it is true, but I heard him.

'You feel Miss Kersten is a good influence?' asked John Dennis.

'Yes, I do,' I said. 'I am fond of her. She has been a wonderful companion for Miss Ormiston. It's very lonely for a newcomer in this town. She is also helpful with the girls. Without her I doubt if Ella would have settled in so well.'

'That's the boong, isn't it?' said Olaf Denton.

'That's right,' said Graves. 'Belle has a few complaints in that quarter, too.'

'If you mean our Aboriginal pupil,' said Philippa, 'I should like to remind you that you voted to offer the scholarship. As far as complaints go, I am quite sure Ella could make a few of her own.'

Maurice Furlonger tapped his fingers on the cedar surface. He ignored Philippa.

'You feel,' he said, 'that Miss Kersten is very friendly with Miss Ormiston?'

'Very,' I said loyally. 'I am quite sure Miss Ormiston is aware of Miss Kersten's fine qualities. She is in a way her right-hand man.' Olaf Denton gave a silly giggle. He was not worth bothering about. I wondered why Philippa pressed her hands over her face. Her fingers were trembling.

'She likes to have the girls, particularly Ella Middleton, in her workshop?'

'She's willing to have any of us,' I said, 'any time.'

'In fact, you would say she is fond of girls?'

'I cannot follow the point of these questions,' I said. 'Miss Kersten is in no sense unpopular. I should even say she loves the girls. And they love her.'

'Thank you, Miss Hansen. You have been very helpful.' John Dennis rose and opened the door for me. Dido gave a triple snore beneath the table. The next week Philippa Ormiston dismissed Margaret Kersten.

Margaret herself told me. Her work-worn hands were tidying her bench. 'The Council cannot afford a carpenter,' she said. 'At least, that is what I am supposed to believe.'

'There was a Council meeting,' I said. 'They asked me about you.'

I watched the nicotine stains on her fingers rather than the woman herself.

'I see,' she said. 'I hope you gave me a good reference.'

'Of course,' I said.

'So it must be Philippa. She doesn't need me any more. She has Mary Christoe. She was always fickle. Whoring after strange gods.'

'I don't understand,' I said.

Margaret wiped a dirty cloth across the bench. There was a smell of wood, fresh, clean, and of mould decayed and rotten.

'Don't try to understand, Miriam.' She sounded weary. 'Let us say, simply, I must leave. I threw up my job in Victoria at Philippa's request, trundled all the way to this upstart country town, merely to be told I'm not wanted.'

She lit another cigarette from the butt of the previous one, which she stubbed out in a lid filled with water. It floated like an obscene corpse, the remnants of tobacco disintegrating and sticking to the sides.

'You have quarrelled?' I asked.

'I suppose you could say that.' Her face was as hard as a man's, the fair hair slicked back to repress the wave. She stuck one hand in her pocket and walked to the window. She lit a new cigarette even though she had barely started the previous one, pressed it out against the sill and threw it into the garden.

'Why?' she said. 'Why? We have had a good time together these past few months. She enjoyed Fiji. Why?'

'I don't know,' I said. 'You could be wrong to blame Philippa. Maybe the Council . . .'

'Maybe,' she interrupted. 'Councils feel a deep suspicion of women who wear trousers. But surely Philippa can handle her own Council?'

'I don't know,' I said. 'I think she despises them and they know it.'

I missed Margaret. We were not a happy staff-room any more. Ann Denham splashed stencil ink and meths over everyone in her suppressed rage. 'Filthy-minded bastards,' she said.

'Who?'

'The Council.'

'I don't know,' said Linda. 'They have a right to protect their children from perversion.'

'Bunkum,' said Ann. 'The trouble with the young is the perception of perversion in every lonely friendship.'

'You have to admit,' said Miss Cunningham-White, 'she was not normal.'

'Oh, rubbish,' said Ann. She shook the machine vigorously in an attempt to dislodge the paper she had fed crookedly into it. A splodge of purple ink landed on my nose. I wiped it off.

'If you want to know,' I said, 'I think Council is merely economising.'

'Don't be so damn innocent,' said Ann.

'I'm not innocent,' I said. 'I know what some of them say about Margaret, but I agree with you that it is rubbish. I am sure, however, you wrong the Council. They have never thought basically that a woman can do a carpenter's job. They consider it a waste of money.'

Mary Christoe stood in the doorway. Her brown hair hung, semi-teased, to her shoulders. Her dress was so short I could see the curves of her legs run into the broader curves of her bottom. In twenty years' time her rear would be like Gladys Dewey's. She was laughing.

'Jenny Fenwick can take off anyone,' she said. 'She just did a marvellous send-up of the Kersten for the class. Dirty breeches, dangling cigarettes, male voice. I wonder how women get like that.'

There was silence. We stood fixed in our places like a tableau, then Ann Denham wiped her hands on an ink-stained rag.

'And how did Jenny Fenwick happen to be miming Miss Kersten?' she asked.

Mary tossed her long hair out of her eyes, straightened her leather boot, and laughed. 'Oh,' she said, 'I ran a little revue. Told them they could take off the staff if they liked. Christ, it was funny. You should have seen yourself, Miriam. They had Ella dressed up in spotted nylon with a great orange tea-towel tied round her head.'

Ann stood in front of Mary Christoe. Her inky fingers rose. Mary's face was streaked with purple, five definite fingers imprinted on her cheek. 'You bastard,' Ann said. Then she walked out.

For a second Mary stood there. The rest of us said nothing, not even Linda Skaines. To be fair to Linda, I do not think she liked Mary. Suddenly Mary screamed at us.

'Say something. Go on, say something. You pious nits. I wish you could have seen yourselves. The kids have your measure, all right. You ought to hear the things they tell me about you.'

I raised my head. I tried to sound dignified. 'If I were you, Miss Christoe, I'd be silent. Good teachers don't discuss their colleagues with the pupils, nor do they undermine authority in a school. You should also realise that Margaret Kersten has been a good friend to most of us. I suggest you wash your face.'

She half sneered. 'Ah yes, wash my face. That will give you time to run to Miss Ormiston with your usual tales, won't it, Miss Hansen? Well, you needn't bother. Miss Ormiston is my friend.'

I did run to Miss Ormiston, even so. Someone had to run. Jenny Fenwick was bad enough without being supported by Mary Christoe. She was an odd girl, even a likeable one. Three schools had already asked her to leave. I have always been opposed myself to Philippa's policy of accepting other schools' rejects.

I knew Miss Cunningham-White dreaded evening duty. She had never dreaded duty in the past. The old girls always spoke of her affectionately as their friend, but the present dormitory mocked her. Later when people said to me, 'What did Jenny Fenwick do? What could a mere schoolgirl do to disrupt a school?', I could never find an answer. She merely created an aura of disobedience, impertinence, wherever she went. Dormitories that had switched off their lights at 10 p.m. without murmur ceased to do so when Jenny joined them; classes that had worked reasonably diligently became bear-gardens of disorder. I felt the time had come to act.

So far I had said nothing to Philippa about this, but now

I felt it my duty to warn her. The aloof Englishwoman so much in evidence at the Council meeting was still with us. She was now wearing tweed suits and twin sets and English brogues. It had the effect of separation, of building a channel of race and hemisphere between us and her. She listened to my story but did not listen.

'Miss Christoe is a good teacher,' she said and picked up her pen to resume writing a report.

I persisted. 'I am not discussing her teaching. It is my duty to tell you that if you keep both Miss Christoe and Jenny Fenwick, your school will disintegrate. We've already lost Mona Edison and Janet Ellis.'

'My dear Miriam,' she said, 'I am grateful for your concern, but it is not your duty to tell me anything. Administration is my concern. Mary Christoe has been a delightful companion in those hours when you return to the comfort of your home. I am a lonely woman. I must have some friends. The evenings are so long. You may not have noticed how long the evenings are. As far as Jenny Fenwick is concerned, she is a difficult girl, I know. But it is not our job as educators to turn our back on difficulties. I agree it was wrong of Mary to allow the children to mock the teachers, but when it comes down to tin tacks it was only a bit of fun. Surely the staff are sufficiently mature to laugh at themselves?'

I said nothing more. How could I explain that no dormitory had ever reduced Miss Cunningham-White to tears before, not once in all the years I had known her? I changed the subject. I suppose lonely evenings suggested the thought. After all, if she were lonely she could have kept Margaret.

'I was sorry we could not keep Miss Kersten.'

'Are you?' she said. 'That is surprising, Miriam, seeing that you took such good care to damn her.'

I felt my mouth fill with nervous saliva. My bewilderment appeared on my face. I felt my hands flutter pointlessly in the air.

'Don't get agitated,' she said. 'I know you did not intend to injure her. You did your best to give her a character reference

according to your own lights. Maybe you and the Council
think alike. I don't know. But you did manage to confirm the
belief of those pompous little men that Margaret is a predator
—a destroyer of young girls. Poor dear Miriam. So loyal.'

I felt anger, anger that rose like a slow fire inside me. 'I
told the truth,' I said.

'You always do,' said Philippa. 'That is the trouble.'

'Anyway,' I said, 'it was you that dismissed Margaret, not
me.'

She looked at me, just looked. For a second neither of us
moved. We were like cats waiting for the hunted to break for
cover. She moved first. She laughed.

'How innocent you are, Miriam! Yes, I dismissed Margaret.
I'm not sorry. I thought she would understand. But she was
vicious. Plain vicious, when I told her.'

I shrugged. I was sick and tired of the accusation of innocence. A decent person can no longer believe in the normality
of their friends. I see no reason to find perversion in every
relationship. But I have lived in a country town all my life
and so I am hardly likely to be ignorant of the meaning of
certain animal facts. I was glad Margaret had been vicious
to Philippa.

'Good,' I said.

Philippa looked at me in surprise. 'I think you'd better
leave, Miriam.'

I felt vicious myself as I drove home that day in genuine
bewilderment. I beat my hands on my steering wheel in sheer
rage. I did not harm Margaret; I would not have harmed
Margaret. I loved her. Philippa was the vicious one. Philippa
was guilty, guilty, guilty. I repeated the word to myself again
and again. She wanted a scapegoat.

I felt very lonely as I drove up past Merrick's store. People
always seemed to blame me for trying to keep the things I
valued. Only this time I had lost something far more precious
than a tadpole. That night I dreamt of Robert and the tadpole. Mother stood above me with a stick. She kept saying,
'Give it to him, Miriam, give it to him. It's your fault he lost

his tadpole. You say such mean things.' Only somewhere in the dream Mother became the Council and the tadpole became Margaret Kersten in a wickerwork cage and Philippa floated from the roof on a huge cello and said, 'I told you so, Miriam. You have to give Margaret to the Council', and I turned to Margaret—only it was no longer Margaret but Mary Christoe, sitting on a glass silver ball, and Philippa leant across her cello and stroked her hair and said, 'We won't let nasty Miriam hurt you, too.'

It was a haphazard period, the period with Philippa and yet, amidst the increasing chaos in junior school, our senior school was gradually improving. There is something about responsibility that is maturing, and even though our girls were far below the self-reliant, self-propelling paragons that Philippa had envisaged on her arrival they had developed some initiative in the carefree atmosphere. Ann, Philippa and I worked hard. Senior classes were no longer handed to junior favourites without experience. We were all good teachers and general results improved. Matriculation, however, was elusive. Philippa was quite incapable of thinking about examinations in terms of university regulations. The girls chose their subjects freely, and too often they sat for the wrong ones. Whims and delusions flourished unchecked until the awful day of reckoning when the tertiary institutions turned them down.

In junior school life hummed. Mr Musket's classes became even noisier. Miss Cunningham-White's mobile little mouth became a taut line as Jenny Fenwick organised her forces against her. Complaints and rumours drifted around town. Etherington girls were noisy in Church, Etherington girls crept out at night, Etherington girls smoked behind the lilac bushes, Etherington girls. . . . Meridale has always been an inventive town, skilled in the destruction of the wrongdoer; but the town is rarely given the raw material of gossip in such abundance.

Did Philippa know? Did she simply not care? I have never been sure. Reports were filtered to her through Mary Christoe.

I tried myself to tell her what was happening, but to her I was Meridale, prone to see things with its eyes, to feel with its bones. She did not believe me. At the same time, I tried to carry out her plans, to build a permissive school, even though I have never believed that people can develop in undisciplined atmospheres. I reproved Mr Musket and Linda Skaines for running to Philippa with complaints. 'You must try to control the children,' I said, 'you must encourage them, give them an incentive.' I suggested to Miss Cunningham-White that she ought to be a little firmer in the dormitories. But I knew in my heart it was useless. With Mr Pilsudski I did not even try. He did not care if his pupils left, and I did not care if he left.

The insidious baiting of staff and prefects would continue while Miss Christoe laughed at it all over surreptitious sherry in the dormitory which she was supposed to control, and while Philippa failed to support her weaker members with her own authority.

At home, Mother and I harried each other with cruel witticisms and suppressed ironies. To escape, I drove away each week-end to our rockiest, most depressive landscapes, seeking a sublimation through paint.

Occasionally I took Ella. For a while her mockery of me had separated us. I looked at her and I saw myself orange-turbaned. I found it difficult to forgive. Finally she came to me, her large brown eyes filled with fugitive timidity like a hunted kangaroo.

'Have I done something wrong, Miss Hansen?'

I scanned her shy face. 'Do you think you have done something wrong, Ella?'

She shuffled her feet. 'Was it the revue?' she said. 'It wasn't very nice, I know. But Miss Christoe said we all had to take part—me, too. She said I had to learn to be co-operative; and Jenny Fenwick said it would only be a joke, anyway.'

'People of your race don't have to learn to be co-operative,' I said. 'You are co-operative—by nature. And it was not a joke, not the way it was done. Miss Kersten's leaving was not a joke.'

'I know,' said Ella, 'but it is hard to know what the jokes are. I don't seem to have the same sort of humour as the others, and then I worry. It is not always easy to understand what the girls here think is funny.' Her eyes were aeons old.

'Very well,' I said. 'I'll forget it.'

Sometimes I took Ella back to her home. I did not find these visits easy. The dogs, the children milling around the house, the curious but not friendly faces, the cries of 'A whitey to see you, Mrs Middleton'. How conspicuous I felt, how sandy beside their velvety darkness! At Bennet Street I could talk to Ella as an equal.

But Mother's eyes breathed hate, even if she dared make no comment apart from an irritating tap, tap, tap on the floor with her stick. Blacks in her home. How dare I? Her hate lent piquancy to the occasion, but it was not the reason for bringing Ella. I was growing to love her. I had no intention of using her as an assertion of independence against Mother.

Enclosed in the warmth of the wood stove, we worked at maths problems, tussled with science. She was not clever. Her examination results had been a disappointment to all of us who wanted the experiment to succeed. Did Ella and I make progress? I do not know. I only know I enjoyed standing in the wooden kitchen feeling the warmth of flame on our backs, while Ella, white apron on brown skin, plunged her arms into flour that lay like snow on a brown field. Together we made scones and cakes. When they were baked, we ate them, and Mother ate them too, inspecting each particle for traces of dirt. At the end of the day we packed what remained for Ella's mother.

Meanwhile in town rumours grew.

'I believe,' said Mena Furlonger, fingering possessively the china in Furlonger's store, 'that carpenter has left you. Good thing. You can't be too careful.'

'I do not understand,' I said. 'If you are referring to Miss Kersten, she was one of our finest people.'

'I think you are genuinely dumb'—she paused. 'Or maybe you're merely an unredeemed innocent.'

'I do wish,' said Della Graves, stroking her synthetically blonde locks in front of the post-office, 'you people would do something about that Mr Musket. Miss Christoe was telling me that Miss Ormiston refuses to co-operate.'

I pushed my letter through the slot marked 'local'. I noted my brown glove was fraying at the finger. 'I can't discuss Miss Ormiston in public,' I said. 'Miss Christoe, being a junior member of staff, is hardly in the position to comment on school policy.'

'My dear Miriam,' said Della, 'she has eyes and ears, hasn't she?'

'To be perfectly frank,' I said, 'I've never taken the trouble to find out. She could be blind and deaf as far as I'm concerned.'

Rumour and gossip, snippets of dissatisfaction. The old story. My daffodil died, and the spring flowers sprawled over our unruly garden. The term was in its last stages when I came into the office on a routine matter to find Philippa, her head on the desk, weeping. The light streaming through the slatted blind fed on the black hair, revealing streaks of silver. Black hair quite often greys earlier. I shuffled my feet in a gesture of departure, but she said without raising her head, 'Sit down, Miriam.'

I sat and waited. I wanted to comfort her, ask the reason for her tears, but I said nothing. The very angle of her head forbade sympathy. She did not even wipe her eyes. The path of the tears streaked down her cheeks as if defying me to notice it. I did notice, however, the letter near her hand. She passed it to me. I took it reluctantly. Grief is private, but as I read I was glad to avoid the verbal impact, to receive the shock through my eyes rather than through my ears.

Margaret Kersten was ill. It was a letter from her aunt. Margaret had collapsed with lung cancer two weeks ago. They had operated and fortunately only a small area of one lung was affected. The other lung was quite sound. With care and luck she would recover, or at the worst there would be a remission.

I looked at my polished shoe under the table and noticed that Philippa was wearing plaited straw sandals. She always anticipates the seasons, I thought; a hint of spring and Philippa floats on the hay of summer. I felt my own sorrow, but my smooth face did not pucker. I have always been inarticulate, particularly in the presence of grief.

I put down the letter. 'You will have to go to Sydney,' I said.

'I can't. We were not speaking when we parted.'

I felt anger replace sorrow, but my face remained calm. 'That is pride,' I said. 'Your feelings are totally irrelevant.'

She nervously fingered the neck of her loosely woven dress. I had a glimpse of breasts, small, childlike. She was undeveloped, a woman without maturity.

'I have killed her. She was my friend.'

'Nonsense,' I said. 'Rejection does not cause lung cancer. You and I both know she smoked incessantly. And she is not dead.'

'She said I hated her.'

'She was disappointed,' I said. 'Rejection hurts. I know. She was probably already ill.'

'How can I go?' She spoke almost to herself. 'How can I say, "I've come even if you think I hate you. I've come because you are ill."'

'You don't say it.'

She revived. 'Don't be silly, Miriam. Of course I don't say it aloud. But it's obvious, anyway.'

'In that case,' I said, 'you'll have to take the risk. If she rejects you, then you leave. She is the one who is ill. It is her choice. But she won't turn you away. She loves you.'

I stood up and tried to look practical. I had no desire to get into a discussion on love.

'I must return to fifth form,' I said.

'Thank you, Miriam,' she answered. 'You are so helpful. Your loyalty is worth a great deal to me.'

'Give my love to Margaret,' I said.

I left the room. I, too, wanted to weep. I, too, loved

Margaret. I taught all day. At night I drove home, cooked Mother's tea, tucked her in bed.

'Robert says you have no right to bring boongs into my house.' She spoke with triumphant malice.

'Robert does not pay the bills,' I said, and left her.

I shut myself in my room. Only then did I have time to weep, to weep for Margaret; but by then I had exhausted all emotion. There were no tears. I burrowed my head in my pillow and, to my shame, I slept. The next morning weeping seemed pointless.

I stood at my window and looked at one of our chronic late frosts. The grass was brittle white as far as the eye could see, the sky was blue, clear blue. The day would be fine. Pointless to weep because a friend was seriously ill. The world would continue. It was like frost in September. On my dressing-table the wooden bird stood in full flight, its structure as delicately fashioned as the crystalline world outside. I balanced it on my hand. I held it high against the pane of glass so that it rode the blue air beyond the pane. A tip of sun lit its wing. I bowed my head.

And so we drifted. Philippa no longer seemed to care what happened. We drifted into summer. Mr Musket's classes grew noisier. Miss Christoe fed the girls sippets of sherry and sippets of gossip. I was busy myself with matriculation class and so was Ann. We both missed Mona. Miss Cunningham-White sat in offended silence in one corner of the staff-room while the current baby spread its crib over at least two chairs. It was the evening of the annual church service that Maurice Furlonger rang me.

'I suppose you have heard, Miriam, that Miss Ormiston is retiring.'

'I have heard nothing,' I said.

'She handed in her resignation at the Council meeting last night.'

I could imagine the flabby face at the other end of the line. My mind said 'hypocrite'. I had been talking to Philippa yesterday about plans for next year. She had no intention of resigning then. I did not tell Furlonger so.

'She will tell me in her own time,' I said. 'I have no doubt she has her reasons.'

'Of course, Miriam.' He tried to sound as stuffed and distant as I did. He did not succeed. Maurice gave mental hand-pats even over the telephone. I listened without comment.

Finally he exclaimed, 'For God's sake, Miriam, show some feeling. Things are impossible. The dog alone is a menace.'

'I am not discussing dogs,' I said. 'I have no doubt Miss Ormiston and the Council have their reasons for their decisions. I shall do whatever the school considers my duty. I am merely an employee. I am not sure why you are ringing me.'

'My dear Miriam, you are senior mistress. It is only fair to warn you. The matter is too delicate to discuss in public.'

'Delicate?'

'For God's sake, Miriam, stop acting the eternal spinster.'

'I am the eternal spinster,' I said.

'As Mena says and Della, we cannot expose the girls to moral danger. It's obvious.'

'Forgive me, Maurice,' I said, 'it would help if you could say precisely what it is that is obvious.'

'Well,' he said, 'well—you know. Girls, women. Things like that. Miss Kersten even looked like a man.'

'She was raised with men,' I said drily.

I heard Maurice put down the receiver and call Mena.

'Hell,' he said.

Mena's voice came over, crisp, pecky, hen-like, scratching as if through a beak slowly. 'Surely, Miriam, you've heard of lesbianism.'

I felt my sandy neck grow red. I was angry. The unsewered minds of these little people! I hated them.

'Can't Maurice pronounce the word himself?' I said nastily.

'You embarrass him,' she said.

I laughed. 'You are ridiculous. You really are. Both of you. You see sexual affairs in every encounter. Philippa and Margaret aren't like that.'

'Aren't they? And I suppose I was wrong about Ina Spurway, too?'

'I'm sure you were, Mena.'

My mind reluctantly turned over the days and hours since Ina left. Rachel, Margaret, Mary Christoe. The loneliness of the unmarried female stalked beside me, too. 'You fatuous, self-satisfied groveller in the dirt,' I wanted to shout. 'What do you know about loneliness? What do you know about love? Philippa loved Margaret. There was nothing wrong with that. I loved Margaret, too.'

Mena was still cackling on about Ina Spurway: '. . . well rid of a painted harlot like her. And now we have an obvious lesbian—'

It was time I said something, and I interrupted. 'Nonsense, Mena. Single women sublimate. Why do you think we make such good teachers?'

'Sublimate!' said the clacky little voice. It was an exclamation of disbelief. 'Well, now that you understand the central issue, I'll put Maurice back on.'

'Don't bother,' I said.

'He hasn't finished,' said Mena.

Silence and silence. Were the hen and cock sparring in the tasteful morning room of their delightful brick bungalow? I hated them. The *bloody* self-righteousness of the married with their intolerable presumptions. Feeling like Ann Denham, I repeated the 'bloody' to myself with enjoyment.

'Are you there, Miriam?'

'Yes.'

'Could you . . . ?' he began. I felt a lifting of spirit. He was going to ask me to take over. Loyalty teetered over into treachery. For a fraction of a second I dealt with the fraction of a dream. I felt the brick of the school become my brick in my school. I saw myself in gown and hood saying the prayers, reading the lesson, commenting on sporting victories, upholding traditions.

'Yes?' I prompted.

'. . . carry on until we get someone suitable?'

Someone suitable? Not old local Miriam, Miriam who did their Latin proses, helped them with their sums, corrected their grammar. Miriam was merely a Hansen, the carpenter's daughter. Miriam knew the backgrounds of their Dads.

'Well, Miriam?'

'I shall do whatever my employers think fit,' I said.

When I put down the phone my hand was shaking.

I remember that Sunday morning was hot. White rabbit fur clung in sticky tufts to the necks of the Sydney Arts graduates. Philippa stood in her ridiculous but dignified Cambridge gown and hat, her face purged of all expression. She wore a plain gingham dress and no make-up. Her hands shook as she began the Bible reading. The scene took on the fine lines of a drawing to become fixed in my consciousness for ever; the sweaty black-hooded staff, the white-frocked girls, and Philippa looking like an educated orphan. I can remember her reading Psalm 27: 'When the wicked, even my enemies and my foes, came upon me to eat up my flesh, they stumbled and fell.'

Her voice rose like a curse and I knew that it was not an impetuous resignation, the offspring of a temperamental moment. It was polite dismissal. Enemies and foes. A few difficult girls, a few cocky young graduates, a couple of ambitious parents, a few dirty-minded mothers. I felt the Church music sink into the pores of my skin. It soothed. I felt sorry for Philippa. She had meant well. Musical evenings, breakfasts outdoors, charity works for the aged. She had tried to extend the unextendable, to take children with ordinary parents into a civilised world. And the majority wanted merely to pass an exam. I could feel for the parents. What price civilisation to those struggling to add up? I looked at the sallow, strained face. Her world was not my world. I had little sympathy with her education principles. But perhaps—perhaps if I had known a Philippa I might have gained from the University more than a bare qualification to teach.

The light in the leaded pane of the window made me think of my own painting. I had tried to probe chasms. So had

Philippa. She had not tried to please the Council she despised; but to keep her school, to placate them, she had denied love, dismissed Margaret Kersten. Did God forgive the sin of betrayal? Did Margaret Kersten forgive her treason? I had not asked Philippa on her return from Sydney and she had not told me.

The long room looked as it had always looked. Her cello stood in the corner. Her hair was tied back by a broad black band of ribbon. Her eyes were as black as the ribbon. I was conscious of shock.

'I came to say good-bye,' I said. She nodded.

'Where are you going?' I asked.

'Margaret Kersten's cousin has offered me her home in Sydney for a few weeks.'

'And then?'

'I shall probably go to South America. If they'll have me. They need a principal for a girls' home in Chile.'

'What about Dido?' I asked. 'Perhaps I can help.' Her face did not move.

'I sent Dido to the vet. this morning,' she said. 'I asked him to put her to sleep.' I struggled with my distress and lost.

'You mean you killed her.' I hated my own cruelty for saying the words she avoided, but I have always disliked the euphemism that owners of pets perpetually use. I had liked Dido.

For the first time she showed emotion. 'You are cruel, Miriam, but as usual you are right. Dido is quite dead. I killed her.'

I blew my nose to hide my embarrassment.

'It's easy to be critical,' she said, 'but no one wanted her. Not even you, Miriam. The Council complained about her sex—she brought the dogs, they said—so undesirable for the girls. They were apparently all conceived in other ways. She also snored.'

I put out a hand to comfort her, then quickly dropped it. I

was not near to Philippa. Any comfort I could offer would be an insult to her grief.

'There is nothing I can do, then?'

She began to say 'No', then changed her mind. 'Ella,' she said.

'Ella?'

'There are those who dislike Ella,' she said. 'They believe Aborigines have no place in a school like this. I want you to protect Ella, to fight for her.'

'Of course,' I said. 'I should do that without your asking me.'

'It may not be as easy as you think, Miriam. Once you're in charge you will be more aware of the whispers, the nastiness.'

'I have lived with rumour all my life,' I said.

She laughed. 'How true. I forgot this was your town, your native land. Does it make your heart burn as you turn your footsteps homeward, or have you never wandered on a foreign strand? Never mind, comparisons are invidious, anyway.'

She must have seen the unease in my face, for she suddenly changed her tone. 'Forgive me. I should be serious. There is nastiness made concrete here. When they get a new headmistress they will do their best to make sure she is my opposite. They must run out of new models sooner or later, but they'll probably succeed this time. She will dislike the very thought of Ella, let alone the sight, the sound, the smell of her.'

'Ella does not smell.'

'You can tell Graves that,' she said. 'Also Denton and Harris. Grazier and dairy-farmer. At least they agree on Ella. All boongs smell. Didn't you know?'

'I shall do my best,' I said.

I stood awkwardly with my hand on the door. Her eyes looked into mine. They held despair too deep for words. I was conscious of the toppling of balance. Somehow I hesitated to leave. She saw my dilemma and moved across to open the door herself.

'Don't worry, Miriam. I am safe. There is no equivalent,

for human beings, to a nice vet. with a needle, and my personal courage is limited. Thank you for your help and your loyalty.'

I heard the door close behind me. I did not see her again.

PHILIPPA ____

4

It was evening when I came to Etherington, or perhaps late afternoon.

Five o'clock is barely evening in an Australian summer. The heat is still on the land, a part of the earth underneath. But five o'clock in Meridale is almost evening. By six the sun will begin to settle and the breeze will catch the cooling edge typical of the mountain plateau. I cannot describe an Australian evening. It has a loveliness born of a hot summer, a sense of cool relief that I associate with no other land I have visited.

Significance is evening. Evening is the muted cello note, the dying fall, the plateau to tension. Evening is the eternal hope of peace, ending ironically for me in the crash of cymbals. I have never liked cymbals. Mine is the mood of the muted strings.

Evening was our home in England, the long twilight in summer. Evening was my return from school in the winter, and my mother waiting at the station with the fog pressed on her face like a comic mask. The chug of the old Morris, her face again with the cool, firm line I loved and longed for in my heart. Winter vacation, with winter-familiar trees and hedges looming out of the darkness; and Mother said, 'You will not be returning to school, Philippa. This time the authorities have failed to trace your father. We have had no letters since Anjou and that was three months ago. We have also had no cheques.'

Who can say how I felt then? I cannot. Grateful to my father for taking me out of school—incongruous, inappropriate emotion. I lie. Not gratitude. Rapturous joy mingled with guilt. I miss things. I always have: home, log fires, my mother, my sisters, days washed with the scent of the gardens and the fresh smell of turning earth. A small girl imprisoned in long corridors and dormitories crowded with jolly, jolly teenage humanity. If I ever ran a school, I thought, it would be like home.

Evening and village life. A small day school in the local town, the pottery club, the music club, the drama club. 'So wonderful, my dear, your scholarship to Cambridge.' Kind hearts, kind faces, kind familiar smiles: the same smiles sped me on my way to the university, the same hands waved me on vacations, before the war to the Continent, the byways of France, the mountains of Switzerland, the lakes of Austria and the sluggish, slow Rhine, although I did not like Germany in the late thirties. My pilgrimages in the paths of Father, footsteps erased long before I arrived. How pathetic! Sometimes I stood in inns, Madrid, Lisbon, Florence, Innsbruck, and I saw the women that stood there with him. A man, my father, unearthed out of the memory of childhood, a vague blur with straight black hair like my own. What self-indulgence! In truth I never interested him. When I was born he telegraphed a friend in London, 'Another bloody girl', before leaving on a jaunt with a local schoolmistress.

It was evening and I returned to our village after the air raid. What joy to leave the evacuated children in North England even for a week-end! I had not been home for months. Anticipation—fire, scones, Mother. There was no one at the station, there were no cabs. I walked two miles, through the devastated village and the wrecked countryside. There was no house: a crumbling brick wall and a debris-strewn garden. One of my cellos stood intact against the wall of a chimney and the collar of one of the dogs, stained with blood, was caught round a lilac bush. I sat on the cairn of broken bricks and played as the moon rose over the wreck of my childhood and transformed me into a pacifist seeking comfort in the Church with its soothing litanies. I did not blame God. I blamed man. There was nothing to keep me in England, and the Continent I had known no longer existed. I do not like propped up ex-super states. The post-war world was drab and hopeless. I taught; I became warden of a girls' home; I learnt to play a flute. But the evenings were foggy, perpetually foggy. There was a job in Australia. Terra Australis del Espiritu Santo, the dream of the old mariners; for me a pilgrimage into sunlight. My own pilgrimage this time, blazing my own tracks instead of following the paths of my father. The war had shattered the dark memory into irreplaceable fragments. He had not only disappeared. He was also probably dead.

It was evening and we touched down at Sydney. Evening edging into night. We came in across a harbour lit by a blazing path of dying sun along the centre of the water and streaked with shadow in the inner bays. Balmoral, Lavender Bay, Rose Bay—old-world names. I remember her standing there, a felt hat pulled down over her cropped fair hair and her hands in the pockets of a tweed overcoat. She organised my luggage and bought me coffee. She is good, I thought.

Margaret Kersten spanned my loneliness. I was lulled into love in the warmth of her room; part of the school, but not of it. Outside time and place. Love is not temporal or spatial. 'Play, play,' her deep voice commanded me, and I played while she fashioned odds and ends from wood in the cocoon of that room. When I wept she comforted me and held me in her strong, tweedy arms, pressing me to her breast like my own mother, and she did not ask why I wept. And later there was a spotted dog on my bed, comic spotted face, wiggling bottom.

'Dido,' I said. 'Dido.' The love of the wandering Aeneas.

I did not like that school. It takes months to adjust to monotony. Superficially Australia is monotony. The monotony

of gums and the monotony of living. Regulations and sylla-
buses and state-wide examinations. Even so, I taught those
girls to weave and I wove myself. Sitting on the slatted chairs
I wove and wove webs of wool for my own imprisonment.
Penelope without Ulysses. And together we made music. I
taught them to sing madrigals in their lovely sun-blessed
voices. On the long summer afternoons I walked with them,
resting with fatigue in the long grass, while the golden light
caressed their young throats and the trees cast patterns of
leaves older than time itself on their skin. But they were griz-
zlers. Grizzle, grizzle, grizzle. I can't weave today, I have my
exams next week; I can't sing today, I have to swot; I can't
walk, it's too hot. Waste of time, waste of time, and in the
end their golden music was lost, and after four or five years
I was lost, too, for I had learnt to call the evening meal 'tea'
and to know that the girls were not interested in education
or, for that matter, in music or art. But there were vacations.

In vacations I explored the country with Margaret. We
crawled in our tiny car across the western plains of New
South Wales and through the forests of Victoria. We even
pushed north one hot summer to the Barrier Reef and I grew
sallower as the sun hardened my skin, and stringier in the
neck. It did not matter.

And so we abandoned school and made pottery together.
The coastal mountains of Queensland rise above the coastal
plain, but look back at the blue sea and alienated hills. There,
with the blue sea in our lenses and the grotesquerie of the
mountains in the distance, we spent a year, fashioning pots
and jugs and mugs, carving figures in wood, weaving scarves
and skirts. Dido came, too, and we explored the local forests
together. It was a haven, a bliss; but I was later ill, and the
heat of summer worried me and the doctors' bills depleted our
savings and Margaret poured out her own money to bring
me back to health. The doctors were vague about my disease. Some semi-tropical fever or perhaps merely a breakdown
born of that evening after the air raid. I was conscious of
little except those rough, kind hands smoothing my blankets,

straightening my bed, and later guiding me back to the sun through the weeks of convalescence. Dido sat beside me and Margaret fed me.

When I recovered, she said, 'I'll have to go back to school, Philippa. We're broke.' And so we returned to teaching; but authority oppressed me like shapes of night. I began to retreat with my cello and not even Margaret could penetrate my solitude. And so Etherington.

Margaret and Dido saw me off and I kissed Margaret, feeling as if my own self were separating from me, and said, 'I'll send for you'; and she gently removed my hand from her arm, picked up Dido who smothered my face in slobbery kisses, and said, 'I'll be waiting, Philippa dear.'

Meridale was the new world, but it was an old world. Its stunted, winter-deformed trees made me ache for my last school and the tall gums of the Queensland hills. The ultimate monotony of landscape was there: my early Australian impressions had been wrong. Those landscapes were miracles of variety. Here was the ultimate monotony of land and sky and human dwelling. The railway station was ancient, almost derelict. Its stone painted surface sprawled along the platform, to run into deserts of tin roofs. Again it was evening, and there at Etherington I met Miriam. Honest, sandy face. I felt rather than saw the ugly frock, the bulky laced shoes, the thick stockings. A figure as rural and as dowdy as the cows in the nearby paddock. I had an uneasy feeling of nemesis: dreariness; dreary train, dreary school, dreary Miriam.

Colour and youth. Where were they? I began to pursue them consciously. Fill the rooms and corridors with paint, I thought, and youth. Fresh faces, girls in short frocks and long hair. Mona, Ann, Janet, Miriam, Cunningham-White. What a batch they were! Dreary, middle-aged.

With Miriam's help I painted the walls and ceilings and staircases, everything within sight. She had no knowledge of any world beyond Meridale. A hasty unhappy brush with Sydney, then the local scene for ever. Her ideas of education were confined within the scrappy hills of Meridale and her mind marched doggedly along in the tracks laid down by the local coterie.

But she was willing and she was intelligent. She stayed day and night to help me organise the new programme, arrange the new time-tables, interview the new parents. She made no move to thwart my plans, and it was only at the back of her eyes I could read the layers of disapproval. I did not like her; but I could trust her.

In the early months I neither liked nor trusted Ann Denham. We met and it was morning: promise of a new day, vistas of futures. She ran her eye over my plans for school clubs, new courses, sniffed the new paint, and said, 'And I suppose good old Miriam did the lot without asking for a bloody penny overtime.'

Ann superficially was regulation mould, the convention of professional hairdressing, surplus flesh pressed attractively into fashionable dressing. Delusion. Her mind and spirit brooked no regulation whatsoever. At first the spirit of Ann eluded me completely, although the remark on overtime was typical. A hard-working, efficient trouble-maker with a gift for humanity. I can hardly be blamed if I retreated in silence from her obvious cynicism.

There were all those watching eyes in the staff-room, waiting, waiting, waiting. Thinking of salaries, old ways, vague injuries. I avoided contact and took up my weaving. I wove —skirts, scarves, head-bands, and I had to wear them. I was a stalking horse of personal industry. Again I played, alone in a lovely old-fashioned room with a soaring ceiling and an ornamental cedar fire-place; and my fingers quivered over the strings thinking of the pioneers of this country who used cedar and pine and oak as freely as matchwood. I felt their loneliness in their cold farm-houses in a strange land peopled with the names of their childhood. I reached out to their isolated spirit and knew isolation myself, searing, deep-rooted. I was lonely until Rachel came.

Lovely Rachel. Such pleasure you gave to me, my darling. Simply to look at you was pleasure. I could forget those

middle-aged faces. I could leave Miriam ticking like a clock,
tick, tick, tick, tick, tock. I was air-borne on the knowledge
of your nearness. At night I shut out Meridale with music,
playing while the light of the fire played on your hair and
mirrored itself like a rising phoenix in your blue eyes.

I like youth, particularly feminine youth. There is nothing
strange in that. I have always lived with women. My mother,
not my father. How could I know my father, vanished and
untraceable in Europe? I had only sisters, not brothers. Perhaps Rachel reminded me of my sister Alison, with hair like
crystallised honey and eyes blue-flecked green like the sea.
Although they were not alike. Rachel was coarser, bouncier,
built from Australian sunlight; Alison was moulded from the
softness of English springs.

Rachel was morning, and in those mornings I shook the
sluggish livers of the Cunningham-Whites with breakfasts in
the open air. There was bite in the air, scented pine crossed
with the pungency of gums, and the streams were swollen with
grey-bellied boulders. Girls imprisoned too long flung themselves on the grass or hung from the branches of trees, and
we fried eggs over wood fires and I sizzled in butter the fungi
the pupils collected. What startled eyes! My staff ate delicately, anxiously, murmuring polite approbation with the fear of
poison in their bones. Such busyness; spirit-freeing activity. I
watched the wood smoke spiral above the trees into the cloud-
hung blue of the tableland sky and I planned a school that
would be home; happy, busy girls making music and weaving
clothes, conducting their own discussion groups, caring for
others. I had not yet plumbed their rural ordinariness, their
ability to chew the cud like the cows on their fathers' properties. Perhaps Ina Spurway was to blame. She had allowed the
ability of her junior school to waste away so that the present
seniors were uniformly mediocre. Girls. I had to attract clever
girls, bright girls, gifted girls. And dear old Miriam agreed,
of course. Into her capable hands drifted my ideas to be returned as advertisements, programmes, written suggestions.
She helped me introduce policies and ideals whose meaning

and intention she could not even glimpse. I tried to like Miriam, country town personified, personality repressed eternally into role of dutiful daughter. She had not even thought of buying herself a car. In good sensible Victorian shoes and inappropriate sensible nylon frocks, she trudged or rode her bicycle winter and summer up and down the hills of Meridale.

It was evening when I visited her home and her mother. Curious hotch-potch of architecture. Wood, wood and more wood, stuffed into ornamental cross-pieces and architraves, curved into decorative corners on unnecessary verandas, shaped into inner walls and stained dark brown, topped by picture rails and tiers of shelves; and fire-place after fire-place. A cluttered, stuffy house, where light barely penetrated the inner rooms and, if it did, was carefully hurried out again with dull, heavy curtains. The walls dripped with old paintings, conventional prints and Victorian originals perpetrated by long dead aunts and uncles. And there were the family portraits, sexless relatives in old-fashioned wedding clothes. Miriam's father framed in walnut, Miriam's mother framed in oak. There were the animals that Father carved, the chairs that Father carved, the table that Father carved. And the sofa struggled for identity amidst the festoons of lace doyleys and antimacassars that Mother had created in a long dead past.

Nasty, vicious little woman. She eyed me up and down, her crooked hands resting on her stick, her eyes wide, malevolently beautiful above a penetrating nose. Her mouth smiled, harsh mockery that became embedded in lines of wrinkles stretching to her chin. She knew I did not like her house.

'Do you mind if I open a window?' I said.

A flutter of anxiety in Miriam's cheek. 'You find it stuffy?' said Mother.

'A bit,' I said. 'It's so crisp out.'

'It will be crisp in here if you open the window,' she said.

'A little air wouldn't hurt, Mother.'

She glanced malevolently at her daughter. 'I fear I haven't your tough Hansen constitution.' She turned to me, all charm.

'I'm sure you won't mind putting up with a little inconvenience. I suffer from rheumatism, you see.'

I nodded politely and continued to suffocate amidst the bric-a-brac of that encumbered world. It had to be endured. I could not manage without Miriam's help; but I knew I simply could not face that house again. I decided then that Miriam would have to buy a car and learn to drive. Difficult? Not really. The records showed she was grossly underpaid. She protested, but not too hard. There is joy in freedom and Miriam began to enjoy it. She could escape at night, even attend our musical evenings. There she sat on a straight-backed chair, her feet pressed firmly together, while the girls sat on mats and Rachel leant against my chair, her hair falling over her shoulder. Pleasant evenings with the feeling of youth around me and the soft silkiness of my long skirts against my legs, a buffer against the cello. Curiously, I think Miriam rather liked the music. I almost liked her.

At first, success. There was more life, more colour. The young faces in staff and schoolroom multiplied. When the young were unavailable I looked elsewhere. What gaiety a sari can lend to a dull room, what exotic romance the intonation of a new voice. The children had a little difficulty with foreign rhythms but Miss Nikolides's French was excellent even if her English was somewhat bizarre.

How jovial was the Council in those early days. 'I feel as if I belong,' Jim Graves said. 'Miss Spurway took care to make me an outsider. The girls are delighted with their new freedom.' 'So cultural,' said his wife.

I laid on the table Miriam's carefully drawn plans for improvements, blueprints for an Assembly Hall, a music room, squash courts. They purred and purred like great fat cats—or should I say bulls? Only bulls don't purr. Even then I did not really like them. The all-male cast, self-satisfied like all such casts and not really appropriate for an all-girl school. And from the start the shuffling of feet, the careful avoidance of eye, the plain rudeness. Never mention the word salary—

not to an Etherington Council. It was embarrassing, awkward. Money was a dirty word in that company. Money affected their hard-earned savings, money to staff became higher fees for them to pay. I suppose, more correctly, money wasn't a dirty word but a holy word. Only the expressed need for it was dirty. Obviously, if Mona Edison needed money, that no-good husband of hers should have provided it. Why was Mrs Denham whingeing? Her husband earned a good salary. She should be delighted to have the privilege of teaching their children. Only occasionally did I extract a few more pence from them. I succeeded with Miriam. Miriam was a good local brake on the desirable yet suspect talent I imported from foreign parts. Miriam was reliable, Miriam was one of them. Inferior, it is true, but for all that one of them.

For the rest, they became pompous, even indignant at the mention of money, and I became reserved, avoiding staff members who raised the issue, withdrawing to be alone with my cello. That was why it took me so long to like Ann Denham. Money shook its nickel fingers between us. The very thought of Mona Edison made my knees shake. Not that the Council was entirely wrong; only their reasons were wrong. A trained teacher, no doubt, but such a narrow little woman. What do you say to a woman like that?

Even so I was conscious of growth. Imperceptible, slow, but nevertheless growth. With Rachel for company, there was hope. Rachel, oh Rachel, how could you betray me? I took you everywhere, the concerts, the art displays; sipped coffee with you during the evening and read my favourite poets. You could have loved David; but you did not need to marry him. You could have loved David without cruelty to me who loved you. The humiliation of rejection. You could have accepted my invitation in front of Miriam even if you spurned me later. Miriam witnessed your selfishness and understood my rejection. She knew. Miriam always knows with that dumb inner perception of hers. Stay out all night. Why should I worry? But Miriam knew I worried. Miriam's knowledge is your unforgivable sin. I had to run the gauntlet of Miriam's

eyes. Sometimes they looked as gritty and sandy as her hair.
Miriam disapproving of me and you, but mostly of me.
'Come, come, no need to worry. I shouldn't ring the headmaster if I were you. He cannot control the movements of his
staff. They are men!' Holy word. But she was right. I should
not have rung him—pompous little provincial man.

And so you left. Again it was evening. I stood coldly in
the school vestibule and shook your hand, Rachel my love,
knowing you were making an unfortunate mistake. Miriam,
bustling righteousness, passed by us on her way to her car.

I remember walking over to my room to find Ann Denham
sitting on my sofa. I almost retreated from my own home, but
she saw my intention and began to speak.

'I knew you wouldn't mind if I just walked in,' she said.
'The corridor is damn cold. I mixed you a drink. Hope you
like brandy. I took the risk, anyway. It's my own staple diet.'

Perhaps I should have been offended, but instead I felt
warmed. I looked at the pudgy hands folded round the glass
and smiled at the streak of stencil purple in the palm. I raised
my eyes, and for a moment they looked directly into her
brown-splotched grey eyes. They were not laughing. They
held mine in an act of sympathy and I took the glass gladly.

'I like brandy, too.'

'Good.'

She wriggled deep into the sofa. She kicked off both shoes
and tucked her tiny feet under her. For a minute we sipped
in silence, then, 'Actually,' she said, 'I came over to ask you
to dinner. Tomorrow night if you can make it. About time
you met Peter.'

I met Peter and enjoyed it. He was a scientist, a self-effacing
kind of scientist, but nice. I also met her two daughters. The
evening wore on and we sat on the mat by a log fire's psyche-
delic embers and talked and talked. God, poetry, novels, films,
music. . . . I was grateful. Whatever happened, there was some
kind of refuge in Ann's house. Only once did our new relationship falter. I had mentioned Miriam's opposing my sugges-
tion for evening lessons. 'Don't let bloody Miriam run you,'

she said irritably. 'Miriam will run every damn thing given half a chance.'

I laughed. 'Wearing, Miriam,' I said, 'she is very wearing. So compulsively local.'

She did not laugh back. Something like a flash of anger lit her eyes.

'Miriam is good,' she said. 'You will find she is the only truly good one amongst us. You're right, of course. She is local. But you would be wrong to despise her on that count. She knows this town thoroughly, backwards, frontwards, past, present and future—and she rejects it. You may not realise it; I doubt if she does; but she rejects it all the same. She flings their filthy gossip and barbed nastiness into those black depressive paintings. I said, "Don't let Miriam run you", and I meant it. But don't underrate her, Philippa.'

Then she laughed, all soft pudginess once again. 'Forgive me,' she said. 'I am presumptuous. I've never sorted out my own feelings about Miriam. I hover between total admiration and complete irritation. Hence I feel defensive. A counter-guilt, I suppose.'

And so Rachel went away and I began to know Ann. But Ann was elusive. Ann had Peter and her home and her daughters. There were moments of contact and moments of exclusion; times when she didn't care whether I lived or died. I missed Rachel. It was lonely. At night I worked with Miriam, time-tables, schedules, plans; but I could not say to Miriam, 'Sit near me. Let me play to you.' She could enjoy our communal evenings; there were the stirrings of response; but individual music is too intimate. I simply could not play the cello for Miriam. There are no cracks in her defences. I did not love her. Sometimes, after she drove away—and she stayed regularly till 10 p.m.—I would draw the instrument from the case, turn out all but a single lamp in the lofty room, open my window to the starred crisp night, and play, trying to feel again all those lost evenings in other places: our village and the fog of winter, my mother's face, the tracks of Europe, the standing chimney and the bloodstained dog collar; and I knew that once again I was weeping internally, taking the journey back into the irretrievable, damnable past.

To save myself I had to find a place for Margaret Kersten and for Dido. 'O God,' I prayed, 'let me survive on this rural island of nowhere!' So I made my plans. The school needed a carpenter. The agreement of Council in principle and then the introduction of Margaret casually, very casually, as if she were someone I just happened to remember.

I wrote to Margaret. And, of course, she came. The evening plane dropped into the one-time paddock and they were both there, Dido and Margaret. I felt my security seep back into me at the sight of the belted leather overcoat and the dear weather-beaten face. She kissed me on the mouth and the warmth returned.

'We'll have to wait until they extract the mong,' she said. Poor Dido. She sat in a kind of wire-enclosed tea-chest, her spotted head peering anxiously at the night. 'Too big for a dog pack,' said Margaret. 'Anyway, I couldn't find one and the airline had mislaid their collection.' Her voice was gruff, deep, with a rasp I did not recall. 'You have a cold?' I asked. 'Not at the moment. The cold air breaks my voice. That's all.' People speak of premonitions but in fact I had no premonition. I did not know then, that the first hint of Margaret's illness had reached me.

How the staff reacted! I kept a straight face at the first meeting, watching the impact of that masculine voice on each and every one of them. What a little snort of disapproval flared Miss Cunningham-White's nostrils; what bourgeois timidity and gossipy curiosity passed through Mona Edison's eyes; what genteel shock palpitated the bosom of Janet Ellis! Mr Pilsudski looked perseveringly non-concerned and inclined his head with European gallantry; Ann Denham merely showed ironic amusement at her colleagues' reactions. But Miriam surprised me. As her bony hand clasped Margaret's I sensed instant liking. Not that Miriam showed any emotion. Miriam does not show emotion. But being sensitive to Margaret I knew what Miriam felt.

I never quite fathomed the attraction of Margaret for
Miriam, or, even more surprising from my viewpoint, Miriam
for Margaret. They had the kind of companionship that grows
in silences, that is aware of nearness. At first it did not worry
me. I was too elated to care. I had the companion I needed.
Outside my door at night I could hear the reassuring grunts
of Dido. Sometimes, when lonely, I slipped across to Margaret's cottage and stayed until morning.

What barnyard minds the rural gentry have! Later one of
the Council was to use this fact against us. They never understood that I cannot bear physical contact, that I withdraw
from caress. Their minds could not conceive pure companionship. I sat curled on the foot of Margaret's bed while she lay
stretched out, head on the pillow. Talk and talk and talk and
talk until dawn greyed the room. Sometimes I looked at her
feet lying near my curled form and once or twice I ran my
finger along the arch, enjoying the start of surprise; but I
rarely touched her. Only when I wept did she put her arms
around me and draw me to her breast. God, how complacent
are the comfortable unhappily married, seeking to bridge their
alienation by physical sensation! Margaret and I had no need
of such union.

She carved a bird for Miriam. I knew that because I had
admired it, too.

'What happened to the bird?' I said. The workshop was her
usual conglomeration of orderly disorder.

'Miriam liked it.'

I said nothing more, but I felt anger. I had thought of that
bird as my bird. I had thought that Margaret would give it
to me. Being Margaret, she offered no excuses, no explana-
tions. Miriam wanted it. That was enough.

She put down her hammer and lit a cigarette. She amused
herself by flicking ash on Dido's head.

'Don't,' I said crankily.

'One more spot won't hurt, will it, Mong?'

'She doesn't like it,' I said, but the brute made me a liar
by licking the hand that flicked her.

'You'll have to behave, Mong,' Margaret said. 'I can hear your dulcet voice over here.'

I laughed. 'I have to leave her outside when I close the sixth-form door to shut out the noise from poor Mr Musket's lessons. They're rather chaotic, I'm afraid.'

'They're bedlam,' she said. I looked anxious. 'For heaven's sake don't let me worry you, Philippa. I was merely stating a fact. The school must be staffed, and presumably even Musket is better than nothing. The girls can put it down to experience.'

'I do worry,' I said. 'Miriam is so disapproving and even Ann thinks something should be done.'

'Neither Miriam nor Ann,' she said, 'have to conjure staff out of nowhere with the offer of an annual pittance and no future.'

I was grateful. I believe in freedom, and I had always disliked snoopy Heads. I patted Dido's head and the ash smeared along my palm.

'The Council don't like you, do they, Dido?'

'You mean her snores,' said Margaret. She lit another cigarette, poked it in the corner of her mouth, and began to whittle a piece of wood into a paper-knife.

I giggled. 'She sits on Maurice Furlonger's foot.' I contorted my face into a jowly likeness of the gentleman, straightening my imaginary tie with great aplomb. Then I squatted on all fours and gazed, adoring, upward. 'She looks on him with rapture, and he is uncomfortably aware of his own image snoring away beside the astringent Mena.'

'And Graves?'

'Graves doesn't like dogs,' I said. 'Definitely not. I'm revising my opinion of that man. He seemed so affable at first. But I suspect he bites. Especially when he's had a preliminary nip from the bitch at home.' I stroked the dog's head. 'Dido never bites, do you, darling?' She grunted.

Margaret frowned. 'Watch them, Philippa. They're not our kind of people. They could make trouble. I doubt if they approve.'

I looked with affection at her blond wavy hair, crisp and short. 'Of you?'

'Of me.'

'They can go to hell,' I said. Roughly I hugged her, then hastened out into the evening to hide my emotion.

There were pleasant days in the next months. My school began to beat with its own tempo and I adjusted my pace to the girls' rural abilities. It was a noisy school, but it was not unhappy. The girls began to sing, automatically, naturally. At meal-times, at assemblies, the hymns they knew flowed in harmonies around the tables and chairs. In chapel the young voices blended and lifted to the rafters. And people began to listen and then to ask them to sing outside the school.

Advertisements of learning amongst its hills and plateaux bring to Meridale a constant stream of teachers and pupils from the city to attend the seminars and conferences at its local colleges. At one we made songs from Australian ingredients—wash-boards, gum-leaves, didgeridoos, and I learnt the ballads of an oppressed people. At another we learnt about the new God: humanist hands outstretched in love, driving the fog of repression out of the Church. Love your neighbour. Love your enemy. Love, love, love.

I reached for the world of humanity, but I crept away to commune with the transcendental as well. Man without God mocked me. Margaret prayed and worshipped, pantheist to the core, but touchable for that reason. But Miriam I could not touch. She attends Church regularly, prays in chapel, knows a limited number of the most banal non-conformist hymns.

'You'd enjoy the Convention,' said Margaret. 'Chops and tea and bread and butter, humming guitars—and God under the stars.'

Miriam shrugged her bony shoulders. 'The stars are so chilly in Meridale,' she said.

'Take a blanket,' said Margaret. 'Rug up like a Spanish Indian.'

Miriam smiled creakily. 'I prefer God on Sunday and in Church.'

Ann Denham's nice eyes merely laughed at me. 'Don't you recognise a sinner when you see one, Philippa?'

I did not expect to enjoy the science seminar. I went to it merely because I was a headmistress and I believe in the march of education in the modern world. Music and art and literature, the mosaic fabric of human communication—these are my preoccupations. But I had to make obeisance to the other culture.

To my surprise, I was fascinated. The test tubes shone, the pumps pumped, the levers levered and at the core of reality the atoms and their parts pulsated like pulsars. The march of the universe rumbled out beneath the lecturer's magnificent beard and I saw that a modern school would have to march with it.

Ann opposed me, bitterly, vehemently, at times blasphemously. 'Be reasonable, Philippa,' she said. 'These bloody men live in a world where the 130 IQ represents the dumb. A good dose of a couple of histories, geography, and perhaps a little biology, and our girls may pussyfoot their way into a higher education. Push them into physics and chemistry and you'll bloody well drown them.'

My eyes still shone with the glory of science. 'This is the twentieth century,' I said. 'The girls must be given every opportunity to be part of it. What is more, there are government grants for laboratories. They can study history later.'

'You're a damn fool,' Ann said and walked out.

I was hurt, withdrawn, and I found I was quite incapable of talking to her for the next month. It made the school day very lonely. I could not always escape to Margaret.

Miriam was not rude. Miriam is never rude. She merely pursed her lips in a disapproving line, looked fixedly at her bony knuckles, and said in a voice like a knell, 'I hope you're right.'

When a number of the girls failed to pass at the end of the year, she took great pleasure in passing on every abusive remark transmitted by parent and neighbour in daily encounters along the main street of Meridale. As if education were a matter of passing examinations!

I wove myself a new red tweed for winter, transmitted the ironies of Mr Pilsudski's compositions into arrangements for the cello, and continued my fight to take a rural school into the atomic age. I have never understood why Miriam should think I am even interested in the thoughts of a miasmic blonde like Della Graves. I could scarcely be bothered placating Jim Graves. His girls are not bright, merely worthy. He will simply have to accept the fact.

The halcyon period ended with the planting of the roses. Such cold brilliant Saturdays, fashioning into garden patterns the grey and brown rocks we had found on the hillsides— granite-dotted hillsides where the lovely grained stone lay in lumpy chunks like the discarded playthings of some antipodean god. I felt the smoothness of cement as I welded the stones together and smelt Margaret's earthiness near me as she zigzagged the paths across the brown earth that Miriam shovelled so efficiently and dutifully. How the earth froze the fingers, refrigerated by the morning frosts! What blue mornings sharpened our faces as the sun warmed our backs!

The season culminated like a religious festival in the rose planting. Peace and Madame Butterfly for Miriam, Crimson Glory and Iceberg for Margaret, and golden Talisman for me. We were a trinity of love born of hard work and aesthetic fulfilment, and we, each of us, felt our identity with Etherington rooted in that garden. In the evening we packed up, changed our trousers for frocks, and drank coffee and ate biscuits by the fire. Later I played the cello, trying to put our reaching out for one another into the music. The flames lit Miriam's sandy hair until it glowed like gold, and the hand patting the dog's head was streaked with the red light of the embers. The smoke from the fire drifted over the room and mingled with the scent of Margaret's cigarettes. And Dido snored. We were happy that evening.

That spring I attended the Conference for the Assimilation of Aborigines. And I had my brilliant idea. Why not a scholarship for one of the Aboriginal girls? I shall never forget my first sight of an Aboriginal settlement. Fresh from England, I had thought this was the land of equal opportunity. At first these people did not exist for me. No dark figures lurked amongst the gum-trees, there were no humpies on the banks of the creeks. I explored the new landscape on foot, but native flora and fauna were rare. I had come to a white man's settlement—or so I thought.

My first contact with the native population was in a coastal town not far from Meridale where I went to the cinema with Margaret to while away an unwanted evening and witnessed the segregation of black from white. The blacks were neatly curtained off, thrust by the white man's edict into the worst seats, branded as inferior and unwanted. This shocked me.

'Drive me to the settlement,' I said to Margaret the next day. Settlement! On the edges of one of the loveliest rivers in the state they squatted in squalor. Patched galvanised iron, abandoned rubbish-tips from which rose clouds of flies like a stench made concrete; and on the outskirts, shyly watching, stood the lovely unkempt children clad in the cast-off garments of a white population. I was silent as we drove back. There was nothing to say.

That picture was repeated many times in the next few months, and I learnt, travelling to settlements in the north, that prejudice deepens with the warmth of the sun. Queensland, its blue brilliance shining with the gauzy colours of the tropics, remains cold in heart to its own people. Meridale, by comparison with the northern outposts, is enlightened. The frost has edged its heart but has not destroyed the core. Here there are housing schemes, the women's club for Aboriginal children, the kindergarten.

I sketched my idea to Margaret sitting on stony ground in the bleak gorge country, and she said, 'Excelsior, old thing— but seriously, have a go if you'd like to do something. Failure is always relative.'

A hostile Council, in essence. Harris and Denton combined against me. But the respectable middle group was waffling along on a wave of civic reform and so, against the warning quiver of their social antennae, the Graveses and Furlongers supported me. And so Ella came.

And Miriam? How would good Miriam react, bred cheek by jowl with all the prejudices of Meridale? Good, loyal Miriam. Loyalty alone would have meant co-operation, but she was in fact enthusiastic. Duty and pleasure met. She arranged all the details, did the spadework of visiting the mother, shepherded the child through initial insults.

Some evenings I walked with Ella through the grounds watching her firm brown face grow fatter with the good food and her confidence become firmer as she made contact with the mainstream of Australian life. On sports days her firm brown legs twinkled over the hurdles and ropes; around the school her willing hands helped her fellows. Miriam and I knew and watched and felt reward. It was worthwhile even if Ann Denham condemned it.

'It's bloody nonsense, Philippa,' she said. 'Bloody nonsense. They treat the girl like a lackey. She should be at High School learning something definite.'

'She is learning something definite,' I said stiffly.

'To be the perfect servant,' she snapped.

I refused to quarrel with her this time. Not talking to Ann was too much like hard work. I knew Ann was wrong, deceived by subterranean prickles of prejudice she herself never even suspected. I forgave her. I felt fulfilment, and in the bare brick Cathedral I knelt and thanked my God for it: an idea had been planted.

Later that year Mary Christoe arrived. Dear Mary. Saucy insouciance. I watched her short firm legs, so feminine in their masculine boots, and her gay, so gay long dark hair. A witty companion and a new breath of youth. Linda Skaines was young, too, but serious young—one of the new breed of young women putting their husbands through degree after degree. They clutched their jobs to their bosoms protectively, their passport to service. They no longer blacked his boots or warmed his slippers, but they accorded their male the same subservience of mind and spirit that women have accorded since Eve without protest allowed Adam to say, 'The woman tempted me.' Good old serious work-horse Linda. I liked her, I really did; but in comparison free-as-air Mary was delightful.

Gossip is a subtle web of destruction, a trap for the curious, the participators in living; but Mary's mimicry was satire, not gossip. I invited her to join Margaret and me for coffee, and took delight in watching her hands, her arms, her face, as members of staff grew into caricatured life. My suppressed irritations obtained release. She was short and Miriam was tall, but her shoulders could droop with the same resigned effect, her sharp-featured lively face could take on Miriam's duty-pressed gaze.

Margaret was jealous. Poor Margaret was eternally jealous of youth. I followed her back to her cottage, dismissing Mary with a flick of my hand. 'Forgive me, my dear,' I said, 'I think Margaret is not well.' Mary's black eyes twinkled back at me as she slipped her leather jacket over her shoulders. She stuck her hand in her pocket and lit a cigarette with a perfect reproduction of Margaret's gesture. Her voice dropped. 'Blue eyes can be green,' she rumbled through the smoke. And, without thinking, I laughed.

Blue eyes were green. As I came into her kitchen Margaret did not turn round. She merely said, 'Is that you, Philippa?'

'Mm,' I said. 'Are you all right? I thought you looked unwell.'

She lit the gas and flicked the match into her bin. 'I am perfectly well,' she said, 'now.'

'Now?'

She stubbed her cigarette into a pottery tray and lit another. 'For God's sake, Philippa, can't you see? That girl nauseates me.'

'Don't be ridiculous,' I said.

'She's a toad,' said Margaret, 'a slimy little toad.'

'I like her,' I said stiffly. 'She's clever and witty.'

'And unkind. She has no perception of goodness.' Her hands shook as she put the tea into the pot.

'You are jealous,' I said. 'You've always been jealous of the young.'

'Don't talk nonsense. The young are always in my shop.'

'The kids, perhaps,' I said, 'but the mature and the beautiful you hate.'

'For God's sake, Philippa! She's nauseating. Miriam and Ann are your friends. But you sit there and laugh at them without compunction.'

I raised my hand. 'Excuse me, Margaret, I don't despise Miriam, but she is absurd. Surely one can laugh at absurdity.'

'One can,' she said. The tea slopped on the table as she picked up her cup. 'One can. But with toads, one doesn't.'

'I'm sorry,' I said. 'I'm sorry I came. I thought you might need help.'

She pushed a cup of tea towards me, but I did not take it. 'I don't need help,' she said, lighting another cigarette. '*You* do.'

I did not drink the tea. I left and she did not see me out. Somehow the night seemed blacker, colder as I walked across the playground back to my rooms. I decided to ignore her, but the oppression of foggy nights returned. The chimney of the school stood black, outlined against the black night. Black on black. Dido ran out to greet me and almost subconsciously I felt for her collar, rubbing my fingers along the leather. It was a cold town.

Maybe that quarrel weakened my defences. Defences can crumble so easily in the face of pomposity. Twelve pompous little men with the destiny of a girls' school in their hands, men whose knowledge of women was minimal, despite the possession of wives and daughters. How do you face an objectionable occasion? By now I can sense disaster, smell it in the air. I dressed for high tragedy—a long gown that flowed —remote, indefinite in time. It removed me from those grubby little Australian men.

I swept in with Dido at my heels and I could read the
startled expressions in their eyes. But they recovered. Probes
and questions, hints and insinuations, Denton trying to be
nice—so vulgar. I tickled the back of Dido with my toe so
that she fell into a heavy slumber.

Miriam can be perceptive, awkward bony Miriam, trying
to do the right thing, but sensing as no one else in that room
sensed the purpose of my gown. She gauged my remoteness
from them and from her and, being Miriam, she made no
attempt to bridge it.

Good solid Miriam, doing her duty but too wilfully innocent to sense the drift of their questions, the import of their
probings. I sat almost unconscious, letting the words flow, the
words punctuated by the vibrations of Dido's snores. It amused
me to watch the creases of annoyance deepen in Furlonger's
forehead, the twitchings of Graves's nose. Good old Dido. I
could rely at least on you.

'She loved them.' Loved. My God. Dearest Miriam, that is
a forbidden word, more nasty than all the 'Fs' put together.
We can pretend to dislike the latter but we can use them freely
when we are by ourselves. But love is another matter. Love
disturbs us, pulls the onion layers off our personal hypocrisies.
You could not have damned Margaret more effectively,
Miriam dear.

'Thank you, Miss Hansen.'

'It's a simple matter of economics.' How well Furlonger
understands economics. 'We cannot afford a carpenter at the
present time. And if we could, the job belongs by right to a
man. Miss Kersten will have to leave. It's as simple as that.'

As simple as that. Simple to face the chunky, honest face,
angry with hurt, and tell her that she is dismissed, unwanted.
And because we did love each other she knew I had made no
attempt to defend her—none whatsoever.

She smoked one cigarette—saying nothing. Then lit another.

'I see,' she said.

'You don't see anything,' I answered.

'Don't I?'

'Don't fight, don't fight,' I said to myself.

'What will you do?' I asked.

'I have no doubt there are places where my presence is less objectionable,' she said.

'And Dido?'

'Dido is yours. I gave her to you long ago. Remember? Well, I guess that wraps it up. Good night, Philippa.'

I raised a hand to halt her departure. Then withdrew it. If Margaret chose to think I was getting rid of her in favour of Mary, then she chose to think it. I have never begged for love. I did not know she was sick.

Would I have fought the Council had I known? I cannot answer that question. I wish I could. I only knew when I opened the letter from Margaret's aunt that I felt guilt more intolerable than any I have known. And again it was Miriam who resolved the issue.

'You do not matter,' she said. 'Margaret needs you. You must go.' And so I went, visited my loved one at the behest of Miriam.

I have never liked hospitals. The room was cold, painted cement walls, sickly coloured quilts. It was not Margaret, this shell of a woman struggling to breathe in a falsely gay bed. She was beyond conversation. And I could not say, 'Sorry.' It would have been meaningless. Love had been reduced to the smell of Dettol and the camouflaged stink of illness. I wanted to escape. Outside the window the old slums and new high density units of Sydney merged with the blackened stacks of industry to the verge of a sandy blue bay. A plane rose from the horizon to speed across the distant water in a glint of silver sunlight. And the woman on the bed coughed in pain. 'It's not as bad as it sounds. The doctors say I may even re- cover completely provided I never smoke again.'

And so in the end Margaret apologised to me, not me to her. I walked a lost city, streets without meaning. There was no way I could excuse myself to Margaret. I could not say I was too craven to fight the Council. I was not too craven. I was too proud, too proud to humiliate myself in pointless arguments. I could not have won even if I had tried. They had marked me for dismissal, too. Perhaps I sensed it then without consciously facing the inevitable.

To appeal to Margaret in the face of my own desolation would have been unworthy. A woman with one lung. I am not a Miriam. I felt pity but I could not offer duty as a substitute for love. I do not like the sick, the old, the dying. I hankered for the young, the gay, the girls whose hair glistens with the sheen of youth. They reassure me.

I was glad to leave the woman in the bed and return to Meridale. Glad?

It was spring without spring. The clarity of air was a mockery of my spirit. For me, it was a season of fog through which I could find no familiar place, no shape beneath my fingers. I touched my cello and heard only a dirge of the spirit. I shut out the sunlight, seeking my own quarters alone with Dido. The school ticked over and I do not think I neglected it. The months slipped into summer, warm, fruitful with the frost at last disappearing from the air and the examinations creating pockets of excitement within the school.

You would think even men could understand grief, would have the decency to respect my need for a period of recovery; but they plotted behind my back, negotiated, whispered, gathered their numbers, and by the final Council meeting my dismissal was a *fait accompli*. It merely needed my resignation to save the face of the school.

'Your resignation, your resignation, your resignation!' The repetitive clamour of nightmare. Why? why? why? Examinations not up to standard, emotional uncertainty, unsatisfactory teacher-pupil relationships, unsatisfactory staff relationships. You could multiply the reasons indefinitely. The creative imagination was not dead, after all, in those men. Excuses, all excuses, built to cover situations and feelings they did not understand. Not all, of course. I had a small band of supporters led by Dennis and Daley but they were out-manoeuvred, politically guileless in comparison with the natural grafters at the head. Their decency was swamped in the jowly self-satisfaction of Furlonger, the lean petulance of Graves, the righteousness of Denton.

'We have been tolerant, Miss Ormiston. We have allowed many experiments, given you time to develop your ideas.'

I heard myself say, 'I was not aware that you knew the meaning of development, let alone education.'

Dido snored and Jim Graves almost kicked her. 'Let's get down to tin tacks,' he said. 'You've shown no sympathy with our viewpoint. Not even on minor matters. For month after month I've endured that dog at Council meetings. It's not decent, it's not decent. All those dogs at the school. In front of the children.'

'Are you sure you mean the dogs aren't decent, Mr Graves? I thought you meant me.' His neck deepened in colour and he was silent.

'We aren't satisfied,' said Denton. 'How can the girls get on when they're lumped into classes with the semi-literate?'

'You mean Ella?' I asked.

'Yes,' he shouted. 'I mean the Middleton girl.'

'Hear, hear!' said Harris.

'And Musket and Pilsudski,' said Furlonger, 'they're—they're not teachers—they're not normal.'

I forced my hands together to stop their trembling. 'You can hardly bracket them together,' I said coldly. 'They're not in the same class. Mr Pilsudski is a genius.'

Graves snorted. 'They're birds of a feather,' he said. 'Neither of them has done a day's teaching in his life. You had plenty of opportunity to get rid of them.' Dido snored. 'And for God's sake get rid of that dog.'

I felt glacial. 'Control yourself, Mr Graves,' I said. 'Believe me, neither Dido nor I has any desire to stay. I shall write out my resignation tonight.'

I looked at them—flabby, paunchy, middle-aged, with the beer purpling their veins and the juice of rich steaks coarsening their bones. The pupils of their eyes reflected nothing but money. No spark of understanding, no gleam of creation.

I rose and looked at them and I knew my contempt showed. 'You deceive yourselves,' I said. 'No one could do anything with this school. No one. Its keynote is parsimony. Parsimony does not build good schools.'

I walked stonily from the room, Dido at my heels. One of them rushed to open the door, but I walked straight through without looking at him.

'Come, Dido,' I said, 'we are anachronisms, you and I. No one wants us.'

I thought of a recent advertisement for South America, but I knew the mountains of the moon are ever distant and whatever ocean I sailed I should be alone.

Sunday was our annual church service. Furlonger had rung Miriam. What he said I do not know, but she preserved a front of loyalty even though I could sense some emotional disturbance in her. She kept darting a sideways glance at me, a look whose curiosity not even Miriam could control. I put on full academic dress for that occasion. It was hot, oppressive. A blazing day. Cicadas drummed from dawn in the surrounding trees and my ears caught the note of a thousand insects beating above and below the basic hum.

I chose my reading carefully. Psalm 27: 'Though an host should encamp against me, my heart shall not fear.' I lifted up my head to the blurred faces of the congregation and they rose to meet me—white frocks and Ella's black face, the odour of rabbit fur, and the sprinkling of blue and yellow, the mustiness of black too little aired. The speaker was a missionary from Fiji, but I did not hear a word that Sunday. The love of God the Father, the Fellowship of the Holy Spirit —and then the open air. Once more I breathed, but the hill was endless and I could feel the tears running down my face unchecked. Summer morning. Sun on my arms and the mingled scent of flowers and Sunday roasts in my nostrils and the ridiculous wet tears on my cheeks.

She stopped the car beside me. 'Get in,' she said. Dear

Ann. I had wanted to walk, to be alone, but she sensed my need for a human presence. She drove without speaking. I could see her curiously slender legs push the pedals—shapely, beautiful below her pudgy body. At the school I opened the door to get out, but she placed a hand on my knee to restrain me.

'It's a bloody shame,' she said, 'a bloody shame. We were beginning to make progress, you and me and Miriam. Just beginning. We were getting there. I know you did not resign willingly. You should have fought. In the end we could have made a good school.'

Dear Ann. You need resources to fight and I no longer had any resources. I sat in the black loneliness of my room and I thought, you need a belief in the future. I had none. Neither Dido nor I had any future. It was pointless to take her to South America. Who would want a scruffy, wind-broken, Dalmatian bitch? I rang the vet. There was a solution for Dido.

Morning shattered into its component parts as I put her in the car. Each song pulsed with the intensity of heat and I heard the cicadas separately and together entering my mind until the volume rose to an intolerable pitch. I crossed the footpath with the dog and I saw the cracks in the pavement and the leaves of a clover spread in triangular green over the edge. I knelt and put my arms round her neck and hugged her. She rumbled with pleasure. Then I opened the gate. 'Take the dog,' I said to the woman, 'she snores.' I did not even say good-bye. I returned to pack my own things.

Only one more meeting with Miriam, pressed into service by Council to keep the wheels running. It was duty. The school had to continue even if I fell by the wayside. Holy, lovely duty. I was a murderer, she told me. I betrayed Margaret and I murdered Dido. With the cruelty of all Miriams, she expressed the plain facts in plain terms. With the shallow sandiness of her kind, her face showed disapproval, but I did not care. I was not needed in Meridale. Meridale had Miriam.

MIRIAM

5

H. P. Fordess. Heather Patricia Fordess, but H.P. was enough. As far as I knew, she never called herself Heather, or Patricia. She was tall, very thin, and her red hair was pressed close to her head. Her eyes were vivid blue, and she had a mouth that pushed its corners in to form a disapproving line. She looked competent and she was competent.

I was reassured. I looked forward to being part of a well-organised school again. A disciplined routine seemed like the promise of a new heaven after three years of permissive chaos.

Before H.P. arrived, the dreariness of my everlasting round of duties was lightened only by letters from Margaret Kersten. She wrote to tell me that, needing rest, she had joined a settlement of people on the North Coast seeking a simpler life. One of its commitments was to provide a haven for the physically and mentally ill. It was not exactly a commune, for people lived alone if they wished, but most of them worked together on the small property. They were a mixed group—young people with skills such as nursing and teaching who resented the bureaucratic demands of the normal establishment; mothers and fathers who wanted to save their children from urban pollution or unsatisfactory schools; middle-aged exes from almost every profession; and a few of the elderly who desired to be useful instead of rotting in front of TV in some sunset home for the aged.

A carpenter was a godsend to them. Margaret could work as much or as little as she liked. Someone always needed shelter, a table, a bed, a chair; but there was no pressure. She did not join in all the communal activities, for she liked solitude; but it was good to know that other people existed just outside her door.

She had not heard from Philippa. It would be nice if I could write to her occasionally. And I did. But I had little time or aptitude for correspondence and my letters failed to convey my deeper feelings. I told her of my day-to-day activities, gave her scraps of staff news. Her letters were much more vivid, about her new projects, her new companions, comic and tragic, the incidents of her life on the settlement. She never complained, but I could at times sense the will power needed for her to keep going. I looked forward to her letters and, in a way, it was Margaret who helped me to manage that year.

H.P. arrived within three months of Philippa's departure, and the school began to hum with a new vigour. I ought to have been happier. I believed in order, didn't I? Unfortunately Mother remained like an albatross around my neck. She decided to burden my first weeks by returning to her bed, though she was perfectly well. It was her revenge for feeling neglected while I worked till all hours at school, putting the books in order, interviewing parents. And I felt resentment even towards God who rested the seventh day while I laboured.

'I am sure, Miriam,' Mother would say as I looked into her room before leaving for school, 'I'm sure you think more of that school than you do of your mother.'

'You have no cause to complain,' I said. 'I have always done my duty by you. Aunt Myra is coming down today to keep you company.'

Mother pouted petulantly, and I noticed that her sulkiness no longer enhanced her prettiness. She was getting old. 'You know Aunt Myra bores me,' she said; 'so petty, so full of complaints.'

'You mean the competition is a bit stiff,' I observed drily.

She held two books in her hands, but I purposely did not see them. Let her ask if she wanted me to go to the library for her. I was beyond the voluntary offering of favours. Who had ever offered me a favour? I was irritated. So many things irritated me. The noise of her wireless, tuned to the endless telephone conversations in which Mother took an occasional role.

'The young, Mr Announcer, have no sense of responsibility these days. I am a poor lame widow. My daughter refuses to do a thing for me. She puts her job first.' I imagined the syrupy voice at the other end of the line. 'I sympathise, Mrs Hansen. I really do. Probably your daughter has to work, you know.'

'There is no need. Father left us a little to live on. . . .' and on and on and on and on. Poor Father. Who could have guessed your humble provision for us was to become a widow's cruse?

Why should Robert escape scot free? In the dark of the night I wrestled with my resentment of his freedom. Every two days I wrote to him. I pointed out his duty to him. I told him quite plainly that it was time he accepted his share of the parental burden. She was his mother, too.

He refused. Always some excuse. Children's bills, children's illnesses, Muriel's ill-health, his own lack of promotion. Robert had never been lacking in excuses, but he excelled himself in those months. I continued to write. Someone had to tell him the facts and I alone was likely to do so. I increased the letters to one a day, even though it was plain inconvenient with all the work I had to do at school. 'Mother is most upset, Auntie Miriam. Why do you write to Daddy so often?'

'Dear Kerrie,' I wrote, 'You are too young to understand, but your mother must appreciate that sons owe a duty to their mother, too. Your father has never pulled his weight. He was always obstinate.'

'Dear Miriam,' wrote Robert, 'You know quite well I am

not in a position to help. Your everlasting requests are up-setting my wife who has never been as strong as you. I should prefer you not to discuss me with Kerrie.'

'Dear Robert,' I wrote, 'I do not discuss you. I merely answered Kerrie's query which I presumed came ultimately from you not her. What is more I have never regarded your wife as an invalid. It is true she has always appeared wispy and pale, but I have detected a wiry strength beneath the fragility, particularly when she is working in my kitchen. Any-way she had flu last winter merely once, whereas I myself had four colds and two attacks of bronchitis.'

'Miriam,' said Mother, 'what are you doing to Robert? He wrote to me yesterday. He says you are plaguing him with letters.'

I looked at Mother without moving a muscle in my face, even though one began to tick involuntarily in my cheek. 'Mother,' I said, 'you have implied for years that I do not appreciate my brother. Now that I am trying to keep in touch, you complain. In the past you have always desired news of the family. "Have you heard from Robert, Miriam?" "Any news of the children, Miriam?" '

'You appear to be overdoing it,' she said.

Was I overdoing it? I was tired, very tired. I was shut up in this house with a vicious old woman. Shut up for life. Per-secuted constantly by my contemporaries. Neither Robert, nor Jim Graves nor Froggy Daley shouldered the burdens of life. They shoved it onto good old Miriam. Good old Miriam whose mother never thanked her and who had hated her friendship with her father.

I *was* glad to see H. P. Fordess, to place the burden of that school on her shoulders. To celebrate her arrival I took Ella out for the day.

And I wrote to Margaret.

She replied almost immediately. She was glad that Ether-ington had a new principal. Uncertainty was bad for the girls. Maybe I should be able to visit her now. Next vacation there would be more time for my own interests.

But she was wrong. Spare time was not the important factor. Mother bound me and H. P. Fordess gradually undermined my inner being like a white ant. At first I did not foresee the troubles ahead. I did not know I was heading for my bitterest enslavement. Miss Fordess seemed to be my kind of principal, a woman who believed in academic standards and firm discipline. I thought time would soften the more severe aspects of the new regime.

And so I was free again or thought I was. Philippa had told me to look after Ella. I felt it was my duty to do so. That day we painted the old homestead at Felgarah—a white house tucked into a hill against a wall of poplars with their feet in a boulder-strewn, willow-fringed stream. Ella treated it realistically, a white bungalow dreaming on the side of a hill. There was no hint of the broader vistas of her ancestors, although she had a sense of rich, subtle colour. In her painting the almost invisible blues and purples of the boulders were revealed.

I splashed gold everywhere. The poplars were gold in autumn. I splashed my dream of gold onto canvas, and I made the boulder stream clank along the centre, in the shape of money-bags echoed by the shape of the sheep dung in the fields.

Ella looked at me shyly. 'It is gold, Miss Hansen.'

'All the world is gold, Ella,' I said, 'bright harsh gold. We spend our lives trying to spin our straw into gold.'

She looked puzzled. 'Who would spin straw into gold?' she said.

'You don't know Rumpelstiltzkin?'

'No.'

'Well, well. Sit down,' I said. We sat by the stream and she dangled her slim dark feet in the water while I told of the greed of kings and a princess who failed to keep a promise to a little man.

Promise. What is a promise? H.P. began with a clean sweep. Standards must rise, must rise, must rise. Undesirable children must be eliminated. 'Generations have trod, have trod, have trod,' said Ann. Did I take that elimination seriously in the first few months? Should I have foreseen that liquidation would have been a better word for the wholesale reduction in numbers that took place in the next few months? I was glad myself to be rid of Jenny Fenwick. The school could not afford the Jennys. She was rude to H.P. just once—and she left the next week.

I drew up the new schedules, the new scale for marking, organised the new sports practices.

'I appreciate your conscientiousness, Miss Hansen. I am far too busy to convey my instructions personally in every field. I can rely on you. I wonder, by the way, if you would draft a letter to the Fenwicks for me.'

I was her Deputy, and so I agreed. I had never previously written a letter to tell parents that the school found their daughter an undesirable character. It was an agony that left me tossing on my bed hour after hour in the early morning.

I was irritable to Mother when her needs aroused me from a late dawn sleep. As I cleaned her bed and body I knew a weariness of spirit. Mother had never behaved like an un-trained infant before. I felt a cracking of control within myself and in my irritation I slapped her. 'You dirty old woman,' I screamed. 'You have a bell.'

Immediately I was sorry. As she sobbed, I lifted her gently into a chair, but she beat her fists in rage on my shoulders and head. With an effort of will I settled my face into its usual calm lines. 'Forgive me, Mother,' I said. 'I am afraid I am very tired.'

I wrote four draft letters to Mr Fenwick before H.P. was satisfied. The final version sounded cold and stiff, but it was probably the best way. H.P. said, 'Firmness is necessary.' Even so, I am afraid I burnt Mother's tea that night and, while I had begun the evening determined to placate her, we both ended shut in our rooms with our own thoughts.

Recalcitrant students and recalcitrant staff. Mary Christoe had left at the same time as Philippa. The next to go were Mr Pilsudski and Mr Musket. What H.P. said to them I do not know. Thank heaven, I was not asked to draft the interviews. She merely said to me, 'Mr Pilsudski and Mr Musket are both leaving at the end of the month. I am trying to get a good music teacher to raise the examination level.'

'We have never concentrated on examinations here,' I said. 'Many of the parents merely want a little music.'

'My dear Miss Hansen,' she said, tapping her pencil on the table, 'that is quite obvious to the meanest observer. But the public measures a school on results. We shall be taking part in all competitions and all examinations, music, sport, speech, as well as academic, and we are going to come top.'

I wriggled my toes in my square-topped shoes and noted that Miss Fordess also favoured lace-ups. I saw my earlier self, undeveloped, dutiful; or was it my present self I saw?

'Very well,' I said.

I had always believed in academic standards. My own status as a child had depended on academic achievement; but I felt a tinge of unease. Very few of our girls were clever girls. I had a curiously nostalgic picture of Philippa's long black hair falling across her face as her fingers drew love from a cello.

H.P. straightened the papers on her desk, frowning. 'I must do something about the maids,' she said. 'These papers were in strict alphabetical order when I left last night.'

'They probably dusted the table,' I said.

She ran her finger along the under edge and a dark line smudged the skin. 'They were not very successful, then.'

'They have never dusted the blinds,' I answered. 'Never.' This time the picture was Ina Spurway.

'By the way, does Mrs Denham always swear like that?'

'Like what?' I said foolishly.

'I interviewed her yesterday about getting more of the girls to go into the modified course and she used the word "bloody" at least four times in our conversation!' Her mouth tucked in its corners primly like a well-starched serviette.

Without thinking, I said, 'You're lucky it was only "bloody".'

'Then she does swear regularly. Thank you, Miss Hansen.'

I swallowed hard, remembering earlier disagreements with Ann, her accusations of betrayal. I tried to make amends.

'Miss Fordess,' I said, 'Mrs Denham is a very fine teacher. Her swearing means very little. To her it is as natural as talking.'

'It is undesirable,' she said. Another tuck in the serviette mouth. She picked up a ruler from the desk and began to underline her heading in red ink. 'I should like to know if it continues. I shall myself drop her a note deploring the habit.'

I felt my neck flush as I buttoned up my cardigan. 'I do not intend to spy on my colleagues,' I said. I felt within myself a spiritual advancement. I was no longer quite the woman who had been Ina Spurway's lackey.

Her blue eyes twinkled at me in calculated friendliness. 'Come, come, Miss Hansen. We are not children, you and I. It is your duty as Deputy to see the school functions as I wish.'

'If you say so,' I said stiffly.

I think the real trouble began at her first administrative staff meeting when she elaborated on the undesirable character of our present sixth form. 'I cannot have such girls as prefects,' she said. 'I intend to remove their badges and replace them with fifth form.'

I could see Ann Denham's face whiten even across the room. 'They're a bloody sight better than the fifth formers,' she said. I knew what was troubling Ann. She had taught those children for a number of years. Their matriculation examination was less than six months away. She did not want any psychological disturbances. Only a mistress who has taught for a long time in boarding-schools can understand the grass fire spread of psychological upset.

H.P. frowned. 'We cannot continue to discuss the matter if you persist in swearing. I have already asked Miss Hansen to see that it stops.'

I looked uncomfortably at my fingers. 'And I suppose the holy Miriam agreed,' said Ann. I felt tears at the back of my eyes. Why would Ann presume I should betray her? But in my heart I knew the answer.

H.P's voice was clear and rasping. 'It is her duty to carry out my orders.' Ann leant back into her chair. Her stomach, as pudgy as the rest of her, rose into prominence. 'And Miriam always does her duty. Full stop. Do you consider it my duty, too, Miss Fordess?'

'I certainly do,' said H.P. She looked round the room. 'I want it to be quite clear. While you remain in this school I expect unswerving loyalty from all of you.'

Ann smiled. Her voice was deceptively mild. 'Let me put it to you as a human being,' she said. 'These girls are not steady. They have had a chequered career. Good teachers, bad teachers. But they are pleasant and helpful if you take the trouble to treat them properly. They have only a few months to their exams. Some will fail but others will pass, and it will matter to them however meagre the pass. Demotion could upset their work at this stage. After all, you can begin to ease the fifth formers in as helpers—unobtrusively.'

'I do not need to explain my actions,' said H.P. Her blue eyes made me think of frost-rimmed blue crocus pushing out of the winter earth. 'As you are, however, concerned with the human angle, allow me to tell you that individual girls cannot come before the good of the school. The current sixth form is incapable of producing results that rise above a few mediocre levels. They will cast no glory on the school. I have to plan for the future.'

I could feel Ann's anger. I recalled the history prizes—and Gretchen. 'Shit for glory,' said Ann. 'It's children that matter. Remember that, Miss Fordess. Children, nothing else.' She picked up her books and walked out.

I saw H. P. Fordess's brows meet in a straight line. I was praying compulsively. Dear God, dear God, dear God. Not Ann. We can't run this school without Ann. Dear God, not Ann, not Ann.

The moment passed. I wondered what had happened to me. Once Ann's action would have meant ambivalence for me. Headmistresses must be respected. I valued loyalty, duty, the working of a team. But Ann had been superb in those months when I struggled to restore sanity after Philippa's hasty resignation. My thoughts now scattered like confetti—floating in scrappy contradictions—and I knew I had reached the danger point of committing my feelings to individual people. I said to myself, H.P. is right. The school matters above all. The school. She has a right to co-operation and loyalty. Things will settle down—they *will* settle down. Fordess is still feeling her way, trying to carry out instructions to tighten up the school. Be fair. Give her time.

But the next week she imposed the silence rule, and the silence rule caused as much trouble as the expulsions. Those voices that had risen in song throughout our town were beaten into silence.

'They are far too noisy,' said H.P. to the staff. 'Abominably noisy. I cannot stand it. At dinner I want complete silence from the moment they enter the room.'

'They do sing beautifully,' Miss Cunningham-White said. 'The noise doesn't really last long. A sort of natural family chatter over dinner.'

Her eyes were reminiscently moist.

'Miss Cunningham-White,' said Miss Fordess, in a voice designed to silence ladylike rabbits, 'I was given a clear mandate to improve the discipline in this school. I intend to carry it out. The singing encourages them to talk.'

Miss Cunningham-White assented with a sniff.

'The silence of holiness or the silence of despair?' asked Ann.

The next day Linda Skaines brought in a box of silkworms for one of her science classes to observe. H.P. leant over their box, watching the fat larvae nibble their way through mulberry leaves. In one corner a gross grub was already spinning a cocoon of fine yellow silk. H.P. laughed delightedly. 'How quaint, how interesting. I could watch them for hours.'

Linda smiled. 'I could bring you a few for yourself.'

H.P. clapped her hands in emulation of girlish glee. 'I'd love them. Biology interests me. It really does.' Then she pouted like a two-year-old. 'But they are rather noisy. I have such sensitive ears.' Linda was startled. 'Noisy?'

'Eating their leaves,' said H.P. 'Can't you hear them? Such a horrible chewing noise. I couldn't stand it.'

'Oh, damn,' said Ann.

H.P. looked at her with distaste. 'Yes?' she asked.

'Sorry,' said Ann. 'I had a vision of our harmless little girls trying to chew their lettuce more silently than a silkworm.'

'You aren't funny,' said H.P.

'I bloody well didn't mean to be,' said Ann.

I felt flustered. Oil on waters, I thought. 'I'm sure it will all work out,' I said. 'The girls have been noisy lining up for their meal. They could be a little quieter.'

H.P. looked at me with her red hair pressed to her head, her shirtmaker blouse tucked carefully into her skirt. She was amused. Her blue eyes twinkled, but it was like sunshine on frost. 'Thank you for your support, Miss Hansen. Please note, Mrs Denham, I want absolute silence. I shall rely on Miss Hansen to enforce it.'

I enforced it. They no longer sang to bless their food. I had enjoyed their young voices rising in perfect harmony above the steaming dishes. Now they stood at attention until Miss Fordess arrived. They stood without moving an eyelash while she blessed the food. Then they silently drew out their chairs and silently ate.

It is true they failed the first week, but punishment cured them. Long detentions, cancellations of privileges. Maria Denton, who had a sense of humour, allowed a junior to drop a spoon. In that silent room the impact with the floor was like a thunderclap. Maria had an external examination. Maria was an asthmatic child, touchy, sensitive. But her prefect's badge was removed and she sat with her back to the school during meals for an entire week. Maria's mother protested. The Dentons were the school backbone, graziers not shopkeepers, the prime movers in getting rid of Philippa. Mrs Denton was reduced by H.P's unanswering silences to lying on H.P's sofa and behaving like a frustrated small girl.

'I'm not going home until you return my daughter's badge,' she said. 'Her exam is important. We want her to matriculate. You have brought on her first asthma attack in months.'

'Miss Hansen,' said H.P., 'get Mrs Denton a couple of blankets. She will need them if she's going to spend the night on that sofa.'

Maria Denton did not get back her badge and Mrs Denton, in spite of tears that spoilt her expensive cosmetic face, was forced to return home unsatisfied. Mother after mother, frustrated by the Coventry of the central office, tried instead to see me at home, in the hope of reaching the principal through me. I sat at night, tired and powerless, listening to the complaints of angry parents.

And when the door closed on their hysteria, there was Mother. Mother annoyed, Mother grizzling. 'My house is not my own, Miriam. Surely you can see these people at school.'

I tried to say nothing, to keep my temper. I could not explain that I had no desire to see these people anywhere. I remembered how I had hit Mother, and I controlled my irritation. But I lay in bed and reality dissolved around me. The apparatus of my old room assumed new shapes threatening my very stability in the long dark night. I looked through the shadows and saw Margaret's bird trying to rise. The shadows imprisoned its wings and it sank wounded onto the wood of the dressing-table.

That was night. By day I had to admit that school discipline was improving. There was no more noise during lessons, no group rudeness, no bullying of younger or poorer children. The complaints of bad behaviour that used to filter back from town ceased. But there was also a cessation of joyousness, of singing. The feeling of love that had marked Philippa's reign had gone. The silence at meals continued. I began myself to feel depressed. I suppressed an unreasonable desire to clatter my own knife and fork on the plate, to chew audibly. I watched H.P. masticating with decorum the minute slices she transferred to her mouth and I wanted to scream.

When I reached home each evening I could not talk.

Mother and I sat through our evening meals in a silence as deep and depressive as H.P.'s.

'Miss Hansen,' said Miss Fordess, flicking through the examination papers on the desk, 'most of the papers are quite unsatisfactory. Well below standard. I want you to return them to the staff for revision. I have pencilled in comments on the margin.'

I glanced at my own paper. The changes in French would have transformed a level 2 paper into a level 1. We had no level 1 pupils that year; but I was learning not to protest. I knew more French than H. P. Fordess would ever know, but the paper was black with suggested alterations—or should I say 'commands'?

When I gave Ann her history paper, scored likewise in pencil, there was an ominous silence. She did not even swear. 'Where is she?' she said. 'Tell the truth, Miriam, just for once.'

'There is no reason to attack me,' I said stiffly. 'In her office, I should think.'

I have never known what happened on that occasion. I only know that Ann returned to the staff-room half an hour later. She said not one word. Miss Cunningham-White made a half-gesture in her direction, but the malevolence in Ann's eyes stopped her. Ann stood by her desk with her case open, dropping book after book into it until it bulged at the sides. Then she picked up her coat and walked out. She never returned.

The rest of us sat there, stunned, immobile. The duplicating machine stood stolidly on a corner of the bench, its cover purple-smudged. It seemed symbolic. Nothing was said. All that afternoon and the next day Ann's classes sat unattended —little statues—their books open on the desks, their faces bewildered but unmoving. On the third day H. P. Fordess sent for me.

'Mrs Denham has deserted her post.'

I said nothing.

'There can be no excuse for a teacher who deserts an examination class.'

'Mrs Denham would never do that,' I said.

She fingered a red wave, pressing it deeper into her head.

'Mrs Denham has already done that. I shall take over her classes myself. There is no need for panic. In a way, it's a relief. I should probably have been forced to dismiss her.'

I did not flicker an eyelash. I could feel my bones tighten beneath my skin, but I do not think the tension was visible. My mind said, 'Dismiss Ann? Dismiss Ann? Etherington is Ann. Ina, Philippa, Margaret, even H.P., come and go. Head-mistresses all come and go, but Ann goes on.' I saw a bundle of smudgy stencils on the table and I thought, 'No more purple ink.'

The precise voice was impatient. 'Miss Hansen, I must have your full attention.'

I realised that for the first time I had failed to listen to a principal. 'I am sorry,' I said.

She fingered the stencils. 'I have found hundreds of these filthy transcripts in our cupboards. Utterly useless, as far as I'm concerned. I should be obliged if you would burn them.'

'They belong to Ann,' I said.

'I know. We need the cupboard for more important things.'

'I shall return them,' I said.

She lowered her head to signify dismissal. 'Do as you wish. As long as you get rid of them.'

I stacked the bundles in my car. Ann opened the door herself. She was dressed, gloved and hatted.

'Yes, Miriam?'

'I've brought your stencils,' I said.

The not quite brown eyes passed over me. 'How good of you,' she said. 'Still running messages, Miriam?'

'No,' I said. 'It was my idea.'

A glimpse of a smile fluttered on her mouth. 'Poor Miriam. I have no right to be unjust. Forgive my rudeness. Just throw them on that chair. I'm afraid I have to leave immediately. I'm playing bridge with Mrs Dennis.'

I nodded. I should be able to say something, I thought. I

wanted to say, 'We'll miss you Ann, thanks for everything.'
Instead I said, 'You have a matriculation class.'

She stretched her hand in front of her and straightened the
fingers of her glove. It was a contemptuous gesture. 'Are you
telling me my duty, Miriam?'

I stuttered, 'No, no, I was thinking of the children.'

'They'll have to save themselves,' she said. 'God knows, I
can't. I am quite unable to walk on water.'

She left me standing on the veranda. She walked out the
gate, out of my life, without looking back once. That night at
home I did not even say hullo to Mother. I bought her a
ready-made meal, placed it on the table, and shut myself in
my room.

All night I walked up and down, up and down, up and
down. By dawn I was calm again. I took in Mother's egg as
if nothing had happened. She was propped up in bed writing
a letter. She was expectant, waiting for me to ask to whom
she was writing. I didn't bother. I put down her tray, said
'Good morning', and left.

There are times when the tiny threads of tension begin to
destroy the structure of the mind. I have always believed in
duty and the need to obey those in authority over me. But
somewhere something had eroded the unseamed fabric of
my thoughts. Philippa? Perhaps. I did not really agree with
Philippa; I merely did my best to carry out her programme.
Ann? I was not her sort of person. Yet long contact with a
personality has some effect. Perhaps it was a combination of
personalities. Ina, Gretchen, Philippa, and Ann. Without being aware of it, a hint of treason was undermining my old
self.

H. P. Fordess should have been my kind of principal. Academic achievement, hard work, firm discipline, were para-
mount. The weak were ruthlessly weeded out. Were the weak
the flaw in my allegiance?

Day-time, I stood on duty enforcing the law. I gave no sign
of sympathy for Ann. And indeed I had no sympathy. Duty

forbids the desertion of a class in any circumstances. But night. Night was another matter. With the tilt of light through the blind catching the wing-tip of Margaret's bird, my sure allegiance crumbled. The silence of the night reinforced the repressive silence of the school. I wanted laughter, friends. In the silence of my bed I dreamt of Ann kissing me farewell, of Philippa clasping me in her arms. I created waxen images of H. P. Fordess and laughed as I stuck pins into the melting wax. In uneasy dreams I roasted red-haired dolls on spits, and they crashed blackened in the flames, and spilt in grey ash into the lopsided shape of Mother.

At Etherington the rules of behaviour tightened on every side. Stitch, stitch, stitch went the needles, lowering the hems after frustrated excursions into brevity. At the same time the High School and other local schoolgirls raised them. But no mini-skirts were to be worn on our premises. It was an order —signed with a flourish of capitals by H. P. Fordess.

Of course I could not disapprove. When Philippa was in charge I knew the frocks had crept surreptitiously up the long brown legs, but they had never seemed indecent, so I had not checked the tendency.

I watched Heather Denton stitching away on the morning of the sports day like a child demented, to reach the stipulated length before the bus departed, and I said, 'That length is much more appropriate, Heather. Now off you run.' Appropriate for what?

I pitied the parents. Poor old parents! Shut off from their offspring. No treats, no surprise teas, no incidental conversations. Under the new régime their girls left them at the beginning of term and stayed in school until the authorities saw fit to release them.

'You have travelled three hundred miles?' Who cares about three hundred miles? Nothing to a country hick. Hop in the Holden, and belt it hell-for-leather over the country roads. I imagined those red-faced, slow-speaking men, shaded by their wide-brimmed hats, tearing the guts out of the roads from Bourke, Menindie, Coonabarabran, Collarenebri and all places west. And there beside them I saw the little woman (more often big-boned and rangy) enduring the miles with the comforting vision of the youngster at school, sharing her experiences around a restaurant table. Mile after mile, and at the end a crimped redhead, a pair of very blue eyes, and a prim voice: 'School discipline is school discipline. I cannot allow you to disrupt the school routine. No. You may not see your daughter.'

Although it was not my business to dictate policy, I had gained some insight into the feelings of parents in the preceding months. 'The children are leaving,' I said. I imagined our final end: a handful of middle-aged women enclosed in an empty building surrounded by the leering skulls of the ex-pupils who failed to retreat in time.

'Our school,' she said, 'with our girls, our discipline, has no need to fear. We'll have new girls from the best Sydney families.' And I muttered soundlessly, 'Who cares about the best Sydney families? I came to redeem the rural not the urban.'

I schooled my features to tell yet another anxious child that her mother and father could not see her. 'Yes, Helen, that was their car outside the gates. Yes, they wanted to see Miss Fordess. No, they could not upset the school routine.'

Weep, little children, weep. But why should you weep? In the quiet of my own room at home I banged my clenched fists on the wall and wondered why no one had ever rescued me from my mother.

'You are such an ungrateful girl, Miriam. I cannot see why you cannot give up a Saturday afternoon to take Robert to the pictures. You are sure to pass your exam, anyway.' Miriam, Miriam! Do this, Miriam; do that, Miriam; don't sulk, Miriam.

I looked at their young faces limp with disappointment, and I wept for their ignorance. If only there had been an H. P. Fordess between me and my mother.

Stitch, stitch, stitch—or get out. No girl wearing a tunic four inches above the knee could possibly represent *our* school at the athletics carnival. Our, our, our. First person plural.

How chummy we are! How acquisitive of the thoughts and feelings of other people!

I almost laughed as I watched the rout of Mr Harris to the other side of the sports field. 'The staff and students must sit together. No. The girls may not sit with their parents.' Perhaps, Mr Harris, you could look into your own black soul and remember Philippa and Ina whom you routed so heartlessly.

'Miss Hansen, make sure that Barbara Harris sits next to Helen Marriott. Move Ella Middleton over to the other side. Mr Harris does not want his daughter to sit next to Ella.' Black-souled Mr Harris, driving your cows up the misty cracks in the coastal hills; Mr black-souled Harris producing the milk for the big co-operatives—but no co-operative you, Mr Harris!

I watched Ella's brown legs twinkle over the hurdles, June Murphy streak away from the sprinters, while the girls sat sedately in the stands beside the sedate staff and clapped politely. From their exile on the other side of the track, the parents screamed encouragement and cheered wildly when an Etherington girl won. And at home Isobel Graves wept because girls in short tunics were forbidden to take part, and Della Graves persistently nagged her husband about standing up to H. P. Fordess.

I, too, sat primly in the stand beside Miss Cunningham-White, and my thoughts jogged uncontrolled over black souls and repellent mothers, and I could feel my eyelid begin to flick, up and down, up and down. But I forced my hands together and clapped when the girls won.

They returned to school subdued and jubilant, and the victory wreath crowned H.P's head: the victory was personal and the tributes to sportsmanship perfunctory. The important thing was that we won, and the girls could celebrate: an extra hour of unsuppressed activity, while H.P. barricaded herself in her room away from all noise, and good reliable Miriam, aided by good reliable Cunningham-White, coped with the uncaged zoo animals as they screamed and yelled and ran round the buildings.

The phone rang. Jim Graves said, 'I must speak to Miss Fordess, Miriam', and I said, 'I am sorry, Miss Fordess is in bed. She has had an exhausting day.' Then Della's voice cut in: 'You can tell her to get up, then. We shall not allow Isobel to be treated in this fashion. She is one of the school's best runners. And I can tell you, too, that Mrs Harris was most upset at being separated from Barbara.'

I said, 'Like cream and milk. But tell Mrs Harris there is no need to worry. All the separators here are sterilised and in first-class order. They never mix black and white.'

And Della said, 'Are you all right, Miriam? I hope for your sake you are not being funny. I don't feel like jokes.'

I said, 'I was not joking. I was thinking of Ella.'

'Ella?' said Della Graves, 'Ella? For heaven's sake, Miriam, I am not ringing about Ella. I want to speak to Miss Fordess.'

'That is quite impossible,' I said, 'quite impossible.' I put down the receiver and when the phone rang again I simply ignored it.

Next morning H.P. appeared for assembly, neat and ordered. Her trim skirt and grey blouse curved into the trim line of her precise figure. One foolish or merely nervous girl giggled, and annihilation followed. Victory had been celebrated. The moratorium was over.

'What we need now,' said H.P., having completed a precise reading of a Biblical victory chant, 'what we need now is to put our academic house in order.'

And so at Etherington we worked by 'absolute standards'. No encouragement for the unintelligent. Our re-marked examination papers were like a lethal pest exterminator. The thirties and forties who might have crawled through a public examination were eliminated and the prospect of having to repeat a year made many parents withdraw their daughters from the school altogether. Of all the schools in Meridale, Etherington alone had empty classrooms. It was true that our bright became brighter, but those to whom we had offered a watered-down version of literacy disappeared. They were not replaced.

The tension grew. I watched Ella's little dark face trying to cope with the new curriculum, the furrowing anxiety when she knew she would have to reach 50 per cent—the absolute all-time standard—to survive.

But are there absolute standards of ability? Can you measure the worth of the underprivileged alongside those whom God has materially blessed? I found I doubted it. I put my arms around her shaking shoulders, whispered words of encouragement, promised more coaching; and yet I could see quite clearly her recently assessed examination paper lying on the floor where she had thrown it in her despair. Fifteen per cent. What lies I was feeding her! Ella wept and internally I wept with her. I took her home for extra work after school, knowing in my heart of hearts it would avail us nothing.

Mother resented her presence. She threatened and cajoled, banged pots and pans and rang doorbells, in attempts to take my attention away from Ella. If I had not been so disturbed, so busy, I should have guessed her unceasing flow of letters were not all addressed to Robert. Even her hatred of me was not wide enough to cover daily correspondence. Each afternoon as I taught Ella, she wrote away. Each morning I pushed the envelopes into my purse without reading the addresses. I did not even inquire the reason for her sly smile. I was taken aback therefore when I received a letter from the town clerk.

Dear Miss Hansen,

In view of your mother's unusual request, we thought we should contact you for confirmation. It is possible that an error was made in the plotting of the cemetery some years ago, but our surveyor feels it is of minimal importance. It would certainly not be convenient to remove your father's body after such a long delay. I should be obliged if you could call at our office to clear up the misunderstanding.

Yours faithfully,
John Toddy.

John Toddy was related to Mena Furlonger and I suppose in some dim Meridale sort of way to me. I remembered him as a boy, a first year in my final year. Even then he was smooth. Public relations of the non-obtrusive kind were already his hobby. He was always secretary of societies, never president.

As he ushered me into his chambers he did not seem to have changed very much. He was still over-large; the folds on what had once been merely a thick neck now rolled in layers like an African neck bracelet. His hair, still brown, was drawn thinly across his head to hide its sparseness. He shook my hand. 'It's been a long time, Miriam,' he said. I was surprised by the 'Miriam'. I suppose he thought of me that way, but I wondered. He may merely have considered it expedient.

The evidence was there. He took out a stack of Mother's letters. They were all written on the one theme and were accompanied in each case by diagrams and maps. To bridge her loneliness, she had written, she had made a particular study of local charts. Her husband was dead. Her parents were dead. It was natural, therefore, to be interested in the history of the cemetery. Close study of the extensions in the early thirties had led her to a most distressing conclusion. The cemetery and the plan were different. Her husband had been buried incorrectly. His remains lay not in the Hansen plot but in the path between the graves, or at least what should have been the path. It would only need a future council to correct the error and her husband's rest would be disturbed by the constant footsteps overhead.

'Is it true?' I asked.

John Toddy nodded. 'Quite true. We've been aware of the slight error for thirty years. We surveyed the new graveyard in the depression. We were not fussy about who did the work. The path runs a few feet to the north of the original alignment.' He looked aggrieved. 'No one else has complained,' he said.

'Perhaps no one else found out,' I said gravely. 'Who, I wonder, is resting in Mother's plot?'

'Old Mrs Furlonger,' he said.

I nearly laughed. I could see it all now. Mother had hated the Furlongers for years. They not only snubbed her, they also ignored her. Father had worked for them once upon a time. Mother considered that they had systematically robbed him.

'Well, well,' I said, looking at the jelly-like neck quivering below me. 'You're in a mess, aren't you?'

I remembered that Mother had asked Robert to take her to see Father's grave on his last visit to Meridale. Reverence to tombstones has always seemed to me a waste of human effort, so I consistently refused to go. Somewhere, somehow, Mother had become suspicious. She would know that Mena's mother-in-law was resting in the plot reserved for her. Margaret Furlonger had been athletic, beautiful. One of the Dennis family. The antithesis of Mother. I doubt if she even knew Mother existed; but she had been like a gall-stone in Mother's pride, a canker of envy. I can remember Mother's triumph when she died. 'The Dennises were always short lived,' she said.

I turned back to John Toddy. 'It's not the mess,' he was saying abjectly, 'it's the inconvenience. You can see our difficulty, surely?' He raised his hands as if in prayer and I noted the surplus flesh that ringed his fingers.

'I certainly can,' I said. 'Has Mother mentioned compensation?'

He gave me a horrified look. 'We are relying on you to talk your mother out of her request to have your father reburied. It would mean re-burying half the graveyard. You were always an intelligent girl.'

I began to laugh.

'It isn't funny,' he said.

'Oh, but it is,' I replied. 'You mean Mrs Furlonger is half in and half out of the Hansen block, B. G. Daley is half in and half out of the Furlonger plot, and so on and so on.' I remembered that Freddy Daley's fat pink little Daddy who used to keep a sweet store lay next to the Furlonger ground. I had a mental map of that cemetery. Cemeteries are important in a country town. Each denomination has its allotted domain, its own mansion, as it were. I often wondered what happens to the free thinkers. Do they ever listen with foreboding to those daily radio announcements: 'Mr X will be buried in the Presbyterian section of the Meridale cemetery'?

'It is rather funny when you think about it,' I said, 'the whole cemetery re-routed to please Mother.'

John Toddy was cross. His self-importance rose in little bubbles of clothing beneath his shirt. 'It's not funny at all. I don't see how you can find it funny.'

'Don't you?' I said. 'But then you don't know Meridale as well as I do.'

'I've lived here all my life,' he said.

'Ah yes,' I answered, 'but your father was a foreigner, wasn't he?'

'My father came from Sydney.'

'Exactly,' I said. I rose. I extended my hand. 'I shall do my best, but Mother is very obstinate. I shall have to check, of course. Could I have one of those plans?'

Late that evening I took a tape-measure to the graveyard. It was white moonlight. I crawled on my hands and knees checking the white graves. I moved along the grass to the far corner where the new graveyard joined the old. The white stones were grey. The leaves from the old elms lay in tattered abundance on a long-deserted grave. 'Underneath are the ever-lasting arms,' read the ambitious stone. I giggled, then I re-membered my task. I was not there to explore the pretentious, now derelict, past. I retraced my steps to the resting-places of the more recently dead.

In fact, the error was no more than a foot or two either way. Father had no more than thirteen inches of the path and Mrs M. W. Furlonger had barely more than ten inches of the vacant Hansen plot. I walked thoughtfully home. I dawdled above the creek, tracing the pattern of willow leaves on the eddying surface. I had found the practical problem exhilara-ting. A definite release from the tensions of the past month. How clever of Mother to find a way of dispelling boredom. I felt grateful to her. I had enjoyed worrying John Toddy. I stopped near the corner store which had once belonged to his father, and I picked a bunch of grapes that was hanging over the fence. They reminded me of John's neck.

Mother's voice rasped from the bedroom. 'Is that you, Miriam?'

'Yes, Mother,' I said. 'What is more, I come bearing gifts.'

I walked across the room and strung the grapes across her breast. 'You clever, clever girl,' I said.

Her translucent eyes passed over my face.

'Have you gone quite mad, Miriam?'

'No, Mother, no. Not quite. Not yet. I must say you have my absolute support. I have been on my hands and knees for the past two hours measuring the graveyard. You're a clever girl.'

She was taken aback. I had really surprised her at last. She slid six inches further into her bed.

'I think we should start digging tomorrow,' I said.

'Don't be ridiculous, Miriam.'

'Of course,' I said, picking up her hairbrush and brushing my sandy hair, knowing how she hated me to touch her possessions, 'of course it will mean that they'll have to bury you in the soil at present polluted by Mena Furlonger's mother-in-law.'

Her mouth snapped tight. I was not quick enough. She grabbed her stick where it lay alongside her pillow and brought it down across my face. I felt blood trickle into my mouth. She began to weep. I wiped the cut on my cheek with my handkerchief.

'If I were you,' I said, 'I'd write to Robert and tell him the whole story. He'll be interested to know what you do when you visit Father's grave. And don't hit me again, Mother.'

She continued to weep and I began to laugh. I continued to laugh as I sat at the dining-room table marking proses.

Next morning Mother was silent. The graveyard was not mentioned. My own face was bruised and swollen. I felt far from well as I came into Miss Fordess's office. Her blue eyes passed over me. I sensed disapproval. She was dressed in a neat blue suit with neat suede shoes. I thought of Ina Spurway and her beautiful shoes. I had travelled a long way since then. H.P. ignored the bruised face. I did not enlighten her. 'You sent for me,' I said.

She tapped her pencil rhythmically on the table, softly, ever so softly.

'I suppose,' she said more softly still, 'you have seen Ella Middleton's results.'

To myself the pulsing in my throat sounded louder than her pencil. 'Yes.'

'We can hardly continue her scholarship.'

I was disconcerted and showed it. 'But we are committed. The scholarship was offered for the period required to complete a secondary course.'

'Subject to satisfactory progress, Miss Hansen. We cannot call 15 per cent satisfactory progress, can we?'

I felt anger. I hated her slick blue suit, her neat suede shoes, her smug suede voice. 'You cannot expect underprivileged children to compete with the affluent,' I said.

'You worry me, Miss Hansen. I do expect it. Why not? If the girl cannot compete she has no place here with the privileged.'

'I see,' I said.

'Actually,' she continued, 'I am relieved. I am trying to build a new school. There are undoubtedly parents who would be deterred by her presence here. If we wish to be a first-class institution, we cannot take coloured children.'

I said nothing.

'I shall write a note, of course, explaining the circumstances. It would help, however, if you were willing to see the mother, to explain the situation face to face.'

'There is nothing to explain,' I said. 'We are simply throwing her out. We have created expectations which we are now proceeding to destroy. We could take as our new school motto, "Keep Etherington White".'

She tried to look sympathetic. 'I realise you are personally involved, Miriam. I know this is a hard task to set you. But

don't indulge in bitter jokes. It is your duty to give me your
support in this matter and it would help if you gave it willingly. Please, Miriam.'

'My name is Hansen,' I said. 'Miss Hansen. Only my friends
call me Miriam.'

'I am your friend,' she said.

My anger broke. For the first time since I entered that
school I felt uncontrollable anger. Anger with Ina, anger with
Philippa, anger with H.P. It rose in me and spilt onto the dull
ache of my wounded face.

'Do your own dirty work,' I said. I could not believe it was
my own voice.

She was shocked. 'Very well,' she said coolly, 'I shall. But
don't blame me if the Middletons find me a much more unpleasant ambassador than you.'

I saw the trap. Either I went myself or Mrs Middleton
would be insulted. Ella would be hurt.

I felt my anger ebb into the old dull familiar burn of resentment. 'Very well,' I said stiffly. 'I shall go.'

She was efficient, willing to forgive. 'You are a loyal colleague,' she said expansively.

'You overrate me,' I said.

HEATHER PATRICIA FORDESS

6

Monday

Organisation requires good records. I have always kept a diary. It is not possible to tell in advance when a recorded impression may be valuable. I was entrusted with a mission by the Church Council. Pull Etherington together. I had been given a full report of its progress and I had to agree with the authorities it was far from satisfactory.

Accordingly I made my position clear to both staff and girls from the outset. I expected more work, better discipline, absolute loyalty, and objective standards from all of them.

They were not an inspiring staff. The younger members were slack and the older members set in their ways. I saw immediately that Mr Musket and Mr Pilsudski would have to be dismissed. Their very presence bore testimony to the irregularity of the preceding régime. Mr Musket was fat with soft hands and a balding head. His non-existent chin quivered in a way no man's chin should quiver. My own father was a Scot, rugged, square-chinned, immovable. He would not have tolerated bad behaviour from any girl. Quite obviously a girls' school is no place for a failure.

Mr Pilsudski I disliked from the outset. He had a foreign aura at variance with the traditions of our British heritage. He bowed, he opened doors, he pulled out chairs with an assi-

duity I did not trust. My mother used to say that foreigners
thought far too much about sexual matters, and I was not
surprised to find he was separated from his wife. I did not
think it was seemly for the girls to meet such people. I believe,
moreover, that his doctrine of creativity was a sham beneath
which he hid an ineffectual personality surpassed only by Mr
Musket's.

Within a fortnight of my arrival I sent a note of dismissal
to both of them. I did not bother to explain myself. No explanation is necessary when there is sheer incompetence. Our
schools have fortunately been free of the taint of unionism, so
that it is still easy to get rid of the dross. I managed to obtain
two strict but well-qualified maiden ladies to replace them.
They were old but reliable. Miss Harris believed, as I did, in
the necessity of scales and plenty of practice; and Miss Wade
drilled the girls in mathematics tables with old-fashioned
thoroughness. I was able to suppress all new-fangled notions
of easy learning.

From the outset I knew that I could rely absolutely on
Miriam Hansen. It is not easy to take over from an acting
principal, but I think I can say I carried out the manoeuvre
with tact and understanding. The Miriam Hansens never
change. From our first meeting it was obvious that one of my
real problems was Mrs Denham. Every school has one teacher
of this type, a woman of long standing whom everybody re-
veres. Such teachers have the ability to create an atmosphere
of permanency and indispensability. Being good teachers, they
win over the parents. But to those in authority they are sub-
versive. I could feel Mrs Denham's opposition from the outset.
Her language alone would provide any principal with grounds
for dismissal, but I tried to be fair. I explained quite clearly
at my first staff meeting that the retiring seniors would receive
no prizes and no tokens of the school's esteem. From the reports that had preceded my arrival it was quite obvious they
merited no consideration.

'I suppose,' said Mrs Denham, 'that you know more about

the girls in two short weeks than people like me who have
bloody well taught them for five or six years.'

'Judging from their reputation,' I replied, 'I should not boast
of being their guide and mentor, Mrs Denham. Undoubtedly
a few innocent pupils will suffer, but the morale of the school
must be placed before any individual girl.'

'That,' said Ann Denham, 'is a dangerous doctrine. Most
dictators believe it.'

Today I spoke to Miriam about Mrs Denham's language. I
think I can rely on Miriam, even if she is reluctant to take on
the job of warning a colleague.

Before retiring I pinned the new silence rule on the notice-
board. I hoped that in future I could eat in peace, and pass
along the corridors without hearing a single word.

Wednesday

I am not impressed by spoilt parents any more than I am
impressed by spoilt children. The Denton child did not deserve
a prefect's badge and I told her mother so quite clearly. I have
never witnessed such a performance from a grown woman
before. She threatened me with the law, with the Council,
with state inspectors. Finally she wept and screamed like a
frustrated child kicking her legs on my sofa and refusing to
move.

'You must understand,' I said, 'that I cannot change a ruling
once I have made it, not for anyone. Children must know the
limits of their power and they can only respect a headmistress
if she is firm.'

Thursday

I awoke quite refreshed. Mrs Denton did not appear again in
my office, and I was glad I had been firm. And now there was
no more noise. The noise in the corridors had been depressing.
The voices in the dining hall had been deafening, a crescendo
of screaming sopranos counterpointed by the clatter of knife
and fork on plate. I have extremely sensitive ears. The creak
of an unoiled hinge, a typewriter, a cicada, even the stirring

of leaves, is sufficient to leave me emotionally disturbed. I feel like a pendulum off balance and I find it difficult to retain my normal objectivity when dealing with staff and pupils.

When I came across the Aboriginal girl helping the junior girls to clean up for tea, I felt obsequiousness in her dark subservience; and I must admit to a feeling of revulsion at seeing those dark hands in contact with some of my tiny juniors. There is no place for a girl like that in a school like this. I cannot understand why the Council offered such a scholarship. I am a progressive woman. I am myself on a committee that is trying to obtain better study facilities and more scholarships to enable these children to attend state schools. But there is no point in sending them to schools like Etherington. This is, after all, a college for young ladies who will occupy positions as the social leaders of the future. I felt irritated that I should be placed in the invidious position of appearing intolerant.

'Come here, Ella,' I said.

She stood with her non-emotional face turned to mine. She has disconcerting dark velvet eyes.

'You have no preparation for tomorrow?' I asked.

'The little ones were late for tea,' she said.

'Stand up straight,' I said sharply. 'My name is Miss Fordess and I expect you to address me by it. I asked you if you have any preparation.'

'Yes, Miss Fordess.' She shuffled one foot and the sound of her shoe grating on the stone floor sent the nerves in my ears tingling along the back of my neck and along the sinews of my arm. My hand clenched involuntarily.

'Stand up straight,' I said again. 'Feet together.'

This time she obeyed me.

'You are to carry out your own duties, not those of the matron or of the nursing staff. Now go and get on with your preparation.'

She muttered a muffled, 'Yes, Miss Fordess', before slinking out the door like a frightened animal. I admit I was irritated. My father used to say an honest man and an honest dog never cringe.

Monday

Monday is a bad day; the day staff return soaked in the relaxation of their homes, critical of all around them. I had asked for the copies of their examination papers by 9 a.m., but it was 11 before the last of them appeared on my desk. When a job has to be done it should be completed on time. I have myself stayed up all night to complete a batch of examination papers—on more than one occasion. It was part of the general slackness of Etherington that no one apart from Miriam would have considered such a sacrifice.

In general, however, I am not complaining. I have been in the school over two months now and already the improvement in tone is apparent. I have made it quite clear to the part-time staff that the time-table must be arranged in terms of the school's needs and not in terms of their private domestic arrangements. I refuse to cater for mothers who cannot cater for their own children. If they choose to earn a salary rather than to mind their offspring, then they must work like anyone else. I lost one or two teachers, but they were of no importance. I was sufficiently cynical to believe that most of them would revise their home schedules before sacrificing their salaries, however small. I was right.

Undoubtedly the better class of parent is beginning to feel hopeful. I am convinced of it. We are losing the weaker ones, it is true, but the parents of the brighter children are delighted. There are one or two exceptions, but there will always be some who imagine education should be a continuous fun fair. On the whole, parents want results.

Order then is emerging from chaos. Only Mrs Denham continues to defy me, openly and persistently.

'I must insist,' I said yesterday, 'that I am in charge of policy. I welcome suggestions, certainly, but I cannot allow my staff-room to become a forum for free discussion.'

'Not bloody likely,' said Mrs Denham. I decided then and

there that she would have to go. The parents would forget
her in time and there are others capable of teaching her subject with equal skill.

I spent the rest of the day vetting the examination papers.
I was appalled: The questions, the material, the format were
tailored to the abilities of the girls. As long as our papers are
watered-down versions of external papers our academic pov-
erty is apparent to all and the school will continue to be the
refuge of the unintelligent and the retarded. I determined to
take a firm line. Miriam was one of the worst offenders. Her
paper catered for the lowest level. I could see she did not like
my corrections, but she nevertheless accepted them. Mrs Denham was another matter.

Tuesday

I awoke feeling tired. Council meetings tire me. I conduct
them in a businesslike fashion, but the rural advisers remain
rural advisers. They exude such coarse masculinity. Mr Furlonger, well fed and fleshy, oozes delight in material pleasures;
Mr Graves has an air of vague petulance which I suspect has
been accentuated by the approaching middle age of his per-
oxided wife. I have never liked arch women. Mr Daley is pink
and pudgy like his latest paintings, while Harris and Denton
both smell, their clothes exuding an odour of shorn sheep and
cattle on the hoof.

I tried to put our meetings on a businesslike basis from the
outset. I gave their cavalier deference to the weaker sex short
shrift. I expect politeness; I deplore gallantry. I am not interested in sexual attraction in any form. I have felt no sexual
weakness since I was sixteen, when I thought I was in love
with Reggie Carruthers. He went to the nearest boys' High
School and he carried my bag and sat next to me on the bus.
His father delivered my mother's dry cleaning, and sometimes
he helped on the van.

Sixteen is such an unreliable age. It seemed to my immature
mind exciting to lie in the long grass by the river with the
chapped feel of Reggie's lips on mine and his hot hands cup-

ping my bare breasts. It was one of the few occasions when my father beat me as violently as he beat my brothers.

'Next time you wish to act like a bitch on heat with one of your mother's tradesmen,' he said, 'I hope you will recall the pain of this beating. All your life.'

I hated him. I hated him for years, but I kept out of the paddock. There were no more boys. Years later when I saw what a sweaty little man Reggie had become I was grateful. I have never underrated the value of discipline. I disliked my father, but I respected him.

My mother irritated me—whingey, fallible, subjective. She hovered uncertainly between bleating hypochondria and noble-suffering masochism. To her we were children and pain, necessary sacrifices to the human need for reproduction. She liked neither me nor my elder brother. All her love was reserved for my younger brother, Nigel. He was born in a taxi, and in spite of her shame and embarrassment she loved him for making a third excursion into the labour ward unnecessary. She was an illogical woman, basing all judgements on her mood of the moment. My father was remote but just, a man of standards. He dismissed any employee who failed to give efficient service. He treated his children in the same way.

The members of Council were a poor lot compared with my father, but I was grateful, nevertheless, that they were men. On the whole they have an objectivity most women lack. But these men were more than normally stupid. I made it quite clear to them that any child who failed to complete a year satisfactorily would repeat the course.

'You can't ask parents to pay an extra year's tuition fees,' bleated Harris.

'I certainly can,' I said.

'We'll lose pupils,' said Denton.

'We'll replace them with better ones,' I answered.

It had been a difficult evening, but I had won. The new policy of the school had been placed fairly and squarely before them. But I was tired when I got back—and this was the moment Ann Denham chose to make a fuss about the history paper. She walked into my office and flung the paper on the desk in front of me.

'Are these your alterations?' she asked.

'Certainly.'

'I have crossed them out,' she answered. 'I am perfectly capable, after twenty-five years' teaching, of setting a senior history paper.'

'A paper, yes,' I answered, 'but hardly a satisfactory one.'

'What the bloody hell do you mean?'

I blew my nose. 'Really, Mrs Denham, if you insist on swearing we cannot continue to discuss the matter.'

'I am not discussing it,' she said. 'I'm telling you. Maybe you know what you're doing. I don't.'

'Trying to raise the deplorable standards of this school,' I said.

She was quiet for a second, deadly quiet. Then she said, 'Are you trying to suggest that I have no standards?'

'The words are yours, Mrs Denham, not mine. I cannot be satisfied when I see girls like Belle Graves and Ella Middleton passing from year to year unscathed. If I remember correctly, according to you, both of them were worth a pass in history.'

'I was wondering when you'd get round to Ella.'

I ignored the thrust. 'Belle can barely put two words together,' I said, 'yet you maintain she is worth a pass in history.'

She leant across the desk. 'Let me tell you, your highness, I was assessing history papers, not English. Belle's English is immature, I agree, but she is not illiterate. She will pass history in her matriculation exam. I am sure of that.'

'Mrs Denham,' I said, 'I have nothing more to say. I am quite aware that the matriculation standards in this state are low. Our own must be higher. I expect that paper to be altered by lunch-time.'

'Go to hell,' she said.

I said nothing.

'And what is wrong with Ella? Too black for you?'

I said nothing. I drew my paper towards me and went on

with my interrupted work. She bent over and knocked the paper from my hand.

'I was talking to you,' she said.

Again I said nothing. I merely took up another sheet and began to write. She thrust her pudgy face into mine. 'Very well, seeing you have retreated into holy silence there is no point in my continuing. Allow me to tell you the parents are getting sick and tired of this silence act and so am I. Take your bloody paper. Correct it yourself. I'm leaving. Immediately. And I am not coming back unless you apologise. I shall not be ignored while you behave like a sulky schoolchild, and I will not set a paper well beyond the range of the class to please you.'

I did not look up. There is no point talking to either the angry or the rude. Mrs Denham was both. I waited for her return, but when the afternoon passed and she did not appear for a single lesson I considered I was justified in assuming she had left. I spent the evening clearing the room of her remnants—stencil after revolting stencil. For two days during this history period her classes simply sat. Then I sent for Miriam.

I could see that Miriam was disturbed, but I was certain she would co-operate. Miriam's reflexes to authority are automatic. To ensure her loyalty, however, I made a concession to sentimentality. I allowed her to take the stencils with her.

I was happy. There was now no one between me and absolute command. In six months I should be free of all undesirable elements. The examinations would dispose of the unsatisfactory girls.

Wednesday

I write this section in bewilderment and triumph. Bewilderment, because the reasons for the vagaries and petulance of parents elude me; triumph, because today we celebrated the first overt evidence of the success of my policies. For the first time in the history of the school we won at the combined sports carnival. In the final count, it is success that counts.

If we win, the parents will be satisfied, however much some educationists may lament the competitive spirit.

But the road to success is difficult. Parents are so self-centred and so short-sighted. I have never understood why they put their children in school if they are going to pop in and out incessantly in an effort to see them. If they wish to be in perpetual contact with their young they could quite easily keep them at home; and in many areas there are day schools within travelling distance. For the truly isolated of our state the government provides very efficient correspondence courses which even the most unintelligent parent can handle.

When I first came to Etherington I had not expected constant parental interruption.

'We were passing through Meridale. Just popped off to see June for a few minutes. Thought she could have tea with us in town.'

I am now quite firm on this matter. From the beginning I showed my disapproval, although I remained polite. By the sixth month I could barely answer the parents who called.

'No,' I said, 'June (or Jean or Mollie or Helen or whoever it happened to be) cannot leave her preparation for an evening in town.' 'No, you may not see her. This is a school.' By the eighth month I simply said 'No' without explanation. After that I merely rang my bell and sent for Miriam.

Occasionally they threatened me. They would go to the Council, they would write to my superiors in Sydney, they would get an order from the police. On these occasions I rang my bell very hard for Miriam.

Some of them, in pique, removed their children; but they were no loss. They were rarely the best scholars. Miriam, however, was inclined to fuss. 'I don't like to mention it, Miss Fordess, but we are losing too many girls. We are a very small school. I don't know if we can afford to lose so many. I don't like to mention it.'

'Then don't mention it,' I said.

Her face tautened and I noticed a flick in her sandy-lashed eyelid. I had noticed this flicking lid on several occasions in the past few weeks, particularly since Mrs Denham departed in such a rage. I was uneasy. I did not want Miriam to collapse. I could not afford to lose her support.

'The rural illiterate must toe the line or get out,' I continued. 'It is not fair to upset well-established routine for a few girls. If I let one go out for tea, in time they'll all want to go, and their newly acquired study habits will be lost.'

I smoothed my navy skirt and tucked in my blouse. I do not know why I fiddled with my clothes. I am not by nature a fiddly woman, but Miriam stared at me so intently, unblinking, unmoving, that I felt uncomfortable.

'You do understand, don't you?' I ventured. This was a concession. I do not usually appeal to my subordinates.

'Of course,' she said, 'of course. I can understand anything if you say so.'

'Good,' I said and returned to my desk. I wished she did not make me feel uneasy. Once I never felt uneasy with Miriam, but lately I have sensed resistance. I must not let my imagination run away with me. After all, she did carry out my orders implicitly. She kept the parents from my door and explained clearly to the girls the reasons for my decisions.

Our combined schools' sports carnival brought me my first real success. There were the usual irritating upsets precipitated by disobedient girls and thoughtless, interfering parents, but I dealt with them satisfactorily. I simply forbade girls in minitunics to attend even if they were good athletes, and we marched to our allotted place in the stand as a clean, neat, and well-disciplined group. I insisted the parents remain in their area on the other side of the field even though Mr Harris was quite rude about my decision.

The children behaved better than the adults. Mr Harris and his cronies cheered and yelled and waved whenever an Etherington girl won, and he encouraged the other parents to do likewise. We had a wearing day keeping the girls quiet and orderly in view of their parents' behaviour, for we did win—frequently. Ella Middleton is a good runner and so is June Murphy. It was a little humiliating to see Mrs Middleton's sloppy form on the outskirts of the Etherington parents; but I managed to ignore her. But Miriam made a special point of crossing the ground to congratulate her on Ella's success. It was quite unnecessary.

In spite of the day's upsets, I felt a deep satisfaction. The girls ran well today and they ran to win. I could feel a new spirit in them, a rising confidence, a school pride. I have never asked to be liked by my pupils, but I did feel this evening a growing respect for my policies. I allowed them an hour's celebration before bed, although I had to retire to my own room exhausted. I have left Miriam to answer the telephone this evening and to look after the girls. It has been a hard day but I am satisfied.

Friday

The months have ticked away. I have been too busy for diaries. The tone of the school is improving. As I expected, our improved standards produced a long casualty list. I hope by the end of the year to retain only top-grade pupils. 'Like eggs,' said Miriam.

I was worried. I needed Miriam in a way a general needs a good soldier. She had obviously been upset in recent weeks. I detected certain oddities in her behaviour, but I decided to be tolerant. I had no doubt the home situation lay at the root of her trouble. I am inclined myself to believe there should be some humane method by which the senile, the crippled, and the imbecile can be eased out of life. It was ridiculous that Miriam's usefulness should be impaired at the point when I needed her full support. I ticked over the other possibilities. Linda Skaines? Too ethical to be satisfactory. She worked well, accepted advice, but had no Machiavellian guile. To make matters worse, she thought only in terms of her husband's doctorate and the peculiar causes he supported. She was a wage-slave to marriage, and since her intelligence was obviously inferior to her husband's her role was a reasonable one.

Cunningham-White? Too genteel. She considers the name

of your father's aunt more important than examination results.

I looked at the examination results in front of me and began to mark out the failures. Ella Middleton, 15 per cent. I smiled. It was only necessary to be patient. First Ann, then Ella. There was the scholarship, of course, but she had undoubtedly failed to meet the conditions of tenure. I thought of Mrs Middleton. I had no desire to interview her. I never feel at ease with coloured people. And Miriam? Miriam had an old maid's attachment to the girl. However she felt about it, Miriam would have to help.

Monday

It must be admitted Miriam is sandy. And stringy. I looked at her obstinate face, her stick-like legs rising stiffly from her laced boots, her curiously youthful frock. She was flushed, almost scarlet. A pulse in her throat bobbed up and down like the crop of a nervous fowl. She has a male voice box.

'Do your own dirty work,' she said.

I was shocked. Miriam is never rude. I had hoped to keep Miriam until she reached an honourable retirement, but I felt my first doubt. I resented her attitude. I had, however, to swallow my resentment, at least for the moment. Miriam was too necessary to my plans.

'Very well,' I replied coolly. 'But don't blame me if the Middletons find me a much more unpleasant ambassador than you.'

I could feel her anguish. In spite of all her loyal shouldering of duties, she did not trust me. She believed I should indeed insult Mrs Middleton. She agreed to be my messenger. I flattered her in return, praised her for her unswerving devotion to duty.

'You overrate me,' she said and left the room.

I was surprised. I had not thought Miriam capable of irony. I was not worried. I had no doubt, in spite of the symptoms, that Miriam was reliable. Poor Miriam. I suppose even the best of us needs a little revolt occasionally. I was sure it would peter out like a damp squib. Miriam would do her duty as she had always done. You can't break the habit of a lifetime. I could afford to be tolerant. Miriam would effectively dispose of Ella Middleton for me.

MIRIAM

I drove six miles before I turned the car towards the Aboriginal settlement. I drove past the old dump into the eastern fold of the hills. I should do my duty. I was the Head's right hand, I was the Council's rock of strength, I was my mother's anchor in the storm of life. I was, I was, I was. Never *I am*. My hands were chained by the manacles of Meridale: I had been conceived in Meridale, moulded in its classrooms, shaped and reshaped by its prejudices. So be it.

I turned back and nosed the car into the dirt track that was the Middletons' street. The lazy dogs scattered, evading impact by a final twist of their tails. The brown-eyed children did likewise. I could hear them, marching on before. 'There's a whitey to see you, Mrs Middleton, there's a whitey to see you.'

Some days, the days when Ella came too, they crawled round the car talking and laughing, touching the bonnet, the hood, the boot. Today they held back, and I felt I must carry with me the aura of failure, of bad tidings.

Mrs Middleton opened the door. I was aware as never before of the greasy, stringy hair, the almost toothless smile. I thought, I am too early. She hasn't had time to freshen up. But the deepening of my perception of disorder made me realise I had already removed myself in spirit.

'May I come in, Mrs Middleton?'

She stood back for me to enter. 'Is Ella all right? There isn't an accident?'

'Nothing like that,' I said. 'But I do want to talk about Ella.'

The house was already tidy, but the breakfast table had not yet been cleared. The boys were clustered round it licking honey from their fingers. She shooed them out like a flock of chickens.

'Forgive the mess,' she said, 'I've not bin too well—and it's Saturday.'

'I'm sorry,' I said. I sought for words. 'I am here on behalf of the school, Mrs Middleton. You may remember Ella's scholarship was dependent on good progress reports. I'm sorry, but Ella failed her last exam, and I'm afraid her scholarship has been terminated.'

'You mean she's comin' home? You're gittin' rid of her?'

The dark face was impassive. 'Yes, Mrs Middleton, she's coming home.'

'She deserves a good hidin', throwin' her chances away like that.'

I shuddered. 'No,' I said, 'nothing like that. The work was hard. Our standards are very high under the new principal.'

'Other girls failed?'

'Yes,' I said.

'But you want to git rid of Ella. You're not gittin' rid of all failures.'

'No. . . .'

'Why not?'

'Some of the fathers will pay another year's fees. Their girls are not on scholarships.'

'But Ella can't pay fees.'

'I know, Mrs Middleton.'

She stood up and her dignity was like a tribal cloak separating her from me. She was not deceived.

'I've known for some months,' she said, 'that the school didn't want Ella. I understand, Miss Hansen. You can tell your Miss Fordess we won't be makin' any trouble.'

I nearly said, 'It's not like that at all.' I nearly said, 'She's not *my* Miss Fordess.' But I didn't. After all it *was* like that and she had a right to say so.

'Ella will continue at High School?' I asked.

'Not likely. She's had her chance. There'll be a job at the local laundry. She can help her brothers git their chance now.'

I got up. I felt big and awkward. Any intimacy we may once have shared was gone. She now addressed me in the ingratiating tone of the underprivileged everywhere, a voice that tried both to placate the masters and to put them in their place.

'We're grateful I'm sure, Miss Hansen, for all your interest in Ella. We appreciate you callin' on us personally.'

'Good-bye, Mrs Middleton.' I began to put out my hand; but seeing my intention she began to scrape the plates. I let my hand drop.

The kids in the road stood silently in the gutter. They made no attempt to touch the car. As I drove away I heard their chorus of contempt. 'Whitey, whitey, silly old whitey.'

I drove faster than usual. I had reached my climax. I could stand no more. This was the orgasm, the end of my dutiful existence. I shut my eyes and gave myself up to erotic fancies, feeling the electricity of sensual thought run through my body. The climax of duty, the passive body titillated and then revolted—by Ina, then Philippa. It took Heather Patricia Fordess to complete the rape of my independent being. Or was I unjust? Perhaps I had lost my liberty long before I walked up the drive to interview Ina. She had merely played upon the desiccated shell.

I forced my thoughts away from myself to Ella. 'Oh God,' I prayed, 'not the laundry.' My lovely soft velvety Ella buried in that tin mausoleum of chemicals and steam. I stopped the car and I was sick by the side of the road. My hands were trembling. I had done my duty. All that H.P. demanded. I decided she would never have another opportunity to humiliate me.

I went straight to my room. I walked past Mother crochet-

ing some futile doyley and shut my door. She banged on it
with her stick, but I did not answer. She rattled the handle,
but the lock held firm. 'If you're hungry,' I called out, 'there's
plenty of food in the fridge. Help yourself.' It was the only
thing I said, and after a while I heard her uneven steps going
away.

I lay on the bed and looked at the ceiling. I fashioned and
refashioned phrases. Hours passed. Finally I rose. I picked up
my pen and wrote out my resignation. I put it in an envelope
and addressed it to the principal. I prowled round my room,
thinking. I decided to deliver the letter myself, after dark,
but there were hours of daylight to get through. I fingered
Margaret's bird. I balanced it on my hand. 'You shall fly,' I
said, 'you shall fly.'

I had chosen darkness because there were things that had to
be done. There were things in that school that were not part
of Heather Patricia Fordess, things to which she had no claim.
I pulled out a bundle of stencils and spread them on the floor
around me. I thought of Ann.

Mother knocked again. 'Miriam, what are you doing?' I
calculated it was tea-time, so I repeated the message about
the fridge. She grumbled and grizzled for a while, but finally
went away. Later I heard her stumble into her bedroom. When
I was sure she was in bed I crept out. It must have been about
nine. I did not look at my watch. I felt outside time.

I stoked the fire high in the kitchen stove. Mother would
not be able to complain of the cold. I pulled my woollen cap
over my ears and buttoned my longest coat around me. I
picked up a bottle of kerosene from the kitchen and stuffed a
packet of newspaper under my coat. I took my old bicycle
from the shed. I had not ridden it for years and the tyres
needed pumping. The habit of a school lifetime was not, however, lost. The pump was still intact and it was merely a matter of a few seconds before the tyres were firm. I warmed with
the exercise. I put the letter in the pocket of my coat. I then
tied a spade and a sickle on the back of the carrier.

Most of the school was in darkness. Under H.P. the nine o'clock curfew was strictly enforced. I left my bicycle by the rose garden and crept along to the office. Inside a light was shining. I glanced through the window. H. P. Fordess was writing at the desk. She looked secure, comfortable, safe. I laughed to myself and dropped the note in the box outside her door.

I returned to the garden, the garden that Philippa and Margaret and I had created one lovely winter day. I knew what I had to do. This garden was the flowering of my Etherington period. My roots were buried here with Peace and Madame Butterfly; Margaret was the Crimson Glory, and Philippa spilt over the path the multi-coloured gold of Talisman. But Margaret and Philippa had been exiled. And my loyalty had been degraded, my sense of duty exploited for ignoble ends. Our spirits could no longer breathe in this garden. I had to release them. It was my final duty.

I took the sickle and I slashed and slashed, feeling the leaves and thorns brush my hands as they fell. I pulled up the fallen stems with my bare hands and the blood trickled over them in the joyousness of release. I took the spade and uprooted the remnants, digging hard and deep, sensing the pleasure of masculine strength as the brown soil lay bare and purged. I pulled the newspaper from my coat and laid it under the pile of bushes. I poured the kerosene over it and put a match to the soaked paper and twigs. There was a flare of light.

Quickly I swung myself onto my bike. The flame rose like a funeral pyre as I pedalled down the hill, and the shadows of burning light twisted across the road. I imagined I could already hear voices raised in panic within the school grounds, but when I looked back there was only darkness. The bushes had failed to burn after the first flare from kerosene and paper, and I was bitterly disappointed. Then I laughed and laughed. There was no dramatic holocaust, but the garden was destroyed. *Our* roses would never bloom again at Etherington.

I pushed the bicycle into the shed with the empty bottle, the spade and the sickle. Then I tiptoed into the house.

Mother was seated at the table. She must have been waiting for some time. When she saw me she screamed. The mirror opposite reflected my mud-stained face and I raised my hands to wipe it, but my hands were caked with blood.

'You wicked woman,' my mother screamed, 'you wicked woman. You've been digging up the graveyard.'

She swiped at me with her stick and caught me on the mouth. I felt blood on my face. I advanced upon her. She began to scream, dodging around the table and jabbing at me with the stick.

'How dare you,' I said, 'how dare you hit me. All my life you have persecuted me. All my life.'

I moved faster and she tried to run. I pulled the stick from her, and she tripped, screaming, against the stove. I broke the stick across my knee with a resounding crack as I watched the flames sweep up her clothing.

She put out her hands. 'Save me, Miriam, save me!' I did not take them. I was immobilised, lost in the drama of flame and destruction.

Then I saw her terrified eyes and I acted. I beat at the flames with my hands, but they curled around my fingers. I rolled her on the floor over and over. The flames dissipated in a smother of smoke, but I knew even as I lifted the limp form that she was dead.

I carried her body into the bedroom. I pulled the burnt clothing from her skin and dressed her in a clean nightgown.

I stood under the shower and washed the mud and blood from my body. My hands were blistered and the burnt skin crackled like pork. There was pain, but it did not worry me. I began to laugh when I thought of Robert being summoned. The burden was his, at last. He could have everything he coveted: the house, the furniture, the doyleys, the portraits, and Mother.

I dried and dressed, then packed a case with my own clothes. Tomorrow I would throw them away, a bundle in every creek I passed. I decided to drive to the coast, over the hills that Father and I had crossed with a horse and dray so long ago. I would leave the car by the banks of a river or on the sands of the Pacific Ocean. There were plenty of small isolated railway stations in that area, plenty of destinations. I counted my money, and my mother's money. Enough for the moment.

I tied a scarf over my hair, walked to the door, and looked back in farewell. The moonlight struck the wings of Margaret's bird. I picked it up and pushed it into my handbag. I took one last look in Mother's bedroom. She was resting peacefully. Silently I crept down the hall past Father's carved animals, Father's cedar cabinets. I still had several hours of darkness to get out of Meridale. I locked the door behind me, started the car, and drove into the eastern rim of the sky.

The road was like an old-fashioned magic lantern, alternating dark and light. I remembered that Aunt Myra used to own a lantern when we were children. The trees were the light. They slipped past, white ghostly cameos, and the little creeks and bridges jumped up out of the night. Memory extended the sections split by the dark into a continuous film. I knew the country with my mind, my heart, the bones of my being.

It would have been amusing to take the turn to the gorges, those pits of my artistic inspiration. I imagined myself slipping the brake off the car and jumping clear, then hearing it crash into the black depths of those hillsides stratified into rock with the frost of centuries. But it was not practical and I have always been a practical thinker. The turning wheels, the passing trees, the lighted line of tar relaxed my jumbled feelings. I felt the rhythm of peace and I knew I was going to find Margaret. I needed the car to reach the coast, to catch the train north.

I drove fast that night. I had never travelled the curves from the plateaux to the coast in the darkness at that speed, but I drove well, in spite of my stinging hands; and now I was dropping around the last twist into the valley that led to the coast.

It was already daylight when I pushed the car into the scrub, and I smiled with pleasure as I turned back down the road to the station. The last of Etherington.

It was a slow train trip but I did not mind. I had always liked the precise beat of train wheels, the caterpillar pull round curves, the pulsing endeavour to climb the hills. It was a journey to fulfilment through a countryside lit by the gaudy colours of semi-tropical flowers where herds grazed in lush paddocks that had never known the destructive power of frost.

It was almost noon when the train drew in at the station and I knew from the first moment that I had reached my own haven of recovery. It was a tiny town embedded in beauty, guarded by twin mountains. I started to walk towards them. I knew I had at least four miles to go, but it did not worry me. I stood on a road that climbed upward and watched the train line, a perfect parabola across the valley. I passed through a tunnel of red bougainvillea where the shrub had grown thick across the roadway. I emerged from the coloured gloom into the glare of the twin mountains. I knew then how I should paint them: great erotic green breasts mothering the valley, they would leap up the canvas to meet the sun.

When I found the settlement I was tired but exhilarated. A man with a beard, and the narrow strong hips and broad shoulders of a worker was hoeing a field. I thought of my father. He had the same calm eyes, the same sure hands. He was not young—a man in his mid-thirties—but he stood authoritatively at peace with the world.

'Good day,' he said.

'Good day,' I answered. 'I have come to find Margaret Kersten. She is my friend.'

'That is good. She is too much alone.' He pointed to a building farther down the valley. I could see figures working at the walls and roof. I walked to meet them and, then, as the sound of their hammering reached me, I saw her. She was planing a piece of wood. It looked like a floor board. She wore an open-necked blouse and old flannel trousers. She was thinner but brown with health. She worked with a cigarette in her hand just as she had always done and I knew that fear of death had not conquered her.

For a while I stood silently near her, watching with pleasure the smoothed wood slip from beneath her hands. She finished the board and looked up. Then she saw me and dropped the plane in surprise. I looked into the blue eyes. 'I've escaped,' I said.

For a second she said nothing. Then, 'Good for you', in the husky deep voice I remembered.

I suppose I looked a mess—quite unlike my usual well-ordered self. The handkerchief around my burnt hands was filthy, and my dress was covered with sweat and dust. She looked me over. 'A shower,' she said. 'First things first'—and I knew she had not changed. She could accept without question. She called something to the other workers on the building who nodded their agreement. We walked down to a tiny weatherboard cabin. 'All my own work,' she said. 'My very own house.' To me it was perfect, smelling of planed wood, with tables and chairs and walls in their natural grain. It suggested rest and peace and home as surely as her bird had suggested flight. She threw me a towel.

I showered, feeling the water fall in cold stimulation over my tired body. I heard her call. 'Where did you leave your luggage? I could ask Max to carry it down for you.'

'I threw it away,' I said. And then I heard her laugh, peal after peal of deep-throated laughter. I laughed too.

She placed a pair of jeans and a blouse on a chair. 'They'll be too short,' she said, 'and not exactly your type of thing; but I'm afraid we're not nudists here, not yet, anyway.'

I looked in dismay at the unfamiliar denim. I had never worn trousers. Then I shook myself, feeling the water cascade from my wet hair into my eyes. That had been the Miriam of Meridale, not the Miriam who had escaped. I dried myself and pulled on the jeans. They reached half-way up my calf, but they fitted my waist. I felt a kind of excited amusement as I buttoned them up the front like a man and then tied the belt of my dress around them.

I looked at the shoes and stockings and down at my bare feet. Perfectly formed, they were my reward for those dutiful years of sensible footwear. I decided to go barefoot.

When I came into the kitchen, Margaret ran her fingers through her crisp, now-greying waves. 'Perfect,' she said with a grin. I glanced at my bare ankles and feet and felt my dripping sandy hair. I decided then and there to grow it. No more permed ends. My grandmother always wore her hair long and, judging by the folk working on the house, it was quite all right to leave it hanging round the shoulders. I wriggled my toes to feel the air pass between them.

Margaret passed the tea and motioned me to sit down.

'Now,' she said as she poured me a second cup, 'tell me all.'

I did just that. Everything. H.P., Mother, the graveyard, Ella, the roses, the fire, the death, the flight through the night.

She nodded. 'I'm glad you pulled up all the roses,' she said. 'I shouldn't want to stay in that soil.'

It was her only comment. She did not condemn me. I was so glad I began to cry. I felt the hard, firm muscles of her arms on my shoulders. 'Get it over,' she said, 'then forget it. You don't cry, Miriam, and you won't need to cry with me. You know you can stay as long as you like. We always worked well together. This is my house, but I help the others to build their homes. In return I get my vegetables and milk from the farmers and my clothes from the weavers. They'll expect you to contribute some kind of labour.'

'I could make pottery,' I said.

She laughed. 'I guess you could,' she said, 'but I don't want a copy of Philippa. Why not carpentry, like your father? Be my apprentice. I need more skilled help. My own physical strength is limited.'

I knew she had purposely told me that she needed me as much as I needed her. I felt a renewal of purpose. I should look after Margaret as I had looked after Mother, but it would be an act of love.

'I like that idea,' I said.

She turned down the bed. 'You'd better rest.' She gently

brushed back my hair with her work-hardened fingers. 'You must be very tired.' Only then did I realise my own exhaustion. But I felt wanted and secure. I took the bird from my bag and placed it on the table. She touched its wing with her fingers. 'I'm glad you kept it,' she said. She watched me as I lay down. She spread a rug over my feet. 'By the way, there will be some problems. The police will want to know about your mother. But I'll talk to Pete. As you say, it was an accident and you had obviously been driven by the school beyond human endurance.'

'The man in the field,' I murmured sleepily. 'Pete. Is he the leader?'

'Not officially,' she said. 'We have no leader, but he has a kind of natural superiority. He used to be a doctor. Still is, I suppose. He is quite reliable.'

I was glad. I like a man at the helm. I slept like a baby untroubled by fear or nightmares. It was already evening when I awoke. That night we ate with the group around the campfire. Home-made bread, fresh vegetables, creamy milk. 'Good natural creamy milk,' they said every few seconds as they passed it one to another. Straight from the cow via the refrigerator. 'Have a yam,' they said, 'straight from the earth.' Their fresh faces were totally serious, and I thought what good staff members they would have made. They had such a self-conscious desire to establish umbilical contact with the soil, the udders and, I suspected, even the dung. It could be burnt to ward off mosquitoes.

Music drifted from the guitars and flutes of the young folk. I thought of the evenings at Etherington, of Philippa and Rachel and the cello. But this time I was not an outsider sitting upright on a straight-backed chair in lace-up shoes. No one appeared to notice my bare feet and trousers. If I died here and now, I thought, there would be no worry about graveyard plots. They would wrap me up in a grey blanket woven by themselves and simply place me back in the earth from which God had made me. Probably fantasy. There were authorities and there would be health laws that some council had to handle. A natural wooden box made by someone like Margaret would be more likely, and finally just as good as the free earth.

I decided then to find that contact with the earth and grass and wood that they valued, even if I felt a resurgence of my old cynicism, the kind of embarrassment I knew when Philippa persisted in talking about God as if He were really in the room with us.

I should learn to dye and weave in my spare time, and I decided my new clothes would be flowing with embroidered hems and necklines. When that was done, I should paint.

I walked back with Margaret to the cabin. Pete had found a stretcher I could use until I made a new bed. I liked the thought of carving my own bed.

'I'm going to become a carpenter,' I said, 'and I am going to paint. I shall paint the heavy-breasted hills and they're going to be green, so green that the canvas will be resplendent with fertility.'

'No more black.' She laughed and kissed me on the forehead.

'Only for contrast,' I replied.

I lay naked beneath the sheets and rough blankets for the first time in my life. I should make a nightgown. My parents had always stressed the need for night clothing as a protection against bronchitis, and I agreed with them. I had always worn printed flannelette, but in this climate I could wear light cotton. I should dye it pink, bright, glowing boudoir pink like an Ina Spurway painting. I snuggled down.

I enjoyed the feel of the clean sheets on my bare skin. The nightgown would be made, but I should not hurry. I could hear Margaret breathing huskily with the rhythm of sleep.

'No, not pink,' I said to myself. 'Green—bright green.'

What the critics have said about Gwen Kelly's latest novel
ARROWS OF RAIN:

"We are taken in breathless pursuit of a family's loves and
labours at 10-year intervals. . . The emotions and doings of
the characters are delivered with quite explosive force. . .
As satisfying, though devastating, a moment as I know in
modern literature."

A . T. YARWOOD
THE AGE

"Gwen Kelly moves through a generation of lives taking
samples like a geologist . . .and the expectations aroused by the
10-year intervals make for marvellous story-telling. There's the
promise of so much change, so many developments. We want to
read on to find out what it is. The geological samples make a
galloping good yarn."

MARION HALLIGAN,
SYDNEY MORNING HERALD

"Kelly dips into their lives at precise 10-year intervals, painting a
rich and intimate picture of each new present and unobtrusively
filling in the details of the missing years in a most effective and
economical fashion."

KATHARINE ENGLAND,
THE ADVERTISER